HE
FOUND
ME

WHITNEY BARBETTI

4,99

CONTENTS

My hands were red and raw from washing the dishes twice. It was always twice. Twice bought me time and ensured there wouldn't be anything left behind. An errant fleck of food, a spot that hadn't been rinsed – these were things he'd notice.

From the living room came the sounds of some crime drama; the gunshots and screams interrupting the quiet of the kitchen. I didn't mind washing the dishes, because it was a way for me to keep distance from him, from the Monster. "Kitchen is a woman's domain," he would say, while looking me up and down with his beady black eyes, a cruel smile stretching his lips. His only occasional venture into the kitchen was for his usual bottle of cherry vodka, shoved in the back of the freezer behind the chicken I'd bought months ago and had yet to thaw and cook.

My stomach clenched just thinking about the chicken, the chicken that hid his habit. I didn't want to see the vodka; I'd smelled it on his breath time and time again, late at night, in the one place that should have been safe. Sleep was not safe for me anymore; there were far worse nightmares in the land of the living. My life was a series of real-life nightmares. But tonight, I'd leave everything. Leave Cora Mitchell behind in search of freedom.

The sound of feet hitting the wood floor in the living room made my muscles seize in awareness, stomach turn over in revulsion. Not again, I thought. A moment later I felt his shadow fall over my right shoulder. His heavy footsteps rocked the peeling linoleum beneath my feet as he approached. I smelled his cologne when he leaned over my shoulder. "Make sure you don't dawdle," he whispered, his breath hot on my ear. He stayed there for a moment, grubby hands caging me to the counter from behind. I felt a trickle of sweat slide down my spine and tried to act like I wasn't wasting time, monotonously scrubbing the spatula in my hand. I felt him hum, the vibration right by my ear and I swallowed the bile that rose up into my mouth. The humming. He knew that I knew what the humming signified. I gritted my teeth together.

"I'm almost done." I didn't bother turning my head and meeting his eyes. A challenge like that would only encourage him, and I had plans that didn't include engaging him in his favorite activity. He was a creature of habit: dinner, then television, then the bottle of vodka, then me. Tonight would be different.

He slid two fingers down my back, over my tee shirt, pausing just before he reached the top of my jeans. He enjoyed this game, teasing me with the threatening promise of later. He thought he held all the power in this exchange, but I was going to prove him wrong.

He kept his fingers at the top of my jeans for a moment and sighed in my ear before backing away. I heard the sound of the freezer door opening and felt the cool blast at my back. It helped to calm me, and I reminded myself that soon, this would all be over. I heard the crunch of the frozen vegetables as he reached for his vodka, and then the clank as he set it on the counter next to the clean dishes.

Anticipating his next move, I wiped my hands on the towel wedged into the cabinet door and reached next to me to grab the shot glass I'd placed next to the sink in preparation. I don't know why he didn't bother ever drinking straight from the bottle. It wasn't as if it made him more civilized. It was just an illusion, one of many in my life. And soon, I'd perform my own.

I grabbed his bottle and poured the shot, hoping for a steady hand. I didn't want to tip him off to my intentions. I slowly set the glass and bottle back down and moved my hands back into the soapy water.

Thankfully, he didn't suspect anything and grabbed both before walking back across the linoleum, returning to the living room. And, just as I hoped, he nearly tumbled over the full trash bag laying in his way. "You could break someone's neck, leaving this right here. Take it out," he bellowed, tossing back the shot. "Now."

Breaking his neck would have been too easy.

As he returned to the living room, I wiped my hands on the dishtowel and took a moment to steady them. This was the moment.

The silent goodbye I'd been waiting for since the lawyer recited my late mother's words in a room of strangers. I took a calming breath in through my nose and willed myself to act casually.

I bent down and picked up the garbage bag, carrying it the short distance to the door. I paused a moment to look into the living room, taking comfort in that he would be asleep in no less than ten minutes. The sleeping pills I'd crushed and mixed into his mashed potatoes and gravy were a high enough dosage to take him out without the added effect of the evening cold medicine I'd poured into his quad-sized shot glass along with the cherry vodka. I would need the head start.

I opened the door and walked onto the landing of his apartment's four-plex before softly shutting the door behind me. I stood there for a moment and took in a deep breath of the evening air. October was normally a chilly time of year for Michigan, but tonight was actually a relatively warm night and quiet too.

I made my way down the stairwell as softly as possible, to avoid alerting any neighbors to my presence. Once I was on the sidewalk, I wrapped my hand more tightly around the bag and walked purposefully to the dumpster that was situated between two apartment buildings. I looked to my right and left and breathed a sigh of relief for the dark windows that faced the dumpster. I ducked behind the dumpster and ripped open the garbage bag, digging out my tennis shoes that were hidden under the cardboard. I threw off my flip flops and flung them into the dumpster. After sliding on the tennis shoes, I grabbed the black windbreaker I'd also stuffed under the cardboard and then took out the small backpack I'd hidden in there. I pulled the backpack over my shoulders, trying to be as quiet as possible, and then slid my arms into the sleeves of the windbreaker, concealing the backpack.

Zipping up the windbreaker, I looked around once again, to make sure I wasn't seen. My hands were still shaking so I rubbed them against my jeans for a minute before glancing at my soon-to-be former apartment. I'd planned this for months, and knew exactly what my next steps would be. But I was still human, and as far as I knew humans were capable of fear. Fear trickled slowly into my veins, weighing down the confidence I felt at my impending escape.

Despite the fear, I had no apprehension. I pulled my hair into a bun before I set off on a run through the weeds and into the trees behind the apartments. The garbage men would be emptying the dumpster at seven the following morning, taking my ripped-open garbage bag along with them. I knew the sleeping pills would keep the Monster asleep at least until then. I'd tested the pills out several times months in advance. I'd done it initially to keep him from visiting my bedroom, before I'd fully developed my plan. I was nothing if not thorough.

Ten minutes into jogging, I chanced a glance behind me. Even though I felt sure that he would be too incapacitated to follow me by now, I couldn't help the shiver of lingering fear. Then, reminding myself that I would soon be finally free of him, the adrenaline kicked in and I ran another two miles before reaching my destination.

My destination was a former schoolhouse. It sat off a sleepy road and was surrounded by dead trees, with branches from those trees littering the ground around its three-story structure. It was dilapidated and ugly, with brick falling off the sides of the building, exposing the white plaster beneath. Broken windows and a boarded up door were what greeted me as I slowed to a quick walk, making sure to walk around where the piles of leaves sat, neglected. This school was a historical landmark – which is why it wasn't torn down yet – and the nearby neighbors did their best to keep it from looking completely decrepit from the outside by raking the lawn in the fall. This worked in my favor, as I knew stepping on dead leaves might sound my presence.

I'd staked the area out in the summer, made note of the neighbors, their habits, and if they had dogs. Thankfully, most of the neighborhood was home to the elderly and their tiny, ankle-biter dogs, the kind that barked at the wind, or a bug, and therefore posed no threat of alerting their owners to my presence. I listened for any noise, just in case, but I knew this run-down building was perfect for the next step in my plan.

When I reached the side of the building, I looked around just in case and flexed my hands, still tingling from the adrenaline. I tried to keep focused on my task at hand, knowing full well I was not safe yet. I stood on my tiptoes and peeked in a few windows, making sure no vagrants had taken up residence inside, before continuing along to the back door of the building.

The back door was not boarded up, but it did have some pretty heavy duty locks. Luckily, that had not deterred a former squatter, who'd likely broken the bottom window pane and later mediocrely patched with some cardboard. I pulled off my windbreaker and then the backpack before putting the windbreaker back on. I reached into the backpack and pulled out the pocket knife I'd stashed inside, using it to cut open the cardboard. Once through the puny barrier, I carefully reached in and unlocked the deadbolts and the lock on the door knob before quietly easing the door open.

The smell of must greeted me instantly. I snuck inside and used the bottom of my shirt to preemptively wipe away my fingerprints before closing the door, using my hand inside the windbreaker to close it. I traded the knife for a flashlight before putting the backpack back on.

While I had prepared my escape down to the last detail, I had forgotten that it would be dark when I returned to this school. Squeezing my eyes shut, I tried to recall how to get to the basement, where I had stashed my goods. I felt around for the wall, my fingers gaining purchase on the peeling wallpaper and followed it until I felt the door that I knew went to the basement of the building. My flashlight would be too risky on the main floor, but once I took the first few steps into the basement, I snapped on the small light. I couldn't remember there being basement windows from the outside of the building, so I kept the light muffled behind my hand while I made my descent.

I removed the flashlight from being muffled by my hand only momentarily to push away the cobwebs that hung down as I walked to the back of the basement. My yard sale bike sat behind some old filing cabinets, hidden. I wheeled it out and walked it to the stairs. I returned to the back of the basement and dug underneath one of the heavy metal desks for the larger backpack I'd hidden. Strapping it to the shelf on the back of the bike's seat, I picked the bike up and let it rest on one shoulder as I carried it back up the stairs, slowly. When I reached the landing, the eerie quiet of the building initially alarmed me, because it was a huge contrast to the blood pounding in my ears. I paused for a moment to calm my reappearing nerves. My flashlight was tucked away in my smaller backpack, so I waited until my eyes readjusted to the darkness. I could see the light coming through the door I'd first entered, so I cautiously made my way that direction, taking care to pick up my feet with each step so I wouldn't trip.

I opened the door slowly, peeked out, and then proceeded to carry the bike out on my shoulder, closing the door softly behind me. As soon as I was on the back lawn, I moved swiftly to the tree cover.

The nice thing about this town was all the forest land. It made discreet travel possible for me.

The forest floor was relatively flat, which made bike travel easy. The grass was dead and most of the trees did not shed leaves. I spent the first half hour on my bike, making sure to stay as far away from sidewalks and streets as possible. As soon as I ran out of tree cover, I knew I was nearing my next destination.

I could see the faint neon lights of the truck stop ahead and stopped, pulling my hair out of its bun and converting it into a low ponytail. I stuffed the ponytail under my windbreaker and pulled a baseball cap out of the small backpack I'd been carrying. I pulled out the dollar store reading glasses and slid those on as well. I zipped the windbreaker up and adjusted my baggy jeans. I hoped I looked inconspicuous as I set my bike on the ground before strolling up to the payphone on the side of the building, making sure to not look anyone in the eye. It was already 10 PM, but since this truck stop was just off the interstate, I knew it would still be consistently busy. I kept my face down as I'd been instructed, out of the camera lens' views. Luckily, I already knew most of those cameras were aimed at the gas pumps, but I didn't want to risk a single detail.

Picking up the phone and dropping in some change, I dialed the number I'd memorized weeks earlier.

It rang once before the voice I was waiting for sounded on the other line. "Ready?"

I released a breath. "Yes."

"I'll be there in fifteen minutes."

Without responding, I calmly hung up the phone and walked around the back of the building, to the field that was safely out of view of the gas station's employees and security cameras. I shivered, the sweat from my bike ride cooling off under the windbreaker. I kept a steady eye at my surroundings while I waited for my ride.

While I would've liked to say I could have done this on my own, there was just no way. I was barely seventeen years old, with all my blood family long dead or gone. I'd spent the last four years with a Monster, and I needed an escape. I know what you're thinking: "Why didn't you call Child Protective Services?" I did. I was a walking, talking cliché. And after the last time I'd confided in an adult I thought I could trust, the abuse I'd suffered as punishment made me realize there needed to be another way out. A way out that didn't include me baring my soul to someone again, to testifying against the Monster.

I was fortunate to have Six in my life. A long-time friend of my mother's, he was at her funeral and he'd slipped me his contact information after the will was read. I don't know how he knew I'd need him someday, but I did.

When my aunt passed away, it was just the Monster and me left. He sold his house and downsized to the small apartment. It was around that time he started realizing a cure to his loneliness was me.

Six set up a PO Box for us to communicate through, and when he learned what little I would share of the abuse, he helped me hatch the plan for my freedom. On nights I knew the Monster was working late, Six would pick me up from school and we'd plot my steps carefully.

Where the Monster was family in marriage only, Six was family in my heart. He was twice my age, but unlike the Monster in every way. I'd grown up with Six a constant presence in my mother's home for Sunday dinners. He was the only person I trusted in the entire world. He was what I guess a big brother would be, if I had one.

I saw the sports car zip into the gas station and then around the building. The headlights of the silver car flashed at me three times before switching to the parking lights on its approach. Ten feet from where I stood, the car stopped its hum and the driver's door opened. As soon as I saw his tall frame silhouetted against the moonlight, I ran to him and he opened his arms, catching me.

Finally, finally, I allowed myself to cry. Relief, exhaustion, and elation. The flood of emotions were stronger than anything I'd felt.

Until **he** found me, seven years later.

3

I drummed my fingers on the metal desk. A fleck of red polish popped off my nail and slid across the shiny desk top. "Crap," I muttered to myself. I leaned down to inspect my now imperfect fingernail. I wasn't one to care usually, but I had just finished removing the glitter remnants my nails had stubbornly held for over a month before applying the blood red color. My favorite color.

A shadow fell over me, a dark figure reflected on the desk top. I shivered involuntarily. It'd been almost seven years, and I still hated shadows. As if reading my mind, the shadow moved to stand to the side of my desk.

"Annie, if you need something to do, just ask."

The smile formed on my lips before I turned to look up at my friend and, at the moment, my boss. "Rosa, I've just been too busy twiddling my thumbs to do actual work. And besides, you know I hate that nickname. It's just as many syllables as Andra. An. Dra," I enunciated.

Rosa laughed. Her laugh was rich and poignant, sparking the air between us. "I know better than to think you spend your day twiddling thumbs in here. Do you have the report you were working on for me? An. Nie?" Teasing me with a wink, she walked around to face my monitors.

I pulled up the report on one of my two monitors and swiftly stood to allow Rosa to sit at my desk. "Have at it!" I motioned with my hand.

"You could at least pretend to be flustered when I ask you for something important." Rosa said without looking at me, sliding her plum colored reading glasses onto her nose.

Still smiling, I rubbed Rosa's shoulder. "I'll try harder next time."

"Take a break," she replied, while studying the monitor. I knew what that meant. Rosa liked to look things over without me lurking nearby. She knew those reports better than I did, anyway.

I strolled to the front porch from the door to my office and stepped out. I quietly closed the screen door and was instantly slammed with a solid wall of heat. My lips curved. Summer was hitting us sooner than usual, which was just fine with me. I walked to the stairs that led down into the yard and felt the sun kiss my shoulders and what was exposed of my chest. In the distance, I saw Rosa's husband brushing down his favorite mare. The white vinyl fence that separated us was in need of a good cleaning, so I walked around the side of the house to the garage.

Rosa and Clint had recently hired a teenager named Farley to mow the lawn and it was obvious that he was still getting the hang of the riding lawn mower, with all the grass and mud kicked up all over the bottom half of the fence. I made a mental note to show him how to mow more efficiently.

I slid my mud-caked, burgundy polka-dot rubber boots on over my skinny jeans, grabbed a bucket, brush, some old towels, soap, and a giant sponge and lugged it all out to the fence.

Clint lifted his head and saw my determined walk out to where he was. "Are you fixing to play in the mud?" he called out to me.

"Nope, but preparing for it!" I replied, plopping the bucket down. "Are you going to be out here with Buttermilk much longer?" I asked, gesturing towards his honey-colored horse with the brush in my hand.

"Just finishing up. Grab the power washer, will you? I'll power wash the fence for you first to make it easier," he said, leading Buttermilk back to the barn.

"I'll do it, Clint. Gives me something to do." I walked back to the garage and grabbed the power washer and the extension cord. Then I grabbed the hose from the side of the house and brought it all back to the fence. After hooking it all up, I started spraying the fence down. Water splashed back onto my legs and trickled down to the inside of my boots. But I could quickly see that Clint was right, the power washer was taking off most of the gunk from the lawn mowers, tractors, dust, and mud. It might seem like a futile task to clean the fence, but with all our upcoming events at the ranch, I knew we had to spruce the place up a bit.

Though it was still early in the day, the heat was strong and with no trees to provide shade, the back of my neck was starting to collect sweat. I bent over at the waist and pulled my long, chestnut-colored hair into a messy bun on top of my head.

Just as I started running a soapy sponge along the fence, I heard Rosa call from the porch. "Annie, do you not understand the definition of a break?"

She knew how to make me laugh. I turned towards her and shielded my eyes from the sun so I could see her, knowing full well her hands would be on her hips. "Apparently not!" I called back.

She meandered her way down the steps. Her limp was still present as she made her way towards me, though it didn't take any power from her walk. Rosa was in her fifties, short and fit, and the most resilient woman I knew. She'd inherited the ranch from her father and had kept it running like a queen residing over her kingdom. But this queen didn't wear gowns and often spent time cleaning up horse shit. Her black hair hung in a bob to her shoulders, though the top half was pulled back in a style that was entirely functional. Around her neck was a tied handkerchief, something I should have thought to grab myself.

"Get your skinny butt back in there and fiddle with some numbers. I want projections for next month. I have had three inquiries for boarding and I think I need to add more stalls to the barn." The reason Rosa and I worked so well is that we both knew how to be brief. We didn't waste time explaining our thought process because half the time, we practically read each other's minds.

"I'll get to it after I finish this section. I want to finish it before noon, so it has time to dry in the sun."

Rosa allowed me a small smile before swinging an arm around my shoulders. "You're my favorite, you know that?" She laughed and glanced towards the barn, where her ranch hands were taking care of the boarded horses. Rosa oversaw the operations of the ranch, but I was the only one she worked closely with.

"You mean Farley has been demoted?" I laughed, and gestured to where Farley was currently mowing the area around the pond, down the hill from the house. He was zigzagging across the area adjacent to the beach. He kept glancing all around him, the look of "oops" clearly written across his face.

Rosa sighed. Farley, while clearly inexperienced, was a sweet kid and eager to learn. He'd get there, and we both knew it. "That mess is my fault. He needs to be trained. I need to get around to doing that at some point, but for now I 'spose we'll just pretend the zigzags are on purpose."

"I had that on my mental list. To train him, that is. I can do it this weekend before that family reunion pulls in for a week next weekend."

"I completely forgot all about that. We'll have to get the arena ready for them too."

We both glanced to the fenced arena past the barn. "That's why I started on the fence. And Dylan knows. He's going to work on the arena after the rain we're expecting tonight. I reminded him to wear a mask, too." Dylan was one of the ranch hands who helped the most in the arena when we had tourists come through.

Rosa's ranch also boarded horses whose owners couldn't properly house and care for them themselves. The big house served as a bed and breakfast, with outlying cabins that came in handy when a large party like the family reunion rolled through. I lived in one of the cabins. Most of the ranch hands lived nearby, but Dylan was the only one who also lived in one of the cabins, which was convenient if the horses got out, or if any wild animals ventured onto the property. The inconvenient part about him living a few cabins down from me was that he was a former one-night stand of mine. Though truthfully, it wasn't all that awkward now, as a deep friendship had grown from that experience.

When I first came to Rosa six years earlier, I behaved a little recklessly. Six had kept me on lockdown for five months until things died down a little. After he'd procured enough documentation for me to live freely under my new, chosen name, Andra Walker, he sat me down and told me he was going to send me to stay with his mother's friend, Rosa. I knew Six had to get on with his life, and I needed to get on with my own, so he sent me here for employment and a place to live. For a foundation. And, I think he knew I needed a babysitter.

It took me a week before I'd set my sights on Dylan. I know how it sounds. I needed to experience something consensual. I wanted power, I wanted the choice. Call it what you will, but I needed to move forward in all aspects of my life.

Unfortunately, I didn't make my intentions clear to Dylan before the night I followed him into his cabin. I was a "one and done" sort of girl. That night was the beginning and end of our sexual relationship.

I'm not afraid of love. I'm not scared of the big C word: Commitment. But Six and Rosa are the only two people who know me. Not Andra Walker, but the girl I was before. Cora Mitchell. They know the road I've taken. I can't afford to share that with anyone else, so it's not fair to play with someone's feelings if I'm not going to allow them to know the real me. My experience with Dylan reminded me the importance of honesty. I liked having choices, not allowing anyone inside. There was darkness in my soul, abused innocence. My darkness was mine alone to carry; I didn't want to burden anyone else with it.

After the Monster woke up and found me gone, he reported me to the police as a runaway. When my history of complaints to school counselors surfaced, suspicions were raised about what had really happened to me. The media reported every time the Monster was pulled in for questioning. A warrant was issued for the apartment we lived in, but of course, nothing was found.

As tips stopped coming in, the online sleuths started speculating. I spent those five months with Six in his basement guest room, and that gave me a lot of time to study all the blogs that popped up, the forum threads, all with web detectives hypotheses of what could have happened to me. The most popular hypothesis was that my uncle was involved. But my case was cold; the only thing everyone could agree on was that I had disappeared.

Six coached me on what to say and how to act so I wouldn't cause doubt in the minds of anyone I encountered. It was the same rehearsed lines over and over.

"I'm estranged from my parents" – which was less suspicious than having deceased parents. All I had to do was gesture towards my multiple piercings and tattoos and it was assumed that I had strict, disapproving parents.

"I was homeschooled" – which made not having class reunions or close friendships understandable.

"I grew up in Los Angeles" – big city. I studied enough maps to come up with a neighborhood that the fictional Andra Walker had lived in. Rosa and I took a trip to Los Angeles after I'd been working for her for a year under the guise of visiting my family. We chose an easy to remember neighborhood and if I played off the sheltered life story, it was believable. And Six had moved to the west coast a few years after my disappearance, so he was a good frame of reference for me to share experiences that weren't actual truth.

Those were the main answers I used. I used them so often in fact, I was starting to believe them myself. It was a nicer story than the nonfiction version of my life:

I ran away from my uncle after years of sexual abuse. My mom died a tragic death and my dad was a nobody.

I went to a normal school, tried to report my abusive uncle and when it backfired on me, the abuse escalated.

I grew up in a town in Michigan that still believes I was murdered by my uncle.

Don't get me wrong, I didn't host a big, dramatic pity party. My life was good. I had Six, I had Rosa, and once Dylan got over the fact that I essentially used him, we became good friends. I had Clint, I had the other employees on the ranch, the horses, and a cozy little home. But most importantly, I had a life, and choices.

"Girl, what's in your head that's got you so distracted?" Rosa cut through my thoughts.

I shook my head, and tried to focus on something else I needed to think about. "Running over the guest list for this weekend," I replied, looking down at my boots. Rosa was the only person in the world who could tell when I was lying.

She didn't say anything for a moment. I waited for her to call me out on my lie, but she just sighed before asking, "Cabins or big house?"

"Three in the big house and one in the cabins. The cabin rental is for a month."

Rosa shoved her hands in her front pocket and grabbed a sponge from the bucket. "That's right, the writer. Wants a quiet place to finish his manuscript." She frowned as she wrung out the sponge. "He's the one waiting for his fancy new house he just bought to be completed." She started where I left off on the fence, so I grabbed an old rag to work beside her.

"That's him. Julian Jameson. Goes by J.J. He made sure to make note of that on his reservation." I might have said that last part snidely. I experienced my fair share of snobs, being an hour from the popular Coloradan ski resorts. But something about Julian Jameson's email correspondence had turned me off. Writers in general made me nervous, but snobby ones made me quickly lose my patience.

Rosa laughed. "Let's see if he likes when you blatantly refuse to call him what he prefers. Kill him with kindness, sweetheart."

Rosa knew I would never be intentionally rude to someone providing me a paycheck. But I also wouldn't put up with pretentious assholes. "You get me, Rosa. And that's why you're my favorite."

Rosa laughed. "Yeah, and the feeling is mutual. Just don't tell Clint." She winked, before heading back into the big house.

"Or Farley!" I called after her. I heard her laugh before I turned around and finished the section of fence I was working on.

After finishing the fence, I ran another report for Rosa and then went into the supply closet off the kitchen to grab a few things to stock the cabin being rented by the mystery author later that day. All of our guests were treated to a welcome basket that had brochures featuring local attractions, some of Rosa's famous huckleberry popcorn, a keychain with Seven Diamond Ranch's logo, and other Seven Diamond Ranch swag.

Loading some fresh towels and toiletries into my messenger bag, I glanced at my watch. It was just past noon, which still gave me two hours until check in for the cabin's month-long guest.

There were fifteen cabins on Rosa's property, with all of them being set just to the edge of the forest that the entire property was surrounded with. The first fourteen cabins were studio-style, with open areas for the bedroom, living room, dining room, and kitchen. The only actual room in the cabins was the bathroom, which was unusually large. The last cabin, which was the one I lived in full time, had been converted four years earlier with Rosa and Dylan's help. I'd wanted a separate space for my bedroom. I sacrificed having a bathtub in the original bathroom to make adequate space for the bedroom and installed a stall shower in the bathroom instead. I sometimes missed not having the bath to leisurely lounge around in, but living and working on a ranch kept most of my leisure time occupied.

Each cabin was spaced about thirty feet apart with gravel driveways between them, to allow for some semblance of privacy, though they weren't soundproof. Which was why I'd chosen cabin fifteen, so my only neighbors were cabin fourteen and the forest beyond the cabins.

The forest served as a reminder of my escape years earlier, something that comforted me. I didn't often lose myself in thoughts of my former life. I didn't look behind me as much anymore and I didn't let myself think too much about the Monster or what became of him. I was safe here, and I was happy. Six visited a few times a year, and Rosa was the foundation of my life. Six knew what he was doing when he sent me to her.

Unlocking cabin ten, I set the basket on the small dining table and brought the towels to the bathroom, pausing to open the blinds and curtains around the cabin. While in the bathroom, I looked at my reflection for a moment. My hair was still in the messy bun on top of my head, with a few tendrils loose, unintentionally framing my face.

I wasn't naïve or self-conscious about my physical features. I had large, wide, hazel eyes, high cheekbones, and a small mouth, with full lips. I pierced my lower lip on one side and favored a small hoop ring. My mother was Greek, and I had inherited her certain je ne sais quoi that had people pondering my nationality. I still resembled the girl on all the MISSING posters, but I lived far enough away from Michigan to ensure that the chances of someone recognizing me were very minimal. And that lip ring proved enough a distraction that people didn't get too caught up in the rest of my face.

I turned my head towards the mirror. Today I wore my work face, which was little mascara and lip gloss if I remembered to apply it, with a nice smear of dust gracing my jawline. The nice thing about summer was the tan it gave me, making my need for cover-up or foundation nonexistent. I never knew if I would be crunching numbers, cleaning empty cabins, shoveling hay or horse shit, so I found makeup kind of unnecessary. The horses didn't care if my lashes were voluminous and they didn't appreciate lip gloss kisses.

While rubbing the leftover dust on my jawline, I heard the unmistakable sound of tires coming up the gravel road. I knew we weren't expecting any deliveries, so I slung my messenger bag over one shoulder and walked back to the front door of the cabin I'd left open to see if I recognized the vehicle.

A sleek midnight blue convertible came into sight. The driver, clearly unfamiliar with driving on gravel roads fishtailed up the driveway a bit before slowing to a snail's pace. I snorted.

Before I knew it, I was stalking out to the entrance of the big house, where the convertible was pulling in to park. As the dust around the car died down, the top of a very dark head of hair came into view. I frowned, trying to figure out who it could be, when the door opened, and the driver climbed out.

He was wearing shiny, dark grey shoes. His long legs - he had to be well over six feet tall - came into view as he stood up, allowing his light grey slacks to fall just perfectly from his narrow hips. A white dress shirt was tucked into the slacks, which were secured with a thin black belt. I only had the back view of him as he reached in the backseat to grab something, but what a view it was. This man was not allergic to the gym. Even as covered up by clothing as he was, I could see the muscle tone through his shirt, and the muscles of his forearms, exposed by his rolled up sleeves. His dark hair was short on the sides with a little length on top, and I could just make out some facial hair, at least a couple weeks growth, lining his jawline.

Yum. That's basically what I was thinking.

And then he turned to face me. His expression when he saw me was stunned. No matter my lack of naiveté about my attractiveness, I knew I wasn't looking particularly drop-dead gorgeous at the moment, so my guard was up. His expression lasted for just a second before he broke into a smile. The smile crinkled up around his bright brown eyes and his appeal burst through the roof of my suddenly instantaneous desire. I was in trouble.

"See something you like?" he called out.

Big trouble. Clearly, he'd caught me staring. Cocky bastard. Reaffirming my annoyance at his entrance, I stalked closer to him. "Just trying to figure out where you're headed," I replied, stopping ten feet from him, making it a point to eye his vehicle and his clothing, confusion clear on my face.

He cocked his head to the side, "Pardon?"

"Well, I don't know anyone who'd show up to a dude ranch in fancy shoes and clothes fit for an office in a high-rise," I answered, arms crossing my chest.

He narrowed his eyes at me, but the corners of his lips lifted up in a crooked smile. "Would you prefer I show up in obviously brand-new cowboy boots, jeans fresh from the store, and a goofy hat that wasn't even broken in yet?"

He had a point. There really was nothing worse than a fake cowboy. "Okay city boy," I conceded and nodded at his convertible. "Where do you need directions to? I'm afraid we're about forty minutes from the interstate, but I-"

"This is where I'm supposed to be," he interrupted. The way he said it sounded like he meant it in more ways than one. It sounded so sure. The intensity in the way he looked directly into my eyes made the power behind his words that much more affirming.

"Well," I said, rounding his vehicle and leaning over to unabashedly peek in the backseat. "You don't look like the veterinarian." I noted the suitcases on the butter leather seats and continued walking around, running my finger across the layer of road dust that had formed over the beautiful paint job.

His body turned to follow my path around the car. I had to give it to him; he didn't look at me lewdly. Instead, he looked at me like he was trying to memorize my movements.

"No," he said, stepping closer to me as I rounded the hood of his car. He put his palm out. "I'm J.J. Julian Jameson. I'm renting a cabin here for four weeks."

Ah. I eyed him shrewdly. I looked at his hand before meeting his steady gaze and reluctantly put my hand in his. Instantly, I felt the pull that had only been teasing me from afar. His eyes widened for a moment and I knew he felt it too. This wasn't the insta-love of teenage romances. It was totally honest insta-lust. I resisted the sudden urge to lick my lips in anticipation.

"Andra," I said, after discreetly clearing my throat. "I wasn't expecting you for a couple more hours."

Instead of letting go of my hand, Julian stepped closer and lifted his left hand to hold the outside of my right hand, which was still grasped with his. His touch was warm and sure. It only enhanced the electricity around us.

"Andra," he repeated, seeming to roll the word around his tongue. I swallowed hard. He tracked the movement of my throat with his unwavering intensity before continuing. "Well, I hate to keep a lady waiting," he replied, smiling softly while running his thumb over my knuckles. The touch sent goose bumps up my arms. Shaking my head, I pulled my hand away as casually as possible.

"I think you'll find that I don't sit around and wait for anything, Mr. Jameson," I replied pointedly and then gestured to the steps up to the entrance to the big house. "If you'd follow me, I'll get you checked in and set up for your stay."

As I climbed the stairs, I shook my arms, trying to release the tension. I couldn't remember the last time a man had affected me so intensely. I was going to have to keep my hormones in check for this one.

"You can call me J.J.," he said from behind me, interrupting my thoughts.

I grabbed the door handle and turned around to him while opening it. "I prefer Julian." I smiled sweetly at him, in challenge, a little annoyed that he'd affected me so much with just the brush of his thumb over my knuckles earlier.

We stood on the porch just staring at each other for a moment before he grinned widely at me. He stepped closer and I didn't allow him the pleasure of seeing me step backwards in retreat. He lifted his hand to my face and I kept my eyes glued to his as his fingers paused at my hairline for a moment before tucking a wayward tendril behind my ear. His thumb traced the bottom of my ear lobe in a warm whisper before he leaned down to that same ear. "As you wish," he replied before stepping back and walking through the open doorway, the scent of sandalwood following him. My ear tingled.

I lifted my hand to my ear, and felt my fingers trembling. What the hell was that? Three minutes after meeting him and I was practically panting like a dog in heat. I tugged my earlobe stubbornly.

I followed Julian in and rounded the reception desk, making sure to keep a safe distance from him. I grabbed the set of keys from the drawer and slid the signature pad in front of him. I typed his name into the software we used to keep track of reservations. "Since you already electronically signed our rules and policies contract, there's not much I need from you besides your driver's license and credit card for incidentals."

After he fished the two cards out of his wallet and slid them to me, I recited our disclaimers while documenting the license and credit card into our system. After handing both back to him, I grabbed the map of the property we provided each guest. "Here," I said, leaning over the paper and circling a cabin on the map, "is your cabin. This is obviously the big house. Here are the pastures and the horse stalls. Please remember not to go into these areas unless accompanied by staff and please do not feed the horses. Since you'll be here for an extended duration of time, you'll probably see people in the barns, out in the pastures, or training in the arena with the horses. They are the owners of the horses we board."

I brushed a tendril away from my eyes and looked at him to make sure he was paying attention. He was. Completely. My eyes locked onto his chocolate-colored ones for a moment before I swallowed hard. This man was wholly focused on me. It was simultaneously thrilling and terrifying.

"We have paddle boats and mountain bikes available to rent at no cost to all guests. ATVs can be rented, but we ask that you keep them on the trails mapped out on this map," I said, gesturing to the maps to side of the desk. "You can arrange to take a horse on the trails as well, though we require that you hire a guide to join you for your own safety and the safety of our horses. And helmets are supplied and required for riding any bike, ATV, or horse." I straightened to stand and avoided looking back at him.

I passed the keys over and was more than a little disappointed when Julian's hand didn't linger on mine when he took them from my palm. "If you need anything, you can ask Rosa or me. Rosa runs this place; you'll know her when you see her. Any of the ranch hands can help you if you feel inclined to ride the horses. You can usually find me in here, by the cabins, or out by the gardens in the back."

With my arm extended, I motioned for us to move back onto the porch. "You're in cabin ten. Cabin one is used as a full-time residence for the lead ranch hand, Dylan. If something goes bump in the night, he's the one you call. Just dial 01 for his cabin." I walked down the steps, heading towards cabin ten. I heard his footsteps crunching the grass behind me, and lengthened my stride. I hesitated for a moment before saying the next part. "I'm in cabin fifteen. Call me if you need something more basic." I heard Julian cough-choke behind me before I turned around to face him.

"Basic?" he choked out.

I smiled up at him and walked closer, happy I finally had the upper hand in our verbal challenge. "Yes," I said huskily. I ran one finger down his sinewy forearm and licked my lips. "Like..." I started, inhaling his sandalwood and Julian scent. I locked gazes with him and then dropped my hand from his arm and grinned, "Towels, shampoo, more pillows, etcetera." I turned my back to him and opened the door back up to his cabin before turning back around to where he was, affording me a smile for my blatant flirting.

Julian hadn't moved from his spot. He started to laugh, a rich, full-bodied sound punctuating the air between us. "There's a lot of promise in that etcetera, Andra."

Despite the teasing, I knew I couldn't ignore the innate pull I felt whenever I caught his intense gaze. One thing I didn't like was playing games. If I was attracted to someone, I didn't make them guess what my feelings were. I respected and appreciated that Julian understood where we were inevitably headed.

"Perhaps," I replied with a small smile before turning around and sauntering back to the big house.

I'd been staring at the computer screen for seven hours and was in serious need of a break. I leaned back in my office chair and stretched my arms, staring at the ceiling above me. I put my feet up on my desk and leaned forward, stretching my legs and arms as I grasped my toes. And then, when I felt the stretch deep in my muscles, I let out a deep breath and leaned back again.

Leaning in the chair as far backwards as it would go, I bent my head towards each shoulder, trying to stretch the taut muscles of my neck when my eyes wandered to the cabins out my picture window. Cabin ten was lit up like a Christmas tree, and Julian's shadow passed in front of the windows every once in a while, indicating he hadn't left the cabin since I'd shown it to him. Not that I was paying any attention to him.

I didn't realize how long I'd been staring out that picture window until Rosa spoke from behind me.

"What do you think?"

I dropped my feet from the desk and straightened my chair in supersonic speed, embarrassed at having been caught staring.

I turned my face back to my computer screen and rubbed my neck. "Insurance is coming due on the ATVs and cabins soon, so that's going to eat a solid chunk next month. But that family reunion will more than make up for that, as will the wedding the weekend after they leave. I did the bank reconciliation for our main checking account and we are ahead anyway, thanks to the unseasonably warm weather we've had. Utilities have been lower than they were last year."

Rosa leaned over my shoulder to see the figures I was showing her. "Hmm," she said, peering through her glasses. "That's good to know, but you and I both know that's not what I was talking about."

Crap. I couldn't play innocent on this one. I looked at her, trying to hold back a smile. Rosa threw her head back and laughed. "Annie, honey, you're about as discreet as an elephant in a chicken coop." She put her hand on my shoulder as we both looked out the window at Julian's cabin. "Besides," she said before sighing, "he's got one hell of an ass."

Laughing, I shut the computer down and turned off the screens. "It's not bad."

"Don't pretend you haven't been staring at his cabin since he got here. I heard him pull in and saw your interaction with him. He's a charmer, that's for damn sure."

I rolled my shoulders as I stood up, trying to alleviate the tension from being hunched over my desk for so many hours. "You need to remind Clint I need his receipts for this week," I said, yawning.

"Go to bed, Andra. Receipts and reports can wait," she said, nudging me out the side door. "I'll lock up."

Impulsively, I turned around and wrapped my arms around Rosa. I was reminded of how my life had been without her in it, and couldn't imagine not waking up and coming to work with her every day. Best friend, confidant, mother. I felt her arms wrap around me and I closed my eyes, relishing the feeling of home Rosa gave me, and silently thanking whoever upstairs was keeping an eye on me, and bringing me this goodness.

"If this is you buttering me up for French toast on tomorrow's breakfast menu…" she started. She pulled back from me and set her hands on my shoulders, "You can count on it. And not because I'm moved by hugs or any of that nonsense, but because hugging you is like hugging a sack of bones," she said with a raised eyebrow.

I laughed out loud, knowing she didn't mean that. While I was fit from working on the ranch, I was far from being a sack of bones. But I knew emotions made Rosa uncomfortable, and we both knew she had a soft spot for me. "My plan worked then, I see." I winked at her and walked out the side door, down the steps.

I ran down the stairs and walked along the cabins, smiling to myself. There was nothing better than a warm summer night. And living as far out in the wilderness as we did granted us the most amazing view of the sky at night. I slowed my steps after passing Dylan's cabin and lay down on my back in the grass. The yard was silent except for a few noises from the stables and crickets that took shelter in the tall grass around me. The grass felt cool beneath me and I blew out a breath, enjoying the peace that settled over me. This was a ritual for me, on warmer nights. Lie in the grass, close my eyes, and soak up the comfort of the noises that made my home. This was my meditation, my church, my choice of relaxation. The fact that I had a choice at all was something I never took for granted. This life, this place, these people – all choices I'd made.

I took a deep breath in and out and closed my eyes before sending up my nightly prayer, in a whisper.

I wasn't a big fan of organized religion. I didn't attend church services or participate in Bible groups. I believed in God, but I didn't believe in taking everything the Bible said so literally. More than anything, I believed in goodness. And I believed that all the goodness around me was something to be thankful for, and the least I could do was honor the one I believed had brought the goodness to me.

"That's beautiful." His voice came out from the dark, right after I'd whispered my Amen. The interruption startled me and I quashed the instant embarrassment that he'd heard me pour my heart out in my prayer. No one was ever a witness to my nightly prayers, not since I was a child. Instantly, tension took hold of me and I turned my head to see him standing ten feet from me in the darkness, illuminated only a little by the lights on the big house.

His gaze, while ever intensely focused on me, was soft. I wasn't sure if it was a trick of the muted light on his face or his expression itself.

I sat up and looked down to pick at the invisible lint from my jeans. "How long were you standing there, Julian?" I asked, refusing to look at him.

I heard him move through the grass towards me before he swiftly and gracefully sat beside me. He had changed from business attire into sweats and a fitted tee. Still yummy, perhaps even more so.

"I heard a door shut from the big house," he motioned towards the porch I'd departed from minutes before. "I watched you walk across the grass and then you were gone. I was worried, so I came out."

I tamped down the instant pleasure I felt from his words and tried to turn his words into a joke. "Watching me, huh? Kind of creepy." I grinned at him. It didn't meet my eyes, I knew. I still felt uneasy, suddenly thrust into an awkward situation with a complete stranger. I never shared this part of myself with anyone. It would be like giving them a looking glass to the inside of my brain. I suppressed the shudder I felt at that. Even I didn't relish spending too much time inside my own head.

Julian didn't return the forced smile. He looked at me for a long moment with bemused brown eyes before reaching his hand down between us to pull up a blade of grass. "It's nice out here," he said, examining the blade of grass in his hands, holding it up so the light from the house washed over it. "I spend so much time inside, on my computer; I forget that there is another world outside of the machines I surround myself with."

I looked at his profile, silhouetted by the light. His eyes were focused away from me, out into the blackness of the forest we faced. The stubble on his jaw made him appear more effortlessly handsome than I remembered.

"This is my entire world," I said, gesturing the land, the big house, cabins, and the forest. It was a brave thing to admit to him, but after being witness to my nightly prayer, he might as well have seen me naked.

"It shows."

I looked over at him. His eyes were on me again, steady, sure. I was unused to such singular concentration by any man. He didn't look at me simply to look at me; it was as if he saw the holes inside and wanted to reach his hands in and open them up, to get a better look. But all he'd see was darkness.

I pulled my knees up to my chin and wrapped my arms around them, trying to stifle the tingle I was suddenly feeling.

"Cold?" He asked.

I shook my head. "You disarm me," I admitted, out loud, looking at my nails. Chipped nail polish. Perfect metaphor for how my armor felt around Julian.

When he didn't say anything, I turned my head his direction. He was staring at me like I was a puzzle he couldn't solve. I laid one side of my head on top of my knees, face turned towards him. "What?"

"Do you always talk this way? Openly, honestly?" he asked, turning his body so that he was fully facing me.

"I don't much care for playing hard to get," I said while shrugging, not completely answering his question.

"Why? Don't like being chased?" he asked, mouth quirked up in a half smile.

My head snapped up off of my knee in alarm and blood boomed in my ears before I blew out a breath. *Chill out, Andra.* "No," I answered, more firmly than I intended to. His eyebrows rose at that, so I scrambled for an answer. "I don't run very fast."

He laughed, brushing away my unease at the idea of being chased by anyone. He scooted closer to me. The hair on my arm stood on end.

"What about delayed gratification?" he murmured, now close enough to hear my sudden intake of breath.

I turned my body so we were now facing each other. "I'm afraid I prefer instant gratification, actually. I already know what the end game is, so why spend so much time getting there? Why hold back? Why wait?"

Julian frowned. It did delicious things to the shape of his mouth. "What are you saying? That we might as well hit up your cabin and knock boots?"

I laughed out loud at the phrasing. "Well, no, of course not," I started. "It would be your cabin, naturally. I'd feel bad booting you out of mine when this-" I gestured with my hand back and forth between Julian and me "was done. And besides, you don't have boots to knock."

Julian looked at me thoughtfully before rubbing the facial hair lining his jaw. "You've just made yourself a challenge."

I stopped smiling. "What do you mean?"

"I am going to challenge you to find pleasure in delayed gratification," he said. "Come on a date with me. Tomorrow. I can prove to you that some things are worth waiting for." His gaze on me was intensely focused. As usual.

One date wasn't a total deal breaker for me on my path of avoiding commitment. "Okay. What time?"

Julian grinned, eyes crinkling at the edges. He was a beautiful man, but when he smiled, he was absolutely dazzling. I felt my stomach clench with impatient desire. "I'll pick you up at seven."

"Perfect," I agreed before launching up off the grass onto my feet. I brushed my hands over the back of my jeans before instinctively reaching a hand down to help pull him to his feet. As he reached his hand up to clasp mine, I pulled back like I'd been burned.

His hands on me did scary things to my composure. "Never mind, you're capable."

Julian stood and faced me. "Quite capable, I assure you. Walk you to your door?"

I snorted. Ladylike was my middle name. "Sure, let's do that." We walked to my cabin in comfortable silence, the only noise being the crickets and general forest noises.

When we reached my door, I grabbed the keys in my pocket to unlock the door. When the door swung open, I reached a hand inside, feeling for the switch, and turned on the porch and main room lights. Julian stood just off the porch, hands in his pockets. "Do you want to come in for some coffee?" I asked, my head tilted to the side in question.

Julian didn't respond for a moment, but stepped closer. "Do you have tea?" he asked.

Damn it. I didn't drink coffee and didn't even own a coffee maker. It was mostly a ruse to get him to come inside. I wasn't absolutely desperate to have him in my bed (only a little bit), but I could stand for first base. "You're in luck," I said, gesturing for him to come inside. "I happen to have a collection of teas."

Julian walked inside my cabin and I followed him in, appreciating the view before side-stepping him into the small kitchen that was open to the rest of the living space, separated from the living area with a small island, long enough to seat three people.

I followed his gaze around my cabin, taking in what he was seeing. It was a large open space, with high beam ceilings. My décor was mostly white and black, with random splashes of color here and there. I had painted the wood floors white one night years before in an effort to brighten up the place. It had worked. I kept the walls their true wood tone, but wrapped white Christmas lights around the exposed beams above. The only wall that wasn't natural wood was the long wall that ran from one side of the cabin to the other, separating this front half from the back half of my cabin, where my bedroom, closet, and bathroom were.

I had half a dozen colorful throws tossed over the living room furniture: a small black sectional and two leather chairs. The walls of my living room were covered in thick frames with various black and white prints of people and places. My coffee table was rectangular and white washed, a bevy of coffee table books stacked in the center. I kept it minimal, kept things neat.

He walked over to the bookshelf I had installed above and around my small sectional sofa. It ran the width of that wall and was crammed with books and wooden trinkets that Six sent me from his travels.

"Your cabin is different than mine," he said, looking back at me.

I filled a kettle with water and set it on the stove. "Set me back a lot of money to make it this way."

"You have a lot of books on the royals," he commented, before pulling one down to examine.

I shrugged, even though he couldn't see me. "It's interesting to me." Several of the photographs on the walls were of the more unknown royals.

Julian moved to the frames hung next to the shelving unit, the only personal photos I kept in the apartment. I saw him focusing on one of Six and me.

"Make yourself at home," I muttered as I grabbed mugs from above the sink. I heard his answering chuckle.

"Is this your brother?"

"Yes," I said without hesitation. When he said nothing else, I grabbed my tray of paper-wrapped tea bags and walked over to set it on the coffee table.

"You look younger here," he commented before tapping the frame.

"Well, I certainly wasn't older," I replied sarcastically, just a few feet behind him.

Julian turned to face me and smiled. I didn't know what to do besides awkwardly stare at his face, his sexy short facial hair, so I nodded my head towards my book shelves. "Sorry, nothing up there is yours," I said, shrugging my shoulders.

"I didn't notice," he replied before sitting down on my sofa.

I sat on the chaise part of the sectional and again gestured with my hands at the collection of books. "What kind of novels do you write?"

"I don't think they'd be your taste," he started. At the narrowing of my eyes, he quickly continued. "Not to say there is anything wrong with your tastes, but judging by all the historical non-fiction you have, I'd say my books haven't been fortunate enough to live on your shelves yet."

Hearing the water sizzling in the kettle I stood up. "Why, do you write romance novels that are constipated with angst?"

Julian's laughter lit up my cabin with warmth. That warmth moved me to smile at him before moving to the kitchen. "Wrong guess?" I asked over my shoulder.

He joined me in the kitchen, leaning against the wall that separated us from my bedroom. Heat burned a hole through my stomach at his closeness, at his gaze. "I write mystery novels," he replied.

I looked up at him as I poured the water. "Oh?" I asked. I already knew that.

"Yes." He didn't elaborate.

"Help yourself to your preferred flavor of tea. I set them on the coffee table." I poured water into the two mugs I'd set out and handed him one before making my way to the sofa.

I grabbed the raspberry bag I favored and dunked it up and down in my mug absentmindedly. Out of the corner of my eye, I saw Julian grab the mint before settling into the leather arm chair adjacent to the sectional sofa.

I watched him as he stretched his legs in front of him. There was a grace in how he did everything, with an undercurrent of confidence and power. Even in sweats, he displayed a definite air of elegance. Probably came from money.

My eyes lingered on his hands as he swirled the tea bag around his mug. His hands held that same power, as if they could crush the mug he held without much effort. His fingernails were short, but clean, probably due to his occupation. "How long have you been a writer?" I blurted out, finally looking away from his hands to make eye contact.

Julian leaned into the armchair's backrest, effectively stretching his tee tight across his chest, defining every muscle hidden behind the cotton fabric. "Ever since I graduated high school and decided I didn't want to make football a career for myself. So, about seven years."

That put him at about twenty-five years old, two years older than I was. I nodded my head in response and drank my tea, settling back into the sofa's cushions. "A football player, huh?" I asked.

Julian rubbed his knee as if lost in a memory before taking a sip of his tea and nodding. "All four years of high school, I played. I was good at it." He winked, a playful grin stretching his lips.

"I'm sure." I took another sip of the tea before asking, "So why quit?"

Julian set his mug on the table before angling his body more in my direction. "Have you ever done something for so long that it becomes second nature to you? So long that you don't know what life is like without it? And that doesn't mean it's necessarily a good thing for you, mentally or physically, but you continue to do it because it's what's expected of you?"

The hair on my arms was standing on end. This was getting deeper than I expected. I nodded my head, unable to speak through the lump that had taken up residence in my throat.

"Well then you can understand, maybe, the need I felt to break free. To prove I could change what I was supposedly destined to be. To do something for myself." He uttered that last word with gruffness in his voice. I met his eyes and saw the feeling behind his words reflecting in his expression.

"Yes. I know what you mean," I said, swallowing hard behind the lump in my throat.

We just looked at each other for a few more moments before Julian stood up, grabbing his mug and making his way to the kitchen to rinse it out. "Thanks for the tea. I should get going."

Despite my attraction to him, the energy from our conversation was making me nervous so I didn't try to dissuade him from returning to his cabin. I followed him into the kitchen and placed his mug into the dishwasher. He was braced with his back against the counter opposite from me, his hands gripping the counter behind him. "Thanks for the company," I replied, smiling softly.

Julian pushed himself away from the counter and made his way to the door while I followed behind. He stopped at the threshold and turned to me, leaning a hand against the frame, putting his face mere inches from mine. "I live a lot of my life inside, writing, editing. It was nice to have someone to talk to," he said.

My body was practically vibrating from the closeness of his body to mine. "It was nice," I agreed, wrapping my arms across my chest.

The side of his mouth twitched up in a half smile before he leaned in, his cheek coming in contact with mine, his mouth at my ear. "Sweet dreams, Andra," he whispered before pushing off the door frame and striding out into the darkness towards his cabin.

I told myself I was watching him to ensure he made it to his cabin safely. But truthfully, and I couldn't explain it, my eyes needed to study him, as he'd seemed to study me. There was no doubt I was drawn to him, drawn to the subdued power in his eyes, in his words.

I tugged the ear he had whispered into when I saw his silhouette, illuminated by the light glowing inside his cabin, climb onto his porch. As soon as he was inside, I went back into my cabin and leaned my back against the interior side of the front door, heaving out a breath I didn't know I had been holding.

Julian Jameson was trouble. But damn if I wasn't enjoying it.

I have always been a little afraid, and a little intimidated of numbers. There is no dishonesty with math. There is only one answer to each equation I work with. There are no options, no escapes. Two plus two will always equal four. If my math is correct but the answer is wrong, I can't lie, I can't choose another outcome. That's a little frightening for a girl who has spent the last six years running on choices. Math is what I could never be: fixed, sure, honest.

Part of me would love to be brave by being honest. But my bravery is the reason for my fraudulent life. A life spun of lies and half-truths, stemming from the one brave moment I had when I doped up the Monster with sleeping pills and cold medicine. So I don't regret my bravery. My only regret is that it took me so long to drown the fear out with adrenaline, to tie my tennis shoes and finally run away.

And this is why I would rather spend my time swatting flies from my face, shoveling horse shit until my arms are aching and I've lost my sense of smell. Because being inside a room faced with numbers that will tell the truth unless I tell them to lie has to be some circle of hell, even if the room is blasting cold with air conditioning. And that's why, when I awoke the following morning, I bypassed the office entirely, seeking out a messy job.

I spent most of that day mucking out the horses' stalls. I needed the manual labor as much as I needed the comfort of the office some days. I'd woken up and immediately decided to clean the stables, needing to expel the excess energy from one of the most restless sleeps I'd had in months. I had no questions as to why I slept so poorly. I knew the answer.

Julian.

I had ear buds in, the melody of my favorite Queen album providing the soundtrack to my self-imposed chore. But not even

Freddie Mercury could distract me from the thoughts that betrayed me, straying towards the ranch's newest tenant.

With a growl, I wiped the sweat off my forehead with the back of my hand. Sweat soaked the long sleeve burnout shirt I was wearing and was collecting behind the knees of my skinny jeans, spilling into the rubber boots I wore.

The ranch hands had taken the horses out for exercise to allow me the space to clean. This was normally a task they took care of, but I'd volunteered earlier this morning as soon as I saw Dylan grabbing the pitchfork and shovel. I wanted to be physically worn out; hoping exhaustion would keep me from losing my head around Julian for our date later tonight.

And there I went again, thinking of him. I lay in bed the night before, remembering his voice tickling my ear, the way tingles had crawled down my arms. The way he had looked at me expectantly while we sat in the grass last night. The way he told me he accepted the challenge I didn't know I'd made him. I couldn't let him affect me so entirely. One and done, that was my motto. Anything more than that would be unfair.

After the floor had dried out in the last stall and I finished spreading the straw, I lifted my head and took a deep breath, pulling my shirt away from my chest, allowing some air to circulate. I glanced at the clock at the entrance of the stables. Three in the afternoon.

As if on cue, my stomach growled, pissed that I'd forgotten lunch. I made my way around the stables towards the big house, stripping my gloves off as I went. The sun was beating down, beckoning me to lie out and soak up some vitamin D. I jogged up the steps into the main entrance, stopped to toss my boots and socks by the door, and headed down the hall towards the laundry room.

Rosa was moving clothing into one of the dryers and looked over at me above her glasses when I walked into the room. "Have you been in the stables all day?" She asked, eyeing my sweat-soaked clothing.

I nodded as I stripped off my shirt, leaving the kelly green bikini swim top I wore underneath. Whenever I finished mucking out stalls, I always headed for the pond. The coolness felt good on my sore muscles, laying out on the floating dock helped deepen my olive skin tone, and the heat usually provided me a nap in the process. I always wore my bikini under my clothing when I knew it would be a manual labor kind of day.

Rosa caught my shirt when I tossed it to her, tossing it right into the wash. I hopped on one leg as I tried peeling the skinny jeans off my legs. Rosa laughed out loud when I plopped my butt on the floor to yank them off. The sweat had glued them to my legs.

Shoving the jeans in the wash, I grinned at Rosa as I moved back out the other side of the laundry into the kitchen. I grabbed two bottles of water from the fridge and a banana from the fruit bowl on the wide, white-marbled island. I sucked down the first bottle of water and tossed it into the recycle before moving out the kitchen door onto the wrap-around deck, banana and water in hand as I headed down the hill to the pond.

The sounds of summer greeted me in my brisk walk down. A circular saw in the garage, the neigh of the horses in the paddock, the sprinkler on the front lawn. The sky was a perfect blue, not a cloud in the abyss. It was an ideal day for a swim. I had meant what I said when I told Julian this was my world. The grass between my toes, the trees casting afternoon shadows over the pond, the dust being kicked up by the horses.

I didn't bother testing the water before getting completely in. Holding the banana and water bottle above the water, I walked in on the shallow side, heading towards the dock. I scissored my legs quickly, keeping my head and arms above water, until I reached the dock and set my snack on the pale wooden planks, pulling myself up next.

The pond was man-made. It was a home for just a few types of fish, but many types of vegetation. Lilly pads and cattails and duckweeds coexisted peacefully in the water. Along the edge of one side were large trees that provided shade over half the pond, along with a few types of wildflowers. Rosa's father had built the pond years ago to provide another kind of recreation for the ranch. In the summer, I spent hours upon hours in the pond, cleaning it or, like today, cooling my overheated muscles.

Opening the water bottle, I took in the view. Off to the right of the big house, I could see the last six cabins wrapped along the edge of the tree line. The sun glinted off the windows, making it impossible for me to capture a glimpse of Julian moving inside his cabin. I'd purposefully slowed my walk passed cabin ten on my way to the stables earlier this morning, but the lights were off and the shades were drawn.

I capped my water bottle before sliding into the pond to swim leisurely, letting the coolness of the pond soothe my tired limbs as I dove to the bottom, dragging my fingers through the roots emerging through the mud. Kicking my legs, I shot back to the surface.

I grasped the black band that held my hair back, undoing the messy bun I'd worn all day. My dark brown tresses fanned around me as I floated on my back, eyes closed. The heat of the sun clashed with the coolness of the water, making me sigh aloud in contentment.

After floating around for a little while, I climbed on to the dock and ate my banana, satisfying the growl of my stomach. After setting the peel on the dock, I twisted my long hair, wringing out the excess water. I left it twisted as I lay down on my back, the warmth of the wood underneath me and the sun above me lulling me to sleep.

I awoke to a large amount of water being tossed onto my body. The contrast of the heat from my sun-warmed skin and the seemingly ice cold water made me sit up with a start, my hair unraveling behind me.

I heard Dylan's distinct laugh in the distance and watched him haul himself onto the sandy beach across from me, his arm wrapped around his chiseled stomach in laughter. "About time you woke up sleepy head!" he yelled in between laughs. "You've been asleep for an hour!"

Shit. I glanced at my watch. It was already almost five, two hours before my date with Julian. As much as I wanted to be annoyed with Dylan, I was grateful for the wakeup call, though his method could use some refining. "Thanks a lot, dickhead!" I yelled back, in good humor.

Dylan slid his jeans back on over his now soaking wet boxers before reaching down with his long, muscled arm to grab his tee. I wasn't blind to his good looks. But our sexual history, however brief it was, was exactly that – history. I appreciated his excellent muscle tone, the way his bright blue eyes sparkled when he laughed, and his sun-highlighted blond hair. But my affection for Dylan was now that of a good friend. And that's all he would ever be for me.

Dylan looked over his shoulder at me, his amusement clear on his face. "Anytime, Andra," he replied, grinning. "I brought you a towel." He gestured towards the beach towel, folded on the sand, before he jogged up the hill.

I pulled my hair back into a bun on top of my head, securing it with the elastic, and slid off the dock, banana peel and water bottle in hand as I swam back to land.

I brushed the sand sticking to my wet legs before wiping down with the towel. I wrapped the towel around my waist and trudged up the grassy hill, not paying attention to the direction I was headed as I shook my arms, freeing the drops of water that had clung to my skin.

In an instant, I'd walked right into a wall. Or, it only felt that way. I was chest to chest with a wall of muscle that belonged to one Julian Jameson, currently clothed in a navy blue fitted tee, lying against his torso so that it was perfectly contoured to his muscles. I barely registered the warm hands that wrapped around my bare upper arms, steadying me.

My breath caught before I tilted my head up, meeting his deep, cocoa powder brown eyes. My eyes moved over that short hair on his beautifully sculpted jawline before meeting his eyes again and I bit my lip. This was the closest I'd been to him, face to face, breathing the same air. I'm not sure how long we stood there, looking at each other. I became aware of his breath, warm on my face. Cinnamon and sandalwood permeated the few inches of air that separated us.

"Andra," he said, the sound gravelly in his throat. His hands left my upper arms, and I nearly stumbled backwards from the loss of warmth. He made a move to grab me again, but I stepped backwards, out of reach. My hands gripped the banana peel and water bottle, grounding me, reminding me of what I was doing.

"I was just swimming," I blurted out. It sounded defensive. Why?

Julian allowed a smile to lift one side of his lips. "I know," he murmured. He looked pointedly at the bikini top before looking back at me. I saw his Adam's apple bob in his neck before he took a hesitant step backwards. The distance felt like an ocean in regards to breathing room, but I was still wrapped up in his presence and felt the goose bumps rise up on my skin instantaneously. "I was coming to find you. Does seven still work for you?"

I nodded, and licked my lips. "I was just heading up to get ready. I'm guessing bikini wear is out for wherever we're going?" I gestured across my body with my water bottle.

Julian's eyes raked over my torso. A muscle twitched in his jaw. "Unfortunately, yes. Dinner in a restaurant is what I'd planned on." His voice sounded gruff and I was pleased that he seemed to be tracking the movement of the droplets of water sliding down my front, disappearing into the towel around my hips.

I smirked, feeling a little more level headed. "What didn't you plan on?" I exaggerated a wink, attempting to lighten the heady tension.

Julian laughed and tucked one hand in a pocket of his khaki cargo shorts. "You. I definitely didn't plan on you." He drew his free hand through his hair and shook his head, an amused expression lightening up his features.

It could have sounded like a line coming from anyone else, but from Julian, it felt natural, and honest. An area deep within my chest bloomed with warmth. I couldn't help the smile that curved my lips. "I'll take that as a compliment."

I stepped around him, intending to head to my cabin before his hand on my shoulder stopped me. I looked at him with an eyebrow raised.

He looked at me with an unspoken question on his lips, eyebrows drawn together in concentration, before reaching behind me, cradling the back of my head. My eyes closed involuntarily and I sucked in breath through trembling lips. I felt his fingers delve into my hair, right under the bun I'd made. And, just as soon as I'd readied myself to be pulled closer, I felt his fingers skillfully remove my hair tie, allowing my hair to cascade down my back.

I opened my eyes, watching his face as he brushed a hand through my hair, resting his hand on my back right where the hair ended, just below the bikini's strings. His features softened, his expression turned appreciative. "Wear your hair down," he murmured, "tonight."

I didn't trust my voice just then. I met his eyes and nodded. His hand slipped away from my back and he smiled tightly at me before abruptly turning away and walking up towards the big house.

I was slicking a baby oil and lotion mixture over my freshly showered limbs when a knock sounded at my door, loud and quick.

"Shit," I muttered, rapidly rubbing the moisturizer over my thighs. My soaking wet hair hung over one shoulder, drenching the towel I had wrapped around my body. I stood up and walked towards the door, clutching the towel tightly around my body as I glanced at the wall clock. It was barely six. It couldn't be Julian already. Unless he was annoyingly early, which was a possibility.

I poked my head in between the curtains shielding the window next to my door. I was able to make out the short black bob hair style and the trademark black clothing. Rosa.

I quickly flipped the deadbolt and opened the door. Even with my state of undress, Rosa walked into the cabin and waved her hands at me. "Kind of an odd time of day to be showering, isn't it?" she asked as she sat in the chair closest to my wood stove. It was an oversized leather armchair, and Rosa's favorite place to relax when she was in my cabin.

I walked behind the kitchen island that served as a seating area, wringing my wet hair into the island's steel sink. "Got a date."

Rosa sighed. I chewed my lip ring nervously, waiting for the speech she had on the tip of her tongue. When she didn't say anything, I walked back into the bathroom to grab the microfiber towel I used to dry my hair before returning to the living area.

Rosa watched me as I scrunched my hair with the towel, not saying anything. After a minute of me standing there, in only a towel, I turned into my bedroom and quickly threw on some yoga pants and a zipped hoodie. I rubbed some Moroccan oil into my hair before grabbing a second microfiber towel, throwing the first one into my hamper.

She was still in the arm chair, eyeing me shrewdly. I huffed a little and sat on my sectional, continuing to towel-dry my hair. When she still remained silent, I gestured wildly towards her with the towel in hand, indicating that I was waiting for her to say what she wanted to say.

Rosa laughed softly. "You're going to break another heart, Annie."

"It's only one date," I scoffed.

"He'll be here for another month. You just met him yesterday. And after tonight, you won't see him again."

Rosa knew me better than anyone, even better than Six. She knew my modus operandi. Though I never dated in the traditional sense, she knew that I never saw the same man more than once. Dylan was the only exception, but I worked with him, and he never asked for more from me after our one night.

"I'll still be here, so of course I'll still see him," I answered, a little defensively. Rosa never actually interfered in my life outside the ranch. But I could understand her concern this time. This was the first time I'd held any interest in a tenant.

"I don't want to get involved, it's your life. But I don't want an unhappy tenant or any sort of awkward-" she waved her hand in the air, searching for her word "-tension."

I sighed and sank further back into the cushions, setting the towel down as I met her eyes. "What do you want me to do?" I asked. Truthfully, I would do anything for Rosa. She was the mother I'd lost, the girlfriend I was deprived of, the protector I never really had. "Should I cancel?"

Rosa sat up in the chair and rubbed her knee thoughtfully. "No. No, don't cancel. But don't let it get serious. Or if it does, don't drop him when you get skittish."

"I'm not skittish, Rosa. I just can't make promises that extend further than the bedroom."

"Ah!" Rosa clapped her hands over her ears. "I don't need to know that!" She said in protest. "All I'm asking is that you don't push him away tomorrow if you actually like him. What is the harm in a summer romance?"

Rosa was visibly uncomfortable having this conversation and immediately guilt flooded in, overpowering the pull I instinctively felt towards Julian. I scooted towards her and grabbed her arm. "Rosa." I waited until she met my gaze. "If we have chemistry on our date, I promise you I won't let it get awkward. If we don't have chemistry, it won't be awkward," I said earnestly.

Rosa smiled at me, still uncomfortable, but patted my hand. "That's all I wanted to hear. Now," she started, wiggling her eyebrows at me, "what are you wearing?"

We spent the next fifteen minutes picking out my dress – a one shoulder black dress that hugged my figure, stopping just above my knees. The top half was black lace, tied with black ribbon over one shoulder, with a thin black belt cinching my waist. I paired it with black platform heeled shoes that had horizontal glittery gold stripes on the heels. I wore my hair, curly and wild, over the bare shoulder and put some quartz dropped earrings in, fingering the delicate gold wire that wrapped around the stone.

Rosa left after giving me a hug and a reminder to tread lightly.

While I usually avoided wearing makeup during the day, I knew enough about it to give me the look I desired. I applied heavy black liner and gold eye shadow, smudging it into the black liner so it wasn't a clean line, and then two coats of mascara. Nude glossy lips completed the look. I spritz on some perfume and twirled in front of my floor length bedroom mirror.

Butterflies flew around my stomach, frantic. I pressed a hand there and looked at myself in the mirror, and saw the nerves reflected in my gold-green eyes. I'd implied to Rosa that chemistry with Julian was hypothetical when I knew it wasn't. There was no doubt that we had chemistry. Which only complicated my promise to Rosa to not cause tension or discomfort.

The knock on the door did nothing to calm the butterflies, but I strode to answer nonetheless. I laid my forehead against the smooth wood surface for a moment, breathing in deeply, bracing myself for what was waiting for me on the other side of the door. I pushed away and then pulled it open with more force than necessary.

Immediately I met Julian's eyes. Our eyes remained firmly focused on one another for a beat before Julian's thickly-lashed eyes swept down. The way his eyes glided down me felt as physical as the touch of a hand. My arms were once again covered in goose bumps. The space that separated us was strained with undeniable, raw tension.

I took the opportunity to take in his dark charcoal suit. It was tailored perfectly to his body and paired with a white dress shirt and skinny black tie. The way he wore the suit hinted at the muscular quality of his body. The hair on top of his head was that perfect mussed-up-but-still-neat style. In his hand he held a bouquet of white roses.

I tried to relieve some of the toe-curling tension by gesturing towards the bouquet. "Where did you manage to find those?"

Julian held up his hand and looked at the bouquet, seemingly embarrassed. "I didn't realize the florist shop in town was closed on Saturdays unless you had an appointment. Luckily, I ran into a cousin – or sister, not completely sure – at the grocery store-"

"Mac's grocery," I interjected. "His sister-in-law owns the flower shop. You probably ran into Mac's wife."

Julian nodded, "thankfully she took pity on me and opened up the cooler for me to snag these." He held them towards me and ran a hand through his hair when I grabbed them in both hands.

I smiled. "Thank you. Let me put these in water before we leave. Come in," I motioned with my hand.

As soon as Julian stepped up into the cabin, his presence invaded the room, stifling what little breathing room I had left. I noticed that the heels I was wearing made us almost the same height. "Whoa," I said a little breathy. "You're…tall." Which sounded stupid, even to me. It wasn't as if it was the first time I'd been face to face with him.

Julian smiled wide, allowing that perfect dimple to dip into his cheek. "I'm 6'4". You must be, what, 5'10" or 11"?"

I nodded, backing up to give myself a little more space. "These heels add several inches, but yes, I'm quite tall."

Julian stepped closer. I backed up another step. The click of my heels on the hardwood brought me back to what I was doing and I turned to fill my favorite blue and white Moroccan vase. It was one of Six's many gifts he sent me on his travels for work. My hand traced the pattern absentmindedly for a moment before I refocused and assembled the roses into the vase.

Julian leaned forward on the opposite side of the kitchen island, bracing his hands on the granite counter. "You look incredible, by the way."

My eyes went straight to his hands. I eyed them almost warily. Not for the first time, I wondered what I was getting myself into.

"Thanks," I replied, fluffing the flowers. "You're not so bad yourself." I peeked at him beneath my lashes, noticing he was ever-intently watching me. He made me feel shy. I was not shy. I turned around, vase in hand, setting it on the counter near my window, and tried to calm my nerves. *This was just a date, Andra. Get it together.*

When I turned around, he cocked his head at me. "Are you ready?" His gaze was curious.

I smiled and grabbed my clutch from the table by the door, waiting for him to join me. When he walked out the door ahead of me, I switched off the lights, turned on the porch light, and locked the door behind me.

Julian's convertible was already on, humming from the narrow gravel driveway next to his cabin. The top was on tonight, which was good because the dust from the road would make us cough violently and our eyes would stream tears. And I wasn't wearing waterproof makeup.

We walked to the convertible without speaking, the sound of my heartbeat loud in my ears. The sun was low in the sky and my heels kept sinking into the soft soil. I crossed my fingers I wouldn't fall and tried for as much grace as possible each time I yanked my heel out of the grass.

He opened the passenger door and I slid in, smiling my gratitude, before he softly closed the door and made his way around to the driver's side. The leather was warm and comforting, and the interior smelled of sandalwood – just like its owner – with a faint trace of cinnamon. My eyes landed on the pack of cinnamon gum in his cup holder.

The driver's door opened and he slid into his seat, smiling at me before rummaging through the center console. He tossed me a small black case. "Here, you pick the music." He started backing out and heading down the driveway before I turned my attention to my lap.

I zipped open the case, pausing for a second at the first disc that greeted me. The CD design was white with yellow and blue paint splatters. OneRepublic. I flipped through the next few discs, noting the eclectic mix of modern day rock/pop, indie, soundtracks to some older movies, and 70s and 80s rock.

Out of the corner of my eye, I saw Julian sneak a few glances at me when I said nothing, still flipping through the pages of CDs. Towards the back, I found what I least expected. I recognized the way the Q was styled immediately. I paused longer on this disc than the others. I let my hand sit on the disc for a moment before looking at him. We approached one of the state highways and Julian headed east, towards the interstate.

"You listen to this?" I asked, tentatively. I worried my lip ring with my teeth, stifling everything I wanted to say.

Julian turned towards me, searching my eyes. "I do." His eyes did not once glance at the disc I was referring to. How did he know?

A moment later Julian slipped a hand to the headrest behind me and gently glided his fingers down the nape of my neck. "I noticed this, yesterday morning. When we met."

I knew he was referring to the tattoo inked on the back of my neck, but the touch of his fingers over the word marked into my skin sent tiny bolts of desire down my spine. He shifted his hand back to the steering wheel, and his eyes to the road. I swallowed hard. Despite the yearning I felt for him, I couldn't help the suspicion that narrowed my eyes. "Did you already have this CD when you saw my tattoo?"

I knew it was probably vain to assume he bought this disc after seeing my neck tattoo, but I couldn't help it. It seemed suspicious. I'd never dated someone who listened to Queen. Well, truthfully, I never really dated anyone.

Julian laughed easily beside me. "Well, if you haven't noticed, your tiny little town doesn't have any music stores. It's not like I made a mad dash for Denver to search high and low for this disc. But," he paused, looking at me again, "I can't lie to you. I didn't have this disc in my car yesterday afternoon."

I drew my eyes together in confusion. "Then where did you get it?"

"I'm remodeling a house about thirty minutes from the ranch. I go up there to check on the progress from time to time. I had the disc in my larger case in the storage there, and I grabbed it when I went up there this morning."

Oh, right. I had forgotten he was remodeling his big fancy house – Rosa's words – not too far from the ranch.

"Do you want to listen to it?" he asked, interrupting my thoughts.

"Hell yes," I said, sliding the disc out of its holder and into the CD player. I zipped up the case and put it back in the center console. A few seconds later, the bass of the stomp-stomp-clap of "We Will

Rock You" reverberated the inside of the car, pumping through the floorboards and the seats. I looked over at Julian with a grin and he laughed, tapping his fingers on the steering wheel in time with the beat.

I regarded Julian for a minute, willing him to look at me. When he finally did, I asked, "Can you please pull the car over?"

Julian cocked his head to the side with worry, but did as I asked, pulling off the shoulder of the highway and onto a grassy area. I didn't wait for him to say anything and instead opened my door, stepping out into the grass, closing my door behind me. I leaned my back against the car, closed my eyes, and calmed my breathing for a moment before Julian had rounded the car to where I was. I opened my eyes again, his presence blocking out everything else.

"Are you okay?" he asked, concern etched into his face, creating lines between his eyebrows.

I nodded, swallowing the tension that had stymied my voice. I pushed off the car, standing just a few feet from Julian. I heard my heart pounding in my ears but I stepped closer to him anyway, paying little attention to the anxiety rushing through my veins. Looking him in the eyes, I murmured, "I just need to do this." Before I could allow the protesting voices in my head change my mind, I reached forward and grabbed the back of his neck. I pulled his face slowly towards mine and took one deep, fortifying breath before I crushed my lips to his.

It took only a second before his arms slid around my waist, pressing my chest to his. He kissed me back with a fervor that rivaled my own. The anxiety in my veins was overpowered by the instantaneous lust that rippled through every part of my body. I thought by kissing him, I'd calm the ache I felt whenever I was around him. Instead, I felt like I was drowning in him, desperate for buoyancy in the sea of my need for him.

I let my hands tangle in the hair behind his ears, dragging my nails across his scalp. Julian's hands moved to the back of my head as he pushed me back against the car with little force. One hand moved into my hair and he twisted his fingers into my curls, tugging on them just enough to tilt my head back.

His lips left mine to travel along my jawline, slowly, kissing just behind my earlobe, before making their way back to my mouth, brushing his facial hair against my skin along the way. All the breath rushed out of my lungs and I gasped for air as his lips crushed against mine. One of my hands moved down to cup his jawline and I drew indefinite shapes into the hair that grew there with my thumbnail. He nipped at my upper lip and then my lower lip before sucking my piercing into his mouth. My knees grew weak and I gripped the back of his neck with more force than before. Something warm and heavy settled deep in my chest, depriving my lungs of the little remaining breathing room.

Julian pulled away and rested his cheek against mine, each of us trying to catch our breath. We were still tightly pressed together, his heartbeat rapidly echoing off of mine. My chest heaved as I gulped air and tried to calm the storm raging within me. His arms had slid over my shoulders, hands braced on the roof of the convertible. His upper arms rested gently on top of my shoulders in this position, sort of like a loose hug, and I ran my hands down his biceps, holding him in place, steadying myself. His weight on me was comforting, as if I was in need of comfort in some way.

I was completely oblivious to our surroundings, and suddenly thankful this road was not a busy one. I felt Julian's warm breath tickle my ear as our breathing leveled out.

"Thanks," I whispered right into his ear. I felt his returning smile against my cheek before he pulled back and looked at me face to face, his hands sliding to my shoulders. "I've wanted to do that since yesterday. And I couldn't wait any longer. I needed to get it over with," I said, smiling softly.

Julian's eyes closed briefly before he let out a laugh. Opening his eyes, he said, "Get it over with? Well, I can tell you that this-"he gestured between us "-is far from over. Especially after that kiss." He shook his head in amused disbelief.

His words should have scared me, but instead the warmth in my chest bloomed, surprising me. I rubbed my hands up and down Julian's suit sleeves, a gesture that was meant to calm myself more than him. He leaned forward and touched his forehead to mine. We were nose to nose, eyeing each other with a quiet hunger. His eyelids closed and I admired his long, inky black lashes, resting against the top of his cheekbones.

He took a deep breath and released it, warming my lips. My lips ached for the warmth of his mouth and I closed my eyes, gripping his forearms through the material. We breathed the same air for a moment longer before he pulled back with a sigh, slowly moving his hands from my shoulders, down over the bare skin of my arm. When his hands reached mine, he brought them both to his lips and kissed my knuckles softly, gazing at me. "Let's go eat," he whispered. He eased me towards him and released one of my hands, opening my door behind me. The end of "Killer Queen" poured out of the speakers.

He held my other hand as he helped me in the car, closing the door once I was safely in my seat. I expelled a deep breath and let my head rest against the headrest. As soon as Julian entered the car, the next track started playing. "Somebody to Love." Before I could change to the next track, Julian beat me to the stereo, changing to the next song and smiling ruefully at me, before pulling off the side of the road, towards our destination.

I flipped the visor down to fix my smeared lip gloss. My reflection showed lips red and swollen, and the skin along my jawline was pink. I touched my fingertips to the inflamed skin, running my fingers up to my ear and smiled, remembering the feel of his scruff on my skin. I peeked at Julian's profile and saw the smile curving on his lip gloss-stained lips.

As soon as Julian pulled into the parking lot of the notoriously expensive restaurant, I decided to have a little fun with him. He didn't know me well enough to know that I'd be happy with the McDonalds just down the road. Cloth napkins didn't impress me. Muted lighting and the din of hushed conversations didn't do it for me.

Julian knew the Andra who grew weak at the knees with his kissing prowess, but he didn't know the Andra who did not fit in at fancy establishments. The Andra who would prefer sweatshirts to slinky dresses, rubber boots to high heels. The Andra who spent more time outside than in, who reveled in the quiet the woods offered. There were reasons why I preferred the company of the animals and insects that lived in the dark to the company of the humans who walked on two feet.

After the kiss we'd shared, I wanted to lighten up the tension that still radiated off of us. I wasn't used to being this absorbed by one kiss. Julian was about to meet the Andra who could hold her own. The Andra I truly was.

As soon as we were seated at our table, I asked for an order of French fries with mayo and ketchup. The waiter looked at me confused before looking at Julian, as if seeking permission. My eyes narrowed a bit in annoyance but Julian looked amused at the exchange and said, "Fries to start and a bottle of the recommended wine." Julian looked to me with a question in his eyes.

"I'll take a beer, please." I smiled up at the waiter with my most charming smile.

"Then just one glass of the wine, please," Julian added. The waiter looked at me, trying to hide his displeasure at my order, but walked stiffly away, just as Julian reached into his interior suit pocket and frowned at his phone. "My agent is calling me. I'll just be a couple minutes. Sorry for this." He gestured to the phone in his hand. I waved him away, all too happy to have a moment to relax.

The waiter returned with our drinks and my fries a few minutes later. I mixed my mayo and ketchup together and dipped a fry into it, closing my eyes and groaning in pleasure when my lips closed around the first bite.

"That's a lovely sound." I didn't notice Julian had returned to his seat across from mine. He was looking at me with one eyebrow raised. "I see you received your French fries," he smiled, nodding his head towards the artfully arranged fries.

"My beer too." I smiled, taking a big sip. Julian's eyes danced in the candlelight at our table, most likely in amusement at my less than dignified behavior.

"Do you always order fries as soon as you sit at a restaurant?" He asked, sipping his wine.

"Actually, I was starving. I saw the golden M up the road and needed to eat something delicious as soon as possible. Fries are delicious." I motioned to the fry in my hand, my face comically serious. "Here's the way I figure it," I started, in between dipping the fry into my mayonnaise and ketchup mixture. I looked up at him, and popped a fry into my mouth before continuing. "Restaurants have a cover charge, but their currency is calories. So every time I walk into a restaurant, I budget for that cover charge. French fries are a preferable way for me to indulge than-" I looked at the menu "-organically-grown Burgundian snails." My nose scrunched up in disgust. "So if I am treated to a very fancy dinner, I order what I love. In this case, these are truffle fries, and are about as delicious as any French fry. So if I'm going to pay a cover charge in calories, I want those calories to come from really delicious fries." I swung a French fry around, gesturing at the very nice restaurant he had driven us to, knowing full well I was not a picture of grace. "And this swanky place is probably hovering around a 500 calorie cover – not including the drinks, appetizer, and dessert, which I will most definitely partake in."

He was sitting back in his chair, arms across his chest, full-on grinning at me. "Which part?"

With a mouthful of French fry, and surely a look of confusion on my face, I asked, "Huh?"

He smiled even wider at me and leaned forward, elbows on the table. "You said 'drinks, appetizer, and dessert.' Which part will you partake in?"

Snorting, I replied, "all of them, of course." And naturally, I shoved another French fry into my mouth. He took a sip from his wine glass, looking right at me the whole time, clearly amused by my ramblings.

I could hear the loud whispers from the tables around us, and realized we had drawn an audience.

"I'm serious, I'm no cheap date. I'm not going to take tiny bites of some kind of rabbit food while you gorge yourself on steak. For one, tiny bites are not happening – I have a huge mouth, in case you haven't noticed, and-"

"Oh, I noticed," he interrupted, smiling seductively at me. Damn him. He was not supposed to listen to me tease him and appreciate it.

Throwing a French fry at him, I continued. "Perv. And two, rabbit food is not proper date food. You should eat what you love on the first date. If you have any hopes for a date number two, or three, or wedding bells, you might as well display your eating habits straight out the gate."

"Whoa, you see us getting married, Andra? Good to know."

"Stop winking, jackass. I'm speaking in general, here. For the girls who go on first dates hoping to get those things from the poor schmuck they've charmed. Not for me. I'd eat steak every day if that didn't mean I'd have to buy wider jeans. I like rabbit food too, but I'm not going to go to some five-star joint that is well-known for its filet mignon and order some lettuce and a fucking tomato and call it good."

His head fell back as he laughed. I tried to suppress the small smile that was fighting its way to my lips. I didn't expect him to enjoy my diatribe, but then again, nothing about him was expected. "For the record," he said when his laughing had subsided, "I like your mouth, big and outspoken as it is. I like that you'll eat in front of me, especially steak."

He paused a second before deliberately leaning closer across the table. I tried not to notice the way the candle light lit up his features, making this meal and this conversation more intimate than I'd like. Speaking slowly, he continued. "There's something very satisfying about seeing a woman eat with pleasure. Seeing her eyes close and hearing that small moan uncurl from the back of her throat. Watching her hands clench involuntarily. Seeing her lips pucker as she savors the taste." His eyes were focused on my face, alternating between my eyes and my mouth. He wasn't smiling anymore. I could feel the pull from his words and couldn't stop from leaning closer to him across the table. "Knowing that I am treating you to such a sensual moment is a very gratifying experience for me. So please," he said and stood up, walking around to where I sat at the table. I could feel my face get warmer as he leaned down, arm on the back of my chair, just slightly brushing his lips against the shell of my ear as he whispered, "Partake." Warmth tickled my ear and I shivered. He straightened.

As he took strong, purposeful strides away, I slumped against my chair and let out the breath I didn't realize I was holding. I grabbed for my glass of water, gulped, and fanned myself. My sleeveless arms were covered in goose bumps.

What the hell was that? I didn't have to wait too long to contemplate what was happening between Julian and I, because he returned just a moment later. I searched his face for any kind of emotion, but was annoyed that he seemed to be unaffected by the pull I was currently feeling. That or he had some serious self-control.

Unbuttoning his dinner jacket, he sat and looked at me across the table with his ever-present mask of quiet amusement. "Did they take your order yet?"

I shook my head and gulped down some of my beer. "No, they were probably waiting for the person who looks like he actually belongs here to return to the table. Not the woman who looks like she already smuggled a set of silverware in her knock-off handbag."

"Just one set?" he asked cocking his head. "You'll need more than one fork if you ever plan on having me over for dinner."

"Oh, look who's presumptuous now! In that case, yes, just one set of silverware is all I'll need," I replied, raising my eyebrows and drinking more beer. I needed to gain my footing back after nearly being seduced by his words earlier.

"Well, if you only have one set of silverware, I guess I'll have to use my hands. I've been told that I am very good with my hands." He made a move like he was going to take my hand in his before he changed his mind and pulled back. My hand itched. Damn.

The waiter came by at just that moment, ruining my chance for a witty comeback. After taking our orders and removing my now-empty fry plate, Julian turned his attention on me and asked "so, are we done with the verbal sparring now? Can I ask questions about you without being mauled by French fries or seeing the threat of death in your beautiful eyes?"

I looked at him dubiously. "You really want to know how old I was when I learned how to ride my bike, what my favorite color, song, food, and movie is?"

"Of course I do. What is the point of dating if I'm not privy to the details?"

"Oh," I said, twirling my first two fingers around the rim of my water glass before meeting his eyes, "Dating? Presumptuous again." I deliberately bit the side of my lip where my lip ring was and looked at him as innocently as possible before continuing. "I thought this was just a prelude to sex."

If I'd thought I'd shocked him, I was sorely disappointed. He merely smiled, winking his stupid, beautiful dimples at me and said "well sure, but while we're waiting for our food, let's get the basics down."

This man was good. Real good. Finally someone who was at my level of humor and wit. "Basics, huh?" I asked, giving him a decadent smile. "I'm pretty good with the basics." I saw his jaw tick, recalling our conversation as I showed him to his cabin the day before. I took a sip of my beer and then crossed my arms across my chest, knowing I was giving him a great view, and leaned on the table. "I learned to ride a bike when I was four – no training wheels; it was quite the accomplishment for someone as clumsy as me. I love the color red."

"Why red?"

I took another sip of my beer. "Red is passion, warmth, love, lust. Red is also the color of rage, blood, power, irritation. Red is the rainbow's compulsory bipolar color." Realizing I just gave him a generous view of my world, I quickly continued. "Favorite song is probably 'Killer Queen' by Queen-" that earned an appreciative nod from Julian. "-and my favorite food is cliché – chocolate. I would happily insert a feeding tube just for chocolate but then I worry about having to buy bigger pants and I haven't worked out the logistics of a 24/7 chocolate-supplying feeding tube. Would it have to go in my nose? Because if so, that changes everything."

I could tell I was engaging Julian, even if I was rambling incessantly. He was making me nervous, true, but his smile and demeanor were so open that it was making it easier for me to spill my emotional guts. His attention on me was unwavering. It was almost terrifying, knowing he was absorbing my every word just as rapidly as my brain was registering the alcohol in my system. I took a large sip of water and looked at him expectantly.

"You forgot to tell me your favorite movie," he said softly.

"Oh! Probably The Princess Bride or The Goonies," I chirped.

"What?"

"You don't know those movies?" I exclaimed. I was pretty sure I heard the clatter of silverware dropping at the table directly behind me.

He shook his head and looked down at his wine, frowning. "Something tells me I should?"

I lifted my hands up in preparation of slamming them on the table in alarm, but stopped myself just before impact. Instead, I whisper-yelled, "You HAVE to see those movies! You just have to!"

"Alright, Andra, looks like you just wrangled me for another date." He smirked his lips and sipped his wine, eyes twinkling over his glass.

I shook my head and narrowed my eyes at him. "Hold up buddy, you're the one who wanted this date, so I don't think saying I wrangled you for another date qualifies. Also, who said anything about another date? Is your middle name Presumptuous?"

He smiled confidently. "Well," he started, watching his fingertips making circles on the tablecloth, "I think you've deduced that it's more likely Pretentious." He looked up at me, and I saw behind the polished veneer for just a moment. Mr. Presumptuous was doubting himself. Or at least his choice of venue for our first date?

Just then, the waiter delivered a plate of beautifully arranged antipasto. I scrunched my eyebrows together, puzzled, and looked up at Julian, who was obviously watching for my reaction. "Did you order this?" I asked, gesturing towards the plate of meats, cheeses, and – be still my heart – olives.

Julian shrugged and said, "Well you asked for French fries as soon as we sat down, but I don't count those as an appetizer. I figured you'd appreciate some meat before your entrée of meat, so when I left the table a minute ago, I asked the waiter for this." His smile didn't quite reach his eyes. It didn't take a psychologist to figure out that he was unsure if he made the right move or not.

I plucked one plump black olive from the plate and put it in my mouth immediately before saying, "Well, I feel bad for you, then."

"Why's that?"

"Because I love antipasto."

"I guess I don't understand why that's a problem."

"Because," I emphasized, cutting into a piece of salmon. "I don't like to share." I quickly slipped the smoked meat in my mouth before winking at him.

His smile finally met his eyes again. "Good to know, because I'm not the sharing kind of guy either." He winked back at me, but it was so blatantly comical that I couldn't help the laugh that flew out of my mouth.

"Something tells me you're not talking about cured meats," I said before slapping his hand away from *my* olives.

"I knew you were smart."

I swallowed the olive I'd snatched from his hand and glared at him, while mouthing, "Mine."

"Funny, that's what I was thinking, too," he said, looking directly at me.

I squirmed a little in my seat. "Don't you think you want to get to know me a little more before you make such bold statements?" I asked, feeling unnerved yet again.

"Andra. I already know so much about you." When I reached to slap his hand away from the olives again, he grabbed my hand and held it still a moment. Turning my hand over, palm up, I watched as he ran a finger from my wrist and across my palm. I looked up to see his gaze, once-again, directly on me. "I know your name is Andra Walker and you love the color red, not because it's 'pretty,' but because it has deep significance for you. You don't mind salad, but given the choice, you'll order steak every time. I know your hair smells like clementines and I don't need to try to impress you with a fancy meal." He started drawing circles on my palm with his thumb. "I know that you choose to cushion your head with grass in lieu of a pillow when you pray. I know you don't deprive yourself the more delicious things in life and you have fantastic taste in music. I know that you are funny, smart, and mesmerizing, the latter especially in candlelight. I know that your eyes betray what you're really feeling, and your pulse jumps when I lower my voice. Just. Like. This." His voice was thick on the last three words, his enunciation forceful. His thumb caressed the skin on the inside of my wrist, proving his last statement.

He pulled back, both in his body language and with the hand that cradled mine, breaking the connection. The physical connection, that is, because the emotional connection was still resilient, stubbornly so. Keeping eye contact with him, not willing to be the first to break, I took the final sip left of my beer.

"My hair smells like fruit?" I asked, effectively breaking the spell he had on me. A smirk played across his lips in response as I tugged the hair I had over my bare shoulder and sniffed it, conspicuously.

He took the final sip of his wine and lifted his eyebrows. "Indeed, it does."

Our waiter came out of the corner he had to be hiding in, refilling Julian's glass without asking and placing another beer next to my empty one. Julian popped some mozzarella in his mouth and chewed, that smirk still tugging at his lips. I snagged a slice of prosciutto and chewed; a mirror image of him.

I sipped my fresh beer and gestured my hand across the table. "So, Julian. I'd like to know more about you. When did you learn to ride your bike? And tell me your favorites."

Julian snagged the last olive before I could stop him, chewing it slowly, blatantly savoring it just to annoy me. "I can't tell you when I rode my first bike – I don't remember the experience. I was young, definitely." He sipped more wine before snagging more mozzarella. "My favorite color is white. Not for any really profound reason." I knew my skin flushed in remembrance of my declaration for the color red. "White is clean, a fresh start. I don't look at a white piece of paper and see it as empty. I see it as the beginning."

"Um, excuse me, but that was actually quite deep," I interrupted, in between bites, one eyebrow raised.

Julian nodded. "I can't pick a favorite song, but one that I listen to often is 'Name' by The Goo Goo Dolls." My face must have displayed uncertainty because he continued on, slowly twirling the stem of his wine glass in his fingers. "'Scars are souvenirs you never lose, the past is never far.'" His eyes shifted to his fingers, still twirling the glass absent-mindedly. "To me, the song is about secrets, but steadfast loyalty too. Losing things you wanted." He shrugged. "I can relate."

I was thankful that Julian wasn't looking at me because the quote he'd recited had put my guard up. The title of the song alone reminded me of who I was, and reminded me of the promises I made myself.

"Also, I just like The Goo Goo Dolls. I grew up listening to their music. Their lyrics are poetic, but unassuming." He seemed lost in thought for a moment before he looked at me again. He cleared his throat. "What other favorites am I supposed to tell you?"

"I…uh…" I tried to remember what questions I'd answered earlier. The discussion of his favorite song and the way it made me feel had rendered me forgetful. "Just tell me whatever favorites you have," I said quickly, taking a large swig of my beer.

Julian sipped his wine. "Okay. My favorite book is actually a series." He held my gaze, eyes serious. "The Harry Potter novels."

"You have excellent taste," I replied. "I've read that series probably ten times."

Julian nodded fervently. "J.K. Rowling is why I started writing. Though our styles and genres are miles apart, she definitely inspired me."

"Where is your favorite place to be?"

Julian pursed his lips in thought. "My mother's sunroom. Floor-to-ceiling windows, warm wood floors, fluffy couches perfect for naps. It's warm and cozy, and smells exactly like home."

I leaned forward slightly. "What does home smell like?"

Before Julian could reply, the waiter returned with our entrees. He held a bottle of wine, intending to pour Julian a refill, but Julian covered his hand over the glass and shook his head. The waiter turned to me and eyed my beer, seemingly asking if I wanted a refill. I shook my head. I needed to clear my head.

I took a knife to my steak and sliced a thin piece. After placing it on my tongue, I moaned in appreciation. It had been cooked perfectly, slightly pink in the middle and seasoned perfectly on the outside. My eyes closed in satisfaction as I chewed. After swallowing, I opened my eyes to Julian's hooded gaze. "Delicious," I said softly.

The dimmed lights of the restaurant blocked out all distractions so that my focus was solely on Julian. And his focus was intently on me. I raised an eyebrow and gestured towards his plate. "Aren't you going to eat?" I asked, slicing another piece of steak. Without a second thought, I held the fork in the air, in offering. "Would you like to try mine?"

I saw his jaw flex before he shook his head. "No, thanks," he said hoarsely. He gulped down some water and concentrated on his plate in front of him.

I couldn't help the smile that stretched my lips.

9

After Julian settled the bill, we walked outside to the car. The sun had long fallen behind the mountains, leaving a slight chill in its absence.

"Normally, I'd spend more time, take you somewhere else." Julian gazed at me. "But I've been informed that you have a curfew of sorts, since you work early tomorrow morning."

I eyed him. "Says who?"

"Rosa." Julian draped his suit jacket over my shoulders and opened the door for me. I clutched the opening of the jacket with one hand and turned to face him, not making a move to sit inside the car.

"Do you want to go on a walk?" I asked, motioning my head down the sidewalk.

The street lamps cast a soft halo of light around him as he looked at me, contemplating. He stuck his hands in his pockets and glanced around before nodding his head off into the distance, in agreement. He closed the door as I stepped away from the car and turned to face me.

I slipped my arms inside his jacket sleeves and gave him a grateful smile as we started down the block. The sidewalks glistened in the moonlight, the crushed stone sparkling like sprinkles in the concrete.

"Why Colorado?" I asked after we'd passed several now-closed stores.

Julian turned to me, eyebrows drawn together. "Colorado is my home. I'm from here originally," he said matter-of-factly. "My sisters and mother live in Denver."

"Oh."

"Same question to you, Andra?"

It was on the type of my tongue to say something that would betray who I really was. "Colorado is home for me too, I guess you could say."

"Where was home before?"

I chewed on my lip ring and looked down at the sidewalk as we slowly walked down the side of the road, feeling guilty for the lies that would start coming from this seemingly harmless question. "California."

"Who is in California?" he asked.

I looked at him. "What do you mean?"

Julian stopped walking and turned to me. "Parents? Siblings?"

Crap. Now to recover quickly. "Yes, my parents live there." I nodded and pulled the jacket tighter across my chest, focusing my eyes on my bright red-polished fingernails. Still chipped.

"Your brother, too?" he asked.

Oh, right. Six. I'd told Julian that Six was my brother. "Yes, he lives there too."

Julian nodded and resumed walking again. I teetered a little in my platform heels, silently berating myself for suggesting the walk. That was not my brightest idea. "How many sisters do you have?"

"Four. All younger. Trouble-makers, too." Julian laughed, seemingly in memory.

I leaned towards him, gently, playfully bumping his shoulder with my own. "Girls are good at that."

He bumped me with his shoulder, and my heels slid, causing me to nearly fall over. He snagged my arm and yanked me towards him, slamming my torso against his. My entire body shivered, remembering this exact same pose earlier.

"Sorry," he murmured. My hands were pressed flat against his chest, the throb of his heartbeat booming against my palms. He exhaled, sending a rush of warmth over my lips. My eyes met his in the moonlight, and I memorized the strong line of his eyebrows, the thick black lashes that framed his deep brown eyes. He looked at me like I was a puzzle he'd yet to figure out. "You are stunning." His hands cupped my jaw, brushing the edges of my lips with his thumbs. Something heavy sat on my windpipe, rendering me incapable of coherent speech. Julian leaned forward and settled his lips on mine. It wasn't as inviting as the first kiss. Softer, more intimate. He didn't try to deepen the kiss, just held me steady, my jaw firmly in his hands.

When he slowly pulled back, I whispered "you're trouble, too." I slowly opened my eyes and saw the smile flash across his face.

"I was going to say the same about you. Come," he said, stepping back and clasping my hand firmly in his. "Let's get you home."

When we arrived back to the ranch, it was nearly eleven. Most of the interior lights of the big house were off, so only the exterior lights greeted us as the car drove up the gravel driveway. This was my favorite view, the big house lit up at night. I'd once told Rosa it was a cabin on steroids, a log mansion. It was three levels, built at the crest of a hill. It appeared much smaller than it actually was, because the back of the house boasted a walk out basement and large picture windows facing the view of the pond and valley beyond.

Julian drove the convertible all the way down the gravel road to my cabin. I laughed. "You could've parked it in your driveway and let me walk the five cabins down."

"Sure." He glanced sideways at me. "But what kind of date would I be then?"

He pulled into the spot next to my parked Jeep and opened my door for me. I shrugged out of his jacket and handed it to him. "Thanks for this." He nodded, and walked beside me up the steps to my porch.

This felt so weird for me. Not awkward necessarily, just different. I didn't date, I wasn't romanced. I never had a desire for any of the extra stuff. I couldn't definitively say I had a taste for it now, but I couldn't pretend that I didn't enjoy myself in his company, either.

The floorboards creaked eerily as we stepped on my porch. My flood light had turned on, illuminating the entrance to my cabin with its unnatural light. I turned to Julian and found him close, one hand braced on the door frame. He looked at me as though he didn't want this night to end and, truth be told, neither did I. I had spent much of dinner teasing him, but he dished it right back. If anything, tonight had confirmed that I couldn't walk so easily away from this one.

"Thank you for tonight, Julian," I said, as seriously as possible.

"Thank you for being a good sport, Andra," he parroted in the same tone.

How did he make me smile so damn much? "I had fun," I said, earnestly, softening. I let my back lean against the door.

"You are…" he said, bringing his free hand up to where my hair hung over my shoulder. His fingers slid through my waves easily. "Unexpected."

It was the perfect compliment, and I'm sure my face told him so. His hands twisted in my hair and slid the mass over behind my shoulder, revealing the strapless side of my dress. His fingers traced the exposed curve of my neck, down over my shoulder, and came to rest at the top of my arm. I was transfixed, wholly focused on his face. I barely registered his lips descending upon mine before my eyes closed instinctively and my arms went lax.

His lips met mine softly. His hand moved to my waist and he pulled me closer while simultaneously coaxing my lips open. I didn't resist, not even for a moment. Before I realized it, my hands found his hair and I dug my fingers in, keeping him close. His tongue traced the opening of my lips and his grip tightened on my waist, probably in reaction to my suddenly weak knees.

This kiss was different. Oh, it was just as intoxicating as the others, but it was more. It was a sleepy kiss, not a kiss of two people getting to know each other, but rather a kiss of reverence. The level of feeling in this kiss was deep, heady, and confident.

My heart beat double time and I felt completely and utterly powerless. Panic set in a moment later and I pulled away, resting my forehead on his shoulder. My breathing was urgent and fractured and I squeezed my eyes shut, suddenly terrified of what it all meant. Julian's hand ran over my hair and down my back soothingly.

What. The. Hell. One date and my self-control was MIA; I couldn't calm down. A million thoughts rushed through my head, fighting their way to materialize on my lips. I pushed them down and pulled away from Julian giving him what I hoped was not a shaky smile. "Thank you for tonight."

His eyes searched mine. He knew something had shifted within me but didn't press. "You already said that."

I laughed. "Right. Well, thanks again."

He nodded and moved away from me, tucking his hands in his pockets. "Goodnight, Andra."

"You too." I smiled once more and let myself into the cabin, closing the door behind me while kicking off the heels. I leaned against the door and slid down until I was fully sitting on the rug that sat flush to the door frame. I knew my dress was going to be covered in dirt, but I didn't care. I needed to catch my breath and figure out what I was going to do about Julian.

I was awake in bed, like usual, staring at my ceiling. The parking lot lights outside my window defined the raised textured pattern around my bedroom's light fixture, looking like tons of islands across the sea of white.

I turned my head to see my alarm clock, the numbers 1:45 bright green, reflecting onto the surface of my shiny white nightstand. I silently prayed for sleep to overtake the person down the hall. It was later than usual. I tugged the comforter up higher over my long sleeve sweater, dread anchoring my chest.

Had I even fallen asleep? I wasn't sure. This was a nightly ritual of mine. Lie in bed for hours, staring at the ceiling, too afraid to allow myself to be pulled into dreams. Sleep was a friend I never visited.

The sound of the television clicking off in the living room should have been hard to hear, but I was as attuned to it as the sound of my heart beat, the latter of which started increasing its boom-boom-boom in dreaded anticipation. My eyes moved to the light that framed my closed door in the doorway and I stared as that light grew dimmer with each flick of a light switch, from the kitchen to the office, to the hallway. Each click of the light brought the shadows across the floor closer to my bedroom door.

Shadows blocked out light in two spots under the door before I heard the click sound of the light switch just outside. My door was completely shadowed now. My heart beat three times, fast in my chest.

I swore I could hear his breathing just outside my door and I prayed that he would continue walking on to his bedroom. My hopes were dashed a moment later when I heard him humming right against the white, hollow door. It was the only sound besides the now rapid beat of my heart. No, no, no, no, I pleaded uselessly, my fingernails digging into my palms, making fists.

The door opened with a creak. That creak was like a security system, alerting me to his presence. The door stopped after two inches, as if he wanted to be stealthier. Then the door swung open fully, his face exposed by the street lights coming through my window.

I screamed.

I sat up in bed, the scream dying in my throat. In a span of two seconds, I'd retrieved the folded knife from under my mattress and held it open in front of me, protecting myself from the nightmare.

Of course, there was nothing in my doorway. My door was closed. It wasn't white, and the Monster was not waiting on the other side. The Monster was states away.

Shakily, I lifted the sheets off my sweat-soaked body and stood up, padding across the floor to my door, double checking the locks I'd installed. The deadbolt was in place, the chain was latched. Nothing was getting through this door without a hatchet.

I blew out a relieved breath and brushed the hair that had clung to my forehead. I hadn't had nightmares like that in a long time. Despite my confidence in having moved on from that part of my life, nights were still occasionally traumatic for me. It took just a few months of nightmares before I pleaded to frame an actual bedroom in my cabin. Rosa, thankfully, was more than willing to come to my aid. The studio style setup the cabin had was too big and too exposed. I needed the assurance of a locked front door and locked bedroom door to assuage my anxiety.

The clock on my nightstand read 1:30 AM. Of course. Gripping the knife in one hand, I unlocked the door and made my way to my kitchen, switching on lights as I passed them. Being in such a small space in the dark bred irrational fears. I glanced at the front door, noting the locks still in place.

I grabbed a glass from the cupboard and filled it with water from my island sink. Taking my glass to the window, I steadily drank the water as I looked out. The big house had one room lit up in changing shades of blue and yellow. I knew the room was Rosa and Clint's, and knew that the light from the television meant Clint couldn't sleep. I needed to remind Oscar, the dinner cook, to serve him decaf coffee.

I angled my gaze to the right as I finished the water, seeing Julian's cabin lit up like a Christmas tree. Did he ever sleep? I looked at all the other cabins I could see from my window, tapping my now-folded knife on the countertop.

I wiped my brow free of sweat and refilled my glass again before turning off all the lights and heading back to my bedroom, locking the door once again. I slid the knife back under my mattress and smoothed down my sheets. As I reached to set my glass down on my nightstand, my phone vibrated across the surface, startling me. I fumbled putting the glass on the table and spilled water across the surface of the nightstand. I huffed out a breath in annoyance before pulling the long sleeve of my pajama shirt down to soak up the water.

I grabbed the phone and slid back into bed. I restarted the movie I'd fallen asleep to before unlocking my phone to view the text message. The number was local, but not in my contacts list.

Good morning, Andra. –J.J.

I smiled to myself before gliding my fingers across the on-screen keyboard.

Me: You're a little early, Julian.

Cool wetness seeped onto my arm from my sleeve and I knew I would have trouble sleeping with a wet shirt. I rolled up the sleeve and a minute later my phone vibrated in my hand.

Julian: I saw your lights were on. And, as I've told you before, I hate to keep a lady waiting.

I laughed and rolled my eyes, typing my reply.

Me: I wasn't exactly waiting with bated breath for you to wish me a good morning.

A moment after pressing "send," a thought occurred to me and I quickly typed it out.

Me: By the way, how did you get my number?

Julian: Well, you won't be seeing me on Sunday, and I didn't want you to feel forlorn when I didn't come find you in person to wish you good morning.

A minute later, his reply to my latest text came.

Julian: Rosa likes me. ;)

A winky face! I tried not to wonder why he wouldn't see me tomorrow, but curiosity got the best of me.

Me: Checking out so soon? And I was just beginning to like you, too. Darn.

Julian: No, unfortunately you are stuck with me for the full month. And I have a meeting in Denver tomorrow morning, sister obligations, and then I'm meeting the tile guys at my home tomorrow evening.

I tried to not let myself feel the twinge of disappointment. It was too soon to get attached to him. I barely knew him. But I enjoyed spending time with him; our verbal sparring, and the physical connection between us was…intense.

Me: Sounds like a busy day. Better get some beauty sleep!

I knew my reply sounded cold, impersonal. But it was a mask, guarding me from getting too close.

Julian: I know it's late, but can I call you?

I hesitated, fingers stilling on the keyboard. After a moment, I worked up the nerve and dialed him myself, not wanting to waste time, and desperately wondering what he wanted to say.

"Andra," he breathed on the other end when the call connected. His voice was gruff from the late hour, and the timbre of it made me bite my lip.

"Julian," I answered, a little breathlessly. Damn it.

"Is it too soon to ask you on a second date?" Wow, he got right to the point. My lips curved and I settled more into my pillows.

"Probably. But I don't care. Sure. When?"

I heard the whoosh of air on the other line. "Tuesday. Rosa said you had that day off."

I rolled my eyes all the way to the ceiling. "Of course she did. What other information did you glean from Rosa?"

His chuckle was muffled by the sounds of paper being rustled in the background. "That you have to be back by Wednesday morning."

I sat up straight in my bed. "Are we talking about an overnight date?"

"No. Well, actually, yes. But not what you're probably imagining."

"It's an overnight date. A sleepover!" I said excitedly.

Julian's laugh was loud and quick. "A sleepover? Are we in middle school?"

"A sleepover!" I laughed.

"Look," Julian said after he finished laughing, "I know what it sounds like. But it's not what you're thinking. Our date tonight wasn't what you would have preferred, but you were a good sport. Date two is going to be more up your alley, and requires an overnight."

I searched my brain for even just an inkling of what kind of date I'd prefer that would require an overnight. However, besides the obvious – let's just say it: sex – I couldn't think of anything. This would be interesting.

"Okay, what do I bring?" I asked.

"I'll see you sometime Monday and will tell you then. Be prepared to leave really early Tuesday morning."

I smirked. "I'm always prepared."

"Why do I feel like that requires a winky smiley face?" he asked. I could feel his smile through the phone and I cradled the phone closer, snuggling back into my pillows.

"Julian," I started, picking at a loose thread in my duvet, "I don't want to lead you on. Dinner was fun, in more ways than one. I don't really do the relationship thing. I had a great time with you, but I don't want you expecting anything more than I am willing to give you."

Julian was quiet for a moment and I felt the nervousness claw up my throat, urging me to back out on date two, back out completely of whatever it was I was doing with Julian.

"This doesn't have to be anything more than what we want, Andra. We don't need to define this. You are warm, honest, beautiful, and full of wit. I appreciate how vibrant you are, and how you challenge me. I want to spend time with you simply because I enjoy being around you." I heard his sigh. "I don't want to suffocate you. No labels, no drama. Just fun. Maybe a kiss or two."

"Or three. Or four," I added.

"Or forty. Or more," he continued.

I laughed again. He was right. We could keep it fun, spend some time enjoying the summer before he moved on. It would be an experiment for me, but one I was willing to test.

"Okay, you have yourself a date."

"Can't wait. Get some sleep. I'll see you at some point on Monday."

"Good night, Julian."

"Good night, Andra."

I hung up the phone, smiling to myself, and snuggled under the duvet, setting the sleep timer on my television. Minutes later, I was asleep.

I stood on the edge, right where the grass died off into pine needles and dirt. It was cool enough that patches of light fog covered small sections of the forest floor sporadically, looking like puffy white blankets. I could see clearly for only about 50 feet before the thick of tree trunks and bush masked what lie ahead.

Of course, I ran these woods hundreds of times. I knew that in approximately two-point-six miles, I would come into a small meadow, filled with overgrown grass and dandelions. And another mile east of that meadow were well-traveled trails that descended into a valley and looped back to the ranch's horse arena. I didn't run those trails, preferring dirt and pine needles to horse shit and dust. I was also less likely to run into anyone this way.

I didn't run to a playlist. These woods, while beautiful and serene, were home to some of the more dangerous four-legged creatures. It was better to let the sounds of my surroundings safeguard me. Instinctively, I reached to the band on my left wrist and fingered the pepper spray and kubotan that hung there. While I knew my way around a gun, I didn't trust that I could use one in a panicked situation. Plus, it made running more cumbersome.

I stretched my legs and arms, still at the edge of the forest. I wore compression tights under my gym shorts, as much to keep my muscles warm as to protect my legs from being beaten by the brutal brush. It was just after six in the morning, which was a perfect time for me to hit the woods. The woods were calmer in the mornings, the morning birds still rousing, and the aforementioned dangerous animals still sleeping. Rosa was cleaning up after feeding the ranch hands, who in turn were starting the morning chores. I liked leaving the noisy ranch for the quiet loneliness of the woods.

I took off in a jog to further warm up my muscles. I'd learned a lot since I first started running into the woods. The first few times I ventured in on my own, I'd started off too fast and ended up pulling muscles, rendering me helpless, scared, and miles away from the ranch. I never wanted to be helpless or scared again, and feeling those things brought my time with the Monster back in stunning and crippling clarity.

I didn't let my thoughts venture to him often, but he was always there in the back of my mind, taunting me with his memory. Whenever I started to visualize him, I quickly named off the colors in my sight until I could focus on something else.

"Green," I whispered. It was the most ubiquitous color in the woods, sure, but it would suffice. "Brown," I said, louder as I narrowed my eyes on the dirt ahead, pounding relentlessly through the pine needles. "Blue." I looked up, only for a moment, at the sky. The morning sky was the softest shade of blue, growing more vivid as the sun moved across the sky throughout the day.

I picked up speed as my muscles warmed, breathing in and out evenly. Even though I'd only slept about four hours, I felt energized, awake. I inhaled through my nose, taking quiet comfort in the earthy and pine scents that flooded my senses. The forest was my form of morning caffeine. The extra oxygen provided by the abundance of trees just felt good. Once I passed the point of my lungs burning from exertion, I had that infamous runners' high and I was drunk with it.

About twenty-five minutes into my run, I circled back towards the ranch, my stomach protesting at its emptiness. I never ran with food in my stomach. I usually drank a glass of orange juice and water prior to running, but never breakfast.

When the cabins came into view twenty minutes later, I couldn't resist my eyes moving to where Julian's cabin was and noted his now-empty driveway. I didn't allow the disappointment I initially felt take root in me, remembering he would be gone all day today. And besides, Sundays were my busiest day, and there was hardly a moment free to entertain thoughts that weren't work-related.

I slowed to powerwalk as I headed for the big house, the blood pumping in my ears as my breathing slowed, my limbs warm. I plopped onto the grass right in front of the steps leading up to the entrance and stretched my legs. I slid off the wrist band that had my pepper spray and kubotan and then grabbed my toes and pulled, stretching.

I felt sweat running down my spine and shivered slowly, my body adjusting to the cool temperatures now that I was no longer in steady motion.

Out of the corner of my eye, Dylan appeared carrying a few egg cartons. Rosa's pet project a few years before had been her hen house. It was still her pet project, but not one she usually had time for. It was one of the many side tasks I usually took care of, so I was surprised to see Dylan carrying the egg cartons into the big house.

When he saw me he changed direction and headed my way. He set the cartons down on the steps just behind me and sat next to me in the grass. "Long run?"

"Eh," I replied, shrugging. I straightened my legs in front of me and leaned my upper body on my legs, hands wrapped on the arch of my foot. "About forty-five minutes."

"That's forty-five minutes longer than I ran this morning. High-five." Dylan held up a hand and I laughed, slapping it with my hand before returning to my stretch. He snagged my wristband that held the pepper spray and kubotan and held up the latter, laughing. "You know what this looks like, don't you?" He asked, waggling his eyebrows.

My kubotan was silver, with indents for finger grooves along the rod. Despite being a useful tool for self-defense, I had to admit I agreed with where his thoughts were going. "It does look like anal beads, doesn't it?"

Dylan tossed the wristband back to me. "Sure, anal beads for the masochist." We both laughed, nearly doubling over, bonding over our immaturity.

"Why did you get the eggs this morning?" I asked, looking over at him when my laughing had died down.

"The guests that checked into the big house yesterday wanted eggs this morning. And after feeding the six of us this morning, Rosa was out." Dylan ran his hands through the grass. "I knew you'd gone for your usual Sunday half-marathon, so I volunteered." Dylan smiled sideways at me.

I laughed. "Well thanks. Hope the hens didn't give you too hard of a time." I slid my legs apart, spreading them to deepen my stretch.

Dylan held the tops of his hands out for my inspection. I noted the many scratches, though none deep enough to be concerning.

"They still hate men, like most women I know," he laughed, but looked at me pointedly.

"What?" I asked, feigning innocence. "I don't hate men. I tolerate you, don't I?" I teased.

Dylan leaned back, using his hands behind him for support. "Rumor is you went on a date last night."

I sighed, rolling my eyes. "Doesn't anyone around here work? Or are they too busy participating in idle gossip to earn their keep?"

"Come on, Andra. We're like a big, smelly, dysfunctional family. We keep tabs on our kin."

"I'll attest to the dysfunctional, but unlike you, I'm not smelly. I shower." I returned his pointed look with mock disgust.

Dylan reached an arm up and pushed me over as I leaned into my left leg, causing me to roll the other way. "If I didn't shower every day, I'd have an entourage of flies after me," he protested.

My friendship with Dylan was close, similar to a brother. Though I didn't confide in him with the deep stuff, we still usually kept up with each other's lives. I knew by the direction of this conversation, that Dylan was a little disappointed to learn about my date from someone else. Our romantic connection was no longer present, so Dylan wasn't jealous; he was clearly feeling down that I didn't tell him myself.

When I sat back up, I turned to face him more fully. "He asked me out late Friday night and I didn't see you yesterday except when you tried drowning me on the dock."

Dylan chuckled, remembering. "Okay, fine." He ran a hand through his wavy blond hair before making eye contact with me. "But you don't date. Ever."

I nodded. "It's weird, isn't it? But I had fun. We're going on another date on Tuesday."

Dylan's eyebrows shot up high at that. "Two dates? I feel like I'm in the Twilight Zone."

"You're not the only one," I mumbled, looking off towards the cabins.

Dylan stood up and reached a hand down to me. When he pulled me up to standing, he grabbed the egg cartons and wrapped his arm around my shoulders. "Still up for Waffle Wednesday?" he asked as we headed into the big house. "I don't want to intrude on your busy dating life."

I grabbed the cartons from him and shoved him away, playfully. "Don't be a dork. I'm always up for waffles."

Waffle Wednesday was a weekly tradition for Dylan and me. Every Wednesday night, we would make waffles and watch movies in Dylan's cabin. It was the only time of the week we had to catch up, and a tradition we had kept up for the last three years.

Rosa came out of the kitchen. "Oh good," she said, taking the cartons from my hands. "Dylan, Farley ran the mower over some barbed wire along the southwest corner. He tried using wire cutters, but can't get it untangled."

Dylan sighed. "What was he doing in the southwest corner anyway? Do we even mow over there?"

The southwest corner of the property was mostly dead grass and tree stumps. There was an access road that led from the stables to that corner of the property and a few steel carports that sheltered the horse trailers that were parked in that area, but otherwise it was mostly unoccupied.

"It's overgrown with weeds, so I asked him to. I'm more concerned about barbed wire being loose back there," Rosa said, leading us into the kitchen.

Dylan poured a cup of coffee for himself and leaned against the counter, facing Rosa. "There is barbed wire fencing back there to keep the coyotes off the property. But last time I checked it in the spring, it was secure."

Rosa washed the eggs before cracking them into a bowl. "So we either have trespassers cutting the wire or a coyote got through and pulled some wire with him. Can you check it out and help Farley untangle the wire?"

"He should've checked the area first anyway. There's a ton of stumps back there, he could have bent the blade." He sipped his coffee and then motioned his cup in my direction. "I miss when Andra mowed. I never had to rescue her."

I grabbed some juice from the fridge. "That's not true." I looked directly at Dylan. "I distinctly recall running over a half dozen sprinkler heads on the front lawn the first few times I mowed."

Dylan laughed, his eyes lit up with humor. "Oh, yeah, that's right. Good job; that was a pretty spectacular mess."

I curtseyed and sipped my juice. "Thank you, thank you."

Rosa pushed a plate of bacon towards me as she whipped up the eggs. "That's why we have flags now." She turned her gaze to me.

I chewed on the bacon thoughtfully before turning to Dylan. "After you get the wire untangled, send Farley and the mower up here. I'll teach him to mark the sprinkler heads up on the front and back lawns and how to mow so we don't end up with zigzags again."

Dylan sipped more coffee and nodded. "It would be nice to look like someone sober mowed our lawn."

Dylan and I laughed. "Hey," Rosa interrupted, "everyone needs a teacher. Farley will figure it out with a little guidance. I remember everything I had to teach you two when you first came to work for me." She poured the eggs into the skillet, eyeing us sharply. "He's just a kid." As if to emphasize her point, she took the bacon plate back from me as I snagged one more piece.

Dylan looked at me guiltily before finishing his coffee. He walked over to Rosa and wrapped an arm over her shoulder affectionately. "You're right. I'll cut him some slack." He leaned down to accommodate her short stature and gave her a loud kiss on the cheek. "See you later." Rosa's head swung in his direction, but he quickly strode to where I was down the counter. I brought the slice of bacon to my lips, but he swiped it from me and popped it into his mouth, grinning at me while he chewed. I slugged his upper arm before he ran out of the kitchen, escaping Rosa's wrath for the kiss and my anger at the bacon thievery.

I reached for a cereal bowl from the cupboard behind me before Rosa said, "I left you extra French toast in the fridge."

She didn't look at me when she said it, but I smiled nonetheless as I grabbed the Tupperware with my breakfast out of the fridge. I heated it in the microwave. Rosa was concentrated on the omelets she was making, so as soon as the microwave dinged, I popped both slices of the French toast onto a paper towel and put the Tupperware into the dishwasher.

"Thanks Rosa!" I sang as I hopped out the kitchen and headed for my cabin to change into work clothes.

After sticking the last flag next to the sprinkler, I turned to Farley.

"After you've marked all the sprinklers, then you are ready to mow. Don't make my mistake of nearly destroying an entire sprinkler system," I laughed, trying to ease the embarrassment Farley already felt after Dylan wrestled the lawn mower for three hours, untangling the barbed wire.

I climbed onto the mower while Farley stood by. "Today I'm going to teach you to how to mow the lawn behind the big house, as it slopes down to the pond." I made sure it was in neutral and the parking break was set before starting the engine while Farley looked on, arms crossed over his rock festival tee. He looked like a rocker farm boy, with his cut off sleeves, ripped jeans and cowboy boots. He wore his Broncos baseball cap backwards over his unruly mop of black curls.

I remembered when we first hired Farley, Clint had given him a hard time as he laid out Farley's duties. Farley kept putting his hand over his eyebrows, shielding his eyes from the harsh sun while he listened to Clint. "You know, that ball cap you're wearing is meant to help shade the sun from your face. We need you two-handed on this ranch."

"But then my neck will burn," Farley had countered.

"Boy, your hair is longer than Rosa's, and I don't ever hear her complaining of a burnt neck."

Farley had laughed it off, knowing he was the new kid and therefore needed to be broken in. And yet, he still wore his cap backwards and always forgot his sunglasses.

I slid my hands around the steering wheel, enjoying the slight pulse from the engine that transferred to my palms. I really loved mowing, but after I took too many projects on, Rosa and Clint had insisted on hiring a local kid to help with some of the easier tasks on the ranch.

I spoke over the engine, "you want to move up and down this slope, not sideways. The surface you're mowing should be as level as possible, so mowing sideways won't ensure an even cut – and it's also dangerous."

Farley's cheeks burned red. We were standing at the crest of the hill as it started to slope down, and the evidence of his last unsuccessful attempt at mowing was obvious in the large patches of tall grass next to chunks of dirt. He was embarrassed, but willing to listen and learn – that was important. Rosa was right, he would do well under a little guidance.

"Slow down when you're going down the hill and as you mow along the edge of the pond. Don't get too close to the sandy edge – just use the edger or weed-whack the taller grass afterwards. And move the blade up to the fifth setting when you're mowing around the pond. The ground is too uneven and if you use the lower settings," I pointed to settings one through four, "you'll end up with a bunch of dirt and no grass. And you'll also end up with a very pissed off Rosa."

Farley nodded. "What about the rougher grass by the trees?" he asked, pointing to the area just between the pond and the trees that shaded it in the back.

"Good question. Slow your speed and use the fifth or sixth blade setting. No one walks back there, but we want to keep it short so it doesn't look unruly, messy. Also less likely to become a home for spiders that way."

Farley peered down the hill at the pond, seemingly absorbing what I was telling him. "Don't be afraid to shift down if you're in a tricky spot, like going down the hill or around the fences. When you get more comfortable, you can increase your speed."

"Yeah, that's probably a good idea," Farley mumbled. I couldn't help the smile that curved my lips. He pulled his hat off his head to run his fingers through the mess of curls. He had a pretty baby face, and I knew from the teasing I heard from the ranch hands that he was quite popular with the young ladies in town. But to me, he was a kid.

I motioned for Farley to hop on the mower so I could hop off. "I'm confident you'll get the hang of it – and honestly," I said, bracing a hand on his shoulder so he looked me in the eye, "this is better than mucking horse shit."

He laughed and nodded. "Thanks, Andra." He ran his palms over the steering wheel.

"You're welcome, Farley. Don't be afraid to ask for help. And don't forget to retrieve the sprinkler flags and store them in the garage when you're done." Farley nodded in acknowledgement, so I jumped off the mower as Farley shifted into gear and rode.

I made my way back to the big house, turning around just as Farley was nearing the bottom of the hill, where it leveled off a bit to the pond. He was driving at a snail's pace, but the zigzags were minimal this time.

I bounded into the kitchen where the afternoon and evening cook, Oscar, was prepping dinner for the ranch staff. After the other guests departed that morning, we currently only had one tenant – Julian – and he was away for the evening, so we'd all be dining together, family-style.

I snatched an apple from the fruit bowl in front of Oscar, not missing his grunt of disapproval. I pulled up a bar stool opposite him and crunched into the apple.

Oscar's eyes flicked up at me, in annoyance. Oscar, aptly nicknamed Oscar the Grouch, was in his fifties, with salt and pepper hair and deeply tanned skin. His eyes were an almost unnatural blue, startling when he looked your way, beneath his fuzzy, black caterpillar eyebrows.

"You're going to ruin dinner," he grumbled, slicing the fat away from the chicken breasts he was carving.

I crossed one leg over the other, and grinned at him, even though he was doing his best to avoid looking at me. "Nah. I'm ruining my lunch."

Oscar slid a few chicken filets to a bowl with what I knew to be buttermilk before scoffing. "You always ruin your lunch. I should know, because Rosa always packs it up for you and personally delivers it to your fridge."

I scrunched up my lips. "Rosa loves me. She spoils me."

"HA!" he exclaimed, pointing his stubby finger at me. "Rosa? Who do you think cooks the food?"

I held back a laugh at his indignation. I was biting my lip while I shook with laughter. Oscar glared at me. "Okay, Oscar. YOU spoil me. I guess that means you love me too, eh?"

He shook his head, seemingly annoyed, but I knew he had a soft spot for me. Oscar had been widowed two years earlier and his daughters were across the country, building their own families. They rarely visited, which I knew was partly why he was such a grump some times.

A few months after his wife died, I'd caught Oscar heading out to go fishing. After he'd declined to invite me along, I had followed him in my Jeep and spent that Sunday at his favorite fishing spot. I don't think we had exchanged more than a dozen words. In fact, the only thing he'd said to me was kind of insulting. "Here, use this. You're not going to catch anything with that crap." He'd shared his lures and bait with me and we drank beer and soaked up some sun.

Oscar turned to the farmers sink in the island and nailed me with his eyes while washing his hands. "Go. Eat. You have food in your fridge and I have potatoes to prepare."

I raised my hands in surrender, still holding the apple and backed out of the kitchen, headed to the cabin for a quick lunch.

When I unlocked my door and let myself in, I noticed a light blinking on my cell phone on the counter. I never took my cell phone with me while I worked, preferring to not have the distraction it created. Ignoring it for a moment, I opened the fridge and grabbed the wrapped sandwich and baby carrots Rosa had left for me. I filled a glass of water and slid into a bar seat at the island, taking a bite of my sandwich before unlocking my phone to view my notifications.

I didn't have any social media presence. The risk wasn't worth it. Besides, apart from Six, everyone in my life lived within a couple miles from the ranch. I had never maintained an online profile anywhere, and I enjoyed the freedom I had. Not that I wasn't curious from time to time, especially about old classmates. But I enjoyed my anonymity.

I had one text and voicemail. I checked the voicemail first. I didn't recognize the number, but there was only one person it could be.

"Hi. Listen, I need you to call me as soon as you get this. I'm not kidding. I will call Rosa if you don't call me right back."

Six's voice sounded troubled and I was immediately aware of the pit in my stomach. Six very rarely called me, and always from a disposable phone with the same area code, so I'd know that it was safe to answer. He was absolutely the epitome of over-protective, and always erred on the side of caution, especially when it came to my safety.

The bite of sandwich had turned leaden in my mouth, and swallowing it past the lump in my throat was more than simply difficult. I took a steady breath and called Six back.

"Can you get out of Colorado for a couple days?" Six never bothered with pleasantries. I know it was partly to keep our conversations short, but mostly because he was a blunt man.

"Yes. Why?"

"There's been suspicious activity. I scoped it myself and just got back, but I need your help. I know you never wanted to go back, but it's necessary."

Six was very level-headed, not easily swayed by emotions or anything else, but I still heard the under-current of concern. I knew he was referring to the Monster. The hand holding my cell phone grew slick with sweat.

"When do we go?"

"Wednesday night. We'll return Friday morning. I already called Rosa."

I swallowed, trying to push the bile down. "What are we going to be doing?"

His answer came almost hesitantly. "Breaking and entering."

My heart picked up pace, slamming against my ribcage like an animal fearfully trying to escape.

When I didn't reply, Six spoke again. "Nothing bad will happen to you. I swear on my life."

I nodded, eyes squeezed shut, before realizing he couldn't see me. "I know. Okay," I whispered.

"I'll be in Colorado Wednesday afternoon. We'll travel together. It will be fine. But this must be done."

I was glad I was sitting down, because my legs were trembling. Fear washed over my body like a wave, but didn't recede. With the phone still to my ear, I heard Rosa come in my cabin.

"I'll see you Wednesday," I said in a small voice.

I heard the click of Six disconnecting the call and put the phone on the counter unsteadily as Rosa came up behind and wrapped her arms around me.

Rosa was warm and smelled of sugar and strawberries. She was not an affectionate woman by nature, but she knew she was all I had, the only person who could provide me the comfort I so desperately needed.

After I had calmed down, I insisted on getting back to work, anything to keep my mind off of the Monster. Rosa had protested, as she usually did, but I brushed it aside, intent on keeping busy. The best way for me to push aside the emotional turmoil I was feeling was to focus my attention elsewhere.

After snagging some beet greens from the kitchen, I grabbed the five-gallon bucket that held my cleaning supplies for the chicken coop and headed down behind the house to the hen house.

Rosa had purchased a beautiful custom hen house and then built a large fenced yard around the coop. She had twenty hens, but her hen house was large enough that it could accommodate another ten or so. Twenty turned out to be a perfect amount as far as egg production went, with around 10 dozen eggs a week. But twenty hens also made a huge mess.

If Rosa was anything, she was motherly, not just to humans, but to animals as well. She insisted on cleaning the stables as often as possible, though I usually took that task. The hen house was cleaned every Sunday, and that was another task I asked Rosa to pass down. She did, albeit reluctantly. The ranch was flourishing on its own, which required Rosa to dedicate her time in other places.

I wasn't much for socialization, at least with other people, so cleaning the stables and the hen house and gardening were chores I enjoyed the most. I didn't prefer to cater to our guests' needs or work alongside the ranch hands. The ranch hands liked to talk and I didn't have much to contribute to their conversation. I was a terrible liar, mostly because it made me feel terrible to look someone in the eye and tell them something untrue. So I adopted being somewhat of a loner, apart from Rosa and Dylan.

So I chose to socialize with Rosa's "girls," keeping them healthy and happy every Sunday late afternoon. I let myself into the chicken run and after distracting the hens with the beet greens, I shuffled into the hen house and spent the next hour cleaning it out before spraying everything with a spray to keep the hens healthy and free of lice.

I left the chicken coop closed up, windows open for ventilation, and let myself out of the chicken run while the hen house dried out.

I sat in the grass just outside of the fenced area while the chickens clucked around the fence, likely wanting more greens. "Sorry ladies, I'm all out."

Now that I was sitting still, my mind went back to my earlier conversation with Six. I hadn't been back to Michigan since Six drove me to Colorado. I'd only seen the Monster in photos published in online news journals. I'd made a life for myself, a life I chose to live. Six didn't bring me to Colorado with the intentions that I'd stick around Rosa's ranch. But the longer I stayed, the more I couldn't imagine spending my life doing anything else. Going back to Michigan was dousing ice cold water on my happiness. It was life getting comfortable, cozy, before it reared its ugly head and suffocated you with reality.

But if Six said it was important, then I knew it was. And that's what scared me the most.

I wasn't sure how long I was spaced out before a shadow fell over me, startling me to my feet as I turned around in defense.

"Hey," Dylan said, palms up in defense. "It's just me."

I laughed, not humorously, and put a hand over my racing heart. "Sorry."

Dylan eyed me curiously and held a water bottle out towards me. "Here. I'm sure you are in need of this." He motioned to the hen house with the water bottle. "I was in there this morning and it stunk."

I nodded and licked my dry lips before grabbing the water bottle. "Thanks," I said, not meeting his eyes, before chugging the water.

I felt him touch my arm. "Are you okay?"

I looked sideways at him, swallowing the last of the water. "Yep fine." Then I grabbed his hand and turned to him, remembering I had plans Wednesday. "My brother called this afternoon and I need to leave town for a couple days."

"Okay…" Dylan said, a note of suspicion in his voice. "When do you leave? And is everything alright?"

"Wednesday. I have to cancel Waffle Wednesday this week. I'm sorry." I squeezed his hand.

"That's fine. There's always next week. But this is kind of short notice, are your folks okay?"

I faced away from him to hide my wince and let go of his hand. I absolutely hated lying, especially to friends. "Yeah, they're fine. It's just been a long time since my brother and I saw them, so we're going to go out that way for a couple days. This was the only time their schedules could line up."

"Hmm," Dylan murmured. "They should come out here sometime. We'd love to meet them."

I didn't know who Dylan was referring to when he said "we" because he was the only person who would want to meet my fictional parents. Another lie would have to slip from my lips. "They hate to travel," I replied. I turned back to Dylan and handed back the water bottle. "I need to finish the hen house."

Dylan nodded, his eyes searching my face. I knew he was concerned, so I tried to play it off with a smile and squeezed his shoulder affectionately before I headed back to the hen house to finish cleaning.

That night I dreamt of the moment I found my mother's body.

My life was a series of befores and afters: before my mother's death and after my mother's death. Before I left the Monster and after I left the Monster.

The first thing I remembered about my mother's death was the minutes after. I'd always dreamt of it this way; remembering the after. It was during the after that I remembered the before.

A paramedic was in front of me, his mouth moving, his warm fingers pressed against my wrist. My head felt heavy as I turned to him, my tongue thick as I tried to form words. "What?" I managed. I was lying flat on my back on the floor.

"Can you tell me your name?" he asked, slowly.

I tried sitting up before he hushed me and coaxed me into lying down again. "Just tell me your name honey."

It felt like I was on a ride, stuck in one spot while the room spun around me over and over. My hand felt like it weighed 100lbs as I lifted it up to my forehead. Every motion required my complete concentration, and my brain felt like it was bobbing in my skull. I couldn't focus on anything. Even the paramedic's features distorted, looking like a watercolor painting.

I licked my lips and tasted something sweet. Grape. I was eating a bagel.

"My bagel?" I asked. What was I even asking? Why was everything so confusing?

"How do you feel?" the paramedic asked.

The ride decelerated; the room around me spun slower and slower. "Um." I closed my eyes and willed the ride to completely stop. When I opened my eyes, the room was still. The paramedic's face came slowly into focus. Blue eyes. They were nice eyes. And concerned eyes at the moment.

I looked around me and saw the blue walls. My mom's bedroom. My brow furrowed while I tried to recall what had happened.

"Miss?" the paramedic asked.

Panic started sliding through my body, though I couldn't figure out why. My hands grasped out and gripped the paramedic's arms. "Please. I need to sit up."

The paramedic seemed reluctant to help me so I pulled myself up into a sitting position and immediately winced, my head pounding.

"Just stay still," the paramedic urged, eyebrows furrowed in concern.

"Ow." It was all I managed to say before I closed my eyes and lifted a hand to the back of my head. What had happened? Another hand moved to my forehead as I rubbed my fingers into the pain. I pushed harder, hoping that aggravating the pain would bring on a memory of what had happened. I bent my head forward and breathed through the pain. A lyric popped into my head from nowhere. "I know it's up for me, if you steal my sunshine."

My eyes opened, resting first on my wet jeans. Why were my jeans wet? My hand touched them to make sure I wasn't seeing things. My fingers came away wet and cold. It was solving a puzzle without having a complete picture to reference.

I felt the cold then, the wet of my shirt against my skin so I reached down and pulled on the loose fabric. It was pink. What an odd color. I didn't own any pink shirts.

I heard the crackle of a walkie-talkie and turned my head in the direction from which it came. There was another paramedic in my mom's bathroom talking to a police officer.

I ran a hand down my face. *WAKE UP*, my subconscious yelled. My head wouldn't stop pounding, bruising my skull. I knew the paramedic was still talking to me but I slowly shook my head and put my hand up, a silent plea to give me a minute while I looked down at my shirt.

Above my left breast was a purple stain. Grape. The jelly. The lower half of my shirt was stained pink and the top half was dry and white.

It was then that my brain clicked, that the shock wore off and I realized my shirt was stained with grape jelly and my mother's blood. I leaned forward and vomited on the paramedic. It was then that I remembered what had happened. The before.

I had just gotten home from school and popped a bagel in the toaster in the kitchen before sliding my backpack to the counter and switching on the radio under the cabinet.

I was in seventh grade, all gangly limbs and frizzy hair, a mouth full of metal. I was a walking cliché of awkward. My jeans had holes from overuse, not from style. My tees were the free tee shirts firefighters tossed into crowds during a fourth of July parade, or the tees given away on the radio station – not stylish. My looks didn't matter to me then. I've always been a bit of a loner, especially then, especially before I became the loneliest I'd ever been.

I smeared grape jelly on my bagel and took a large bite while my foot tapped along with the radio. My head bopped to the beat of "Steal My Sunshine." I didn't catch the glob of jelly that fell from my next bite until it stained my tee shirt, this one saying "Heart of Hanover 5K." I didn't run that 5K, but this was one of the few white shirts I owned that I hadn't stained yet so I plopped my bagel on the counter and ran up the stairs to my bedroom, singing along to the radio.

I bounced down the hallway, the carpet eating up the sounds of my footsteps. My bedroom was at the end of the hallway. I had to pass my mom's office, my bathroom, the linen closet and my mom's bedroom before I reached mine.

I stopped when I got to my mom's door. It was closed. My mom never closed her door, not even when she was sleeping. We often joked about removing our doors from their hinges; we shared everything, never hiding anything from each other.

I didn't know what to do. Knock? I'd never been faced with a closed door before. I turned the brass handle slowly and pushed. The door had expanded in the summer from the humidity, so it took a bit of a shove to get open. I shoved hard enough that I nearly fell into the room and gripped the brass handle for balance. The bedroom was empty, her bed made and tidy. I walked around the armoire on the wall opposite her bed and saw the bathroom door was closed. That wasn't unusual. Everyone needed privacy when they were in the bathroom.

I nearly turned back and headed to my room, assuming my mom was in the shower, but something stopped me.

I knocked once on the door. When there was no reply, I knocked twice. When there was still no reply, I laid my ear on the door. "Mom?" I called softly, tapping the door with my fingernails. "Are you okay?"

Silence. I didn't hear water running or my mom's voice on the other end. Odd.

"I'm coming in," I hollered.

I grabbed the handle and turned it. My eyes took in her clothing on the floor in front of the pedestal sink. I lifted my eyes up and saw my mom leaned back in the claw foot tub, eyes closed, her face serene. "Mom?" I asked, tip toeing further into the bathroom.

The fabric curtain partially obscured her body from my view, so all I could see was her head, her facial muscles relaxed. As I neared the tub, the water came into view and my stomach filled with lead.

Before I knew what I was doing, I had whipped the curtain back and jumped into the tub behind my mom, shaking her limp body, screaming for her to wake up while my hands searched for the open wound.

My mother's body was cold, her pallor unnatural, but I refused to listen to the rational part of my brain that told me it was too late. That I was too late.

I lifted one of her arms out of the water and saw it. The cut from wrist to the inside of her elbow. It was wide enough that I saw a flash a white beneath red muscle.

I dropped her arm and climbed out of the tub and didn't look back. I picked up the bedside phone and dialed 911.

"911 Dispatch, what is your emergency?"

"My mom has a cut. On her arm. I think she'll need some stitches." My voice felt robotic, foreign.

"What is your address?"

"1320 Rosewood Drive. There's a red car in the driveway."

"Okay sweetie. How is your mom doing?"

"She isn't talking. She's asleep in the bath tub." And then I blacked out.

After I awoke from the nightmare, I restarted the Bruce Willis movie I'd fallen asleep to. I don't think I slept for more than thirty minutes at a time after that. Every time I looked at the clock after awakening, I hoped to see that an hour had passed since I last looked at it. Instead, it was never more than thirty minutes. The last time I looked at the clock, it had read 4:45 AM. I wouldn't have the energy or alertness to run that morning, so I resigned myself to a book, hoping sleep would pull me under until I had to get up two hours later.

Unfortunately, I finished the damn book and made it into Rosa's dining room on Monday morning at the same time as the ranch hands. I noticed that Dylan kept glancing my way, but nothing was said as we all ate strawberry pancakes and bacon. I tried to avoid eye contact from everyone, as I knew the bags under my eyes were so exaggerated that they were reminiscent of Halloween makeup for a corpse.

Clint ate next to me in silence as he read the newspaper. There were no other guests on the ranch, besides Julian. I had heard his car pull in at 11:47 PM the night before. It was during one of the many times I looked at the clock. His lights were off when I left my cabin this morning, so I assumed he was sleeping off his long day. Lucky guy.

After clearing my plate, I brought it back into the kitchen and set it in the sink and began to wash the other dishes. The kitchen was completely empty and the ranch hands had long since departed for their chores.

I heard Rosa come up behind me, setting her empty plate on the counter beside me. "Annie honey, you look like hell."

I turned my head in her direction and gave her a dirty look. "That's not very nice."

She put a hand on my shoulder. "Leave the dishes. I'll do them. Go back to bed for a few hours."

I shook my head. "No. I'm leaving you by yourself Thursday, right before the family reunion pulls in. I shouldn't even take Tuesday off."

Rosa walked to the side of me and leaned her back against the counter. "First of all, you are not taking Tuesday off. It's your scheduled day off. I don't want you here that day. And second, what else is there to do that can't be done before you leave on Wednesday?"

I huffed a breath, blowing the long tendrils framing my face away. "I need to air out all the cabins and change the bedding, bring in fresh towels. I need to clean the pond and spray the weeds, especially around the paddock. I have to finish the paperwork and call the insurance agent to go over what needs to be insured and what can be dropped…"

"Ah," Rosa said, holding a hand up in interruption. "Airing out the cabins will take all of twenty minutes to open the windows. You can do that Friday morning. It'll be better weather that morning anyway. I'll have Dylan show Farley what to do with the pond and weeds, since he doesn't need to mow until next week. Call the insurance people today and we will discuss what they say over dinner tonight." She gently tugged me to face her. "You need not worry. You've got enough on your mind, so don't bother making yourself sick over a few weeds and some pond scum." She pushed off the counter. "Just hurry home so I don't have to train Farley on the computer. I don't think my heart could take it." Rosa clutched her chest dramatically, and I laughed.

"Don't worry, I wouldn't even want to imagine that." I set a clean dish on the drying rack. "Six sent me the itinerary last night. We will be back early Friday morning."

Rosa nodded before gently whacking me on the arm. "Now, scram. I didn't buy these fancy dishwashers to waste your talented hands scrubbing strawberry off my steel pans. Get in the office and make those phone calls."

I dried my hands on the dish towel and did exactly as she'd instructed.

Hours later, I'd finished talking with the insurance agent, and my hands cramped from the note taking I'd done on the scratch pad next to me. The sandwich Rosa had delivered two hours before, at lunch, sat untouched, the bread growing hard and stale.

I leaned back in my desk chair, arms over my head, stretching the tension out of my shoulders. No matter how far I pushed the upcoming trip back into the recesses of my mind, it sprang forward stubbornly.

"Think fast, Shorty," came a voice behind me. I spun in my chair and caught sight of Julian right before seeing the backpack that was flying at my face.

"Shorty?" I asked after I clumsily caught the bag. "What kind of nickname is that when I'm an inch shy of six whole feet?"

"It's just my temporary nickname for you. And technically, you are four inches shorter than me, which makes you short from my perspective."

"Yeah, well what should I call you then, Jolly Green Giant?" I asked, while looking over the tactical-looking backpack in my hands.

Julian walked towards me and crouched down, putting him at eye level with me. "I'm afraid the concept of nicknames is too complicated for you. The idea is that it's supposed to be shorter than the person's actual given name," he replied sarcastically.

I sized him up. "Jules?" I asked, sweetly, a smile curving my lips.

"Oh, God no," he groaned. "My mother calls me that. That is not a sexy nickname."

"And Shorty is?" I huffed.

"Like I said, it's temporary," he said, before unzipping the front pocket of the backpack. "This is for our next date. Tomorrow."

I looked over the bag curiously, taking note of the dozens of zippered pockets. I saw an insulated pouch with stretchy bands attached. "Is this for water bottles?" I asked, confused.

Julian reached in and tugged on one of the stretchy bands. "Yes. It will fit two Nalgene-sized bottles in here and keep them cool. And underneath-" he started, before flipping the backpack to reveal the attached straps on the bottom, "-are straps that are made for attaching a sleeping bag."

Realization hit me in an instant. "We're going camping?" I asked, biting my lip, trying to hold in a grin. The glee that filled me reminded me of being a child.

Julian was watching my face for my reaction. He wasn't disappointed. "Yes, we are." He smiled, before sliding his thumb on my bottom lip. He left it there for a moment before tugging my lip out from behind my teeth. My stomach clenched with desire. His face wasn't even four inches from mine. My grip tightened on the backpack.

"Thank you," I whispered to him, searching his eyes. If he wasn't going to make the first move this time, I was. I put both hands on the sides of his face, leaned down, and brushed my lips against his, feeling the bite of his stubble on my palms. He didn't move to grab me back, and just accepted my tender gesture of appreciation. I pulled away and tamped down on my disappointment.

He smiled softly at me and brushed a ubiquitous tendril behind my ear. "My pleasure," he replied, gruffly, before standing back up and making his way to the door, presumably back to his cabin.

I exhaled loudly before turning back around in my chair, fingering all the zippers and straps of the bag. I heard him walk outside, his steps eating up the distance from my office door around the deck, quieting in their departure.

As I started to play around with the bag, I heard those same footsteps clomping back and I turned my chair just as he entered the office.

With determined eyes, he strode to me and cupped my jaw with his hands before kissing me, hard. I sighed into his mouth and brought my hands up to his forearms, trying to hold him in place, while his tongue explored my mouth. His thumb and forefinger tugged on my left earlobe right before he lightly bit on my lower lip. The sensations were overwhelming, and I couldn't prevent the moan that left my mouth. Warmth spread all over my body, rendering me unable to think about anything but of what kissing Julian felt like. He pulled back, breathing heavily, and touched my forehead to his, keeping his eyes closed as we both tried to regulate our breathing. "I forgot something," he said, still cupping my jaw.

"Hmm?" I wasn't yet capable of forming coherent words, it seemed. It felt like an Olympian feat to open my eyes and keep them open.

"Camping," he said, opening his eyes and pulling back to look into mine. "Tomorrow. Tuesday."

I laughed, but before I could reply, he quickly kissed me again. "I'll pack the tent and food. Pack your clothes and whatever girl shit you need."

I started to open my mouth to argue that, wondering at what kind of fancy food he'd bring, but he stopped me with yet another kiss. "I'll take care of it all," he interrupted, before kissing me again. "I've got sleeping bags, too."

As much as I loved camping, I liked sleeping too, and didn't know that I could trust him to bring the right kind for me. But, of course, when I started to interject, he stopped me with another kiss, this time a longer, deeper kiss. "They zip together, to form a big enough sleeping bag for two people," he whispered, caressing my cheekbone with his thumb. I met his gaze and knew the desire reflecting in his eyes was present in my own. I wasn't going to argue about the sleeping bags anymore.

"I'll pick you up at five tomorrow morning," he said, grinning, knowing full well I was just a few cabins down from him.

I laughed out loud as he started walking away, before realizing he said five, as in before sunrise.

"Five?" I asked. He turned around and walked back towards me as I continued talking, "but that's too-"

He kissed me, again, effectively stopping my argument. "I'll make it worth it," Julian said against my lips. Though I knew what he was talking about, I couldn't help but think of his earlier declaration that I was a challenge for him. I was really going to miss him when this was over, I knew. Instantly, my mood changed.

As if Julian read my mind, he kissed me softly, tenderly, before moving his kisses up the side of my face to my forehead. "Stop frowning," he whispered, before kissing my mouth again.

"I'm not frown-" I started before he cut me off with his lips again.

"Stop arguing."

"I'm not arg-" he cut me off with another kiss. I stood up and held him back with a hand. "You can't use kissing as a weapon," I said, not completely seriously.

"I'm not attacking you, Andra." He stepped closer. "And you're not exactly fighting me off," he said, grabbing my hands and pulling one up to kiss, while keeping eye contact with me. "And besides, it's better than arguing about things that are going to go my way anyway."

I laughed. "You're so sure about that, aren't you?"

He tilted my chin up with one hand before leaning down. Just before kissing me, he spoke against my lips. "I'm sure about you." He kissed me again, softly, running his hands down the sides of my neck, over my shoulders and down to my hands, linking our fingers together. I was completely limp under his touch and let myself be pulled under while he kissed me again.

"Tomorrow, five in the morning. Be ready," he said, looking directly into my eyes, before walking back out of the office.

After going over the insurance renewals with Rosa over dinner, I said my nightly prayer in the grass before going into my cabin and tossing things into my new backpack. I packed everything practical for a day of camping and packed my favorite cast iron skillet too. I knew Julian had said he'd take care of food, but in the interest of keeping our meals low maintenance, I wanted to cook with cast iron.

My cabin wasn't decorated with any significant personal touches, but along one wall in my kitchen were a dozen hanging cast iron pans. They provided décor and function, as my kitchen didn't boast a ton of cabinet space.

I heard my phone vibrate across the kitchen counter and I grabbed it, hoping for a message from Julian.

Six: I'll be getting in Wednesday morning. I've got some business in Denver and then I'll be by the ranch. We'll eat dinner before heading to the airport.

I sighed, disappointment and anxiety warring for dominance. It was only then that I realized I'd forgotten about our trip to Michigan. Julian's visit earlier that day had helped exponentially in that regard.

Me: Business in Denver?

Six: See you Wednesday.

I shook my head. Six was secretive about what he did for money. I didn't know much about his life. Even when I lived with him, I was hidden away in the basement. I didn't think he did a lot of legal things – I mean, he assisted in my disappearance after all – but I don't think he caused harm to good people.

Six was the one who had essentially created Andra Walker. He knew my mom well and even carried a torch for her shortly after she'd had me. My dad had never been in the picture; I didn't even know his name. But Six had been there when I needed a father figure the most, as a teenager trying to escape a Monster.

He was quiet, a man of few words and almost no emotions. But he loved me and cared for me the way I needed him to, and I truly couldn't ask for a better stand-in brother.

I crawled into bed and turned on a movie I'd seen at least fifty times. The noise lulled me into a peaceful, uninterrupted sleep.

My alarm went off at 4:30 and I climbed into the shower still half-asleep. It was amazing how a restful sleep could make me feel more exhausted than a night of tossing and turning.

I poured hot water into two travel mugs and then added a tea bag each before grabbing two scones I'd taken from Rosa the night before, warming them up in the microwave right before I expected Julian.

Butterflies erupted in my stomach, and I smiled softly to myself. I couldn't wait for this date. It'd been a long time since I'd been camping. And the idea of spending time out in the wild with Julian appealed to me more than I expected it to.

A soft knock on the hard wood door sounded his arrival and I opened it, smile on my face and mug in hand.

Julian sipped the tea I handed him and took the scone I offered. "I didn't make those," I said at his questioning look. "Rosa."

Julian nodded and leaned back against the counter, putting him exactly opposite of me. I took the moment to take in his appearance. He wore dark jeans, brown work boots and a navy blue cable knit sweater. His hair was wet and curly on the top, his stubble showing more growth than I remembered. His lips were smooth and wet from the tea and I found myself transfixed on his mouth. I couldn't explain the feeling that moved through me at the way he looked early in the morning, but it caused me to walk the short distance to him and kiss him, softly, simply, one hand on his shoulder.

Julian's hand rested on the small of my back before he pulled me closer. I went without hesitation. We didn't deepen the kiss, but just savored it. I pulled back first and met his eyes. Julian smiled at me before brushing his hand over my hair and tugging on my ponytail playfully. "Ready?"

I nodded and reached down to grab my backpack. Julian beat me to it and swung it over one shoulder, scone in his other hand. "I got it," He said, "just grab the teas."

After I locked up my cabin, we walked to the convertible he'd parked in my driveway. I looked over at him and laughed, remembering that he promised to pick me up. He tossed my backpack into the trunk with his. I made out a guitar case before he closed the trunk. We slid into the warmed car and I shivered off the slight chill of the morning.

I noticed he hadn't changed the disc in his CD player, so Queen was still playing. I wondered if he'd listened to it while running errands on Sunday. "How did everything go?" I asked, sipping my tea while we drove off in the dark.

"Good. I'm very happy with the tile work. My meeting was boring, but necessary. My sisters are pains in my ass, but also necessary."

My lips quirked up. "Necessary pains in the ass?"

Julian glanced over at me with a smile. "Yes. Four pains in the ass that I love with obligation as their brother, but also because they are funny, smart, and they keep me on my toes."

"Tell me about them."

"Okay." Julian turned onto a road I wasn't familiar with. "Annemarie is the youngest. She's twelve and absolutely hammers against any youngest child stereotypes. She is far from spoiled, reckless, and isn't a princess. My sister Danielle on the other hand…" Julian looked at me with big, scared eyes. "She's sixteen, and about as intimidatingly beautiful and hard-headed as they come. She's going to give our mother a heart attack."

I laughed. "Sounds like a handful."

Julian nodded his head. "And don't get me started on Elizabeth. She breaks hearts about as often as she changes her major. Which is every month or so. She's gone to school for everything from a nurse to a horticulturist. Both of which she would fail spectacularly at. Keeping things alive is not a strong suit of hers. I shudder to think of her having children."

At my laugh, he continued. "That being said, she probably has the biggest heart of all my sisters and absolutely means well. She's just a bit misguided, hence the constant changes in her major."

"And your fourth sister?" I asked, sipping more tea.

Julian smiled softly. "Rachel. She's the closest thing to a best friend I have. I'm not quite two years older than her, so we grew up together. She is down-to-earth, but she tells it like it is. You don't ever have to worry that she's not telling you the truth."

That caused me to choke on the tea I was sipping, the hot herbal beverage burning my throat as I coughed.

"Are you okay?"

I nodded and smiled weakly at him. "It went down the wrong pipe," I lied. No more talk of truths. I couldn't tell the truths I wanted to, and this was a reminder to keep what I was doing with Julian a casual thing. Guilt settled heavily on my heart.

We reached our destination three hours later after driving on a gravel road for ten minutes. The road ended at a large sandy parking lot surrounded by trees and large boulders. There was no campground office. We were literally in the thick of the forest.

When the car stopped, I got out and stretched my legs, walking to the edge of the parking lot to where the larger boulders shielded what lay beyond.

I looked back and saw Julian following me, so I climbed up onto a boulder and looked out. Down a gradual slope sat a deep blue lake, spanning as far as the eye could see. It was surrounded by mountains, a little oasis in a land of green. The sun was just beginning to rise over the mountains, illuminating part of the lake. I looked to Julian with a grin. "What is this place?"

Julian shrugged, hands in his pockets. "I used to camp up here as a kid. It's mostly a secluded fishing spot, but not so much during the week." He joined me up on the boulder and looked sideways at me. "Wanna swim?" He lifted his eyebrows playfully.

I looked at him incredulously. "That water has to be freezing this early in the morning! And you didn't tell me to pack a swimsuit."

"Is that a no?"

"That's a HELL no."

Julian laughed and headed back to the car. "Come on, we have to hike a little to get to the camp site."

The hike was less than a quarter mile and it was around the top of the hill that sloped down to the lake. Julian stopped at a small clearing about fifty feet from a sandy beach down to the water. It looked like a spot that had been used for tent camping before, based on the primitive fire pit made from stones. The area was surrounded by old pine trees and I wondered briefly what the view was like from the tops of them.

We set up the tent in silence. I noticed Julian had brought the guitar case with him and watched as he set it carefully inside the tent.

"Want a sandwich?" Julian asked, reaching into the cooler he'd brought along. I nodded and spread out one of the blankets he'd packed, laying it over the grass. He sat next to me and handed me a wrapped sandwich. I recognized it as the same kind of sandwich Rosa had made for me the day before. I eyed Julian with a "Really?" look and held up the sandwich.

"What?" he asked innocently. "She likes me."

I rolled my eyes. "You've got Rosa wrapped around your finger. All because you have a pretty face." I shook my head but bit into the sandwich anyway.

"You think I have a pretty face?" he asked, a smirk lighting up his lips.

I rolled my eyes again. "You know you're handsome."

Julian stretched his legs out in front of him. "It's nice you think so."

"Come on!" I was exasperated. "You are the kind of effortlessly good-looking that pisses people right off. And you're charming, intelligent…" I paused before continuing. "And the way you kiss…just wow."

"Well, if it makes you feel better, I've not subjected Rosa to kissing me."

I laughed and pushed him gently. "Good thing too. I don't think Clint would take too kindly to that." And me, too, I thought to myself.

"Well, fear not. There's only one woman I want to kiss." He leveled his gaze on me, brown eyes focused solely on me.

I shivered and tugged on my sleeves. The air was warming up by the minute as the sun rose in the sky, but my shivering had nothing to do with the temperature and everything to do to my body's reaction to the man sitting next to me. I finished my sandwich and brushed the crumbs from my hands before lying down on the blanket.

"So, you have me for the entire day. What's on the agenda?"

Julian finished his sandwich and leaned back on his hands. He looked out on the lake, before leaning his head in my direction. "Well I was thinking we'd hike around the lake, lay out in the sun for a bit, and have a picnic on the beach. Then I thought we could go out on the lake."

My eyebrows drew together in confusion. "Go out on the lake? On what?"

Julian smiled a secretive smile. "You'll see."

I ran my tongue over my lips in a teasing manner and he laughed before standing up and reaching a hand down to me. "Come on, let's go."

He grabbed a smaller cooler and filled it with some things from the large cooler while I changed into my hiking boots and shorts and then grabbed the water bottles I'd packed. I slid a baseball cap over my hair. Julian folded the blanket over his arm and led the way through the trees, holding back branches to keep me from having to duck underneath them. I knew I was strong, capable, but the simple gesture was welcome, another thing I wasn't used to. I was quickly learning that this dating thing wasn't awful. Or maybe it was Julian that made it fun. I forgot my worries in his presence, forgot to hide the dark parts of myself.

After hiking the perimeter of the lake, we returned to the area where we'd started and Julian spread the checkered blanket on the sandy shore, setting his cooler down.

I slid the ball cap off my head and ran the back of my hand over the sweat that had collected there. I plopped onto the blanket and watched Julian as he crouched down to the cooler.

He pulled two beer bottles, a small container of olives, some prosciutto, hard cheeses and crackers from the cooler and set them out on the blanket before opening both beers and handing me one. I looked at him with a small smile and a raised eyebrow. "Recreating our first date?"

He took a pull from his beer and gave me an enigmatic grin as I opened the olives and popped two in my mouth. "Well, I know you go a bit crazy for olives and cured meats, so I thought I'd bring some along, make my company a bit more bearable." The sun filtered through his hair, highlighting the coppery highlights. I ached to run my hands through just then, and swallowed hard, forcing the olives down my throat.

He stared at me, eyes searching my face. I let him stare, unashamed of my makeup free face, surely boasting a fine sheen of sweat. His eyebrows were drawn together, and the way he stared at me was almost as if he was studying a puzzle. My heart thudded in my chest, almost painfully. What was it about him that affected me so deeply?

Before I said anything, he picked an olive from the container and caught me staring. Keeping his eyes locked on mine, he brought the olive to my already parted lips and set the cool, salty fruit just on my bottom lip. I heard his breathing becoming shallower as I opened my mouth more before sucking the olive from his fingers. His eyes were hard on mine, his gaze dominant with desire. I felt that ever present warmth in the pit of my stomach flare up so I set my beer down before I climbed over, straddling his hips, bringing my mouth to his.

Julian immediately wrapped his arms tightly around me, holding me closely as we kissed. The condensation from the beer bottle gripped in his hand soaked the back of my shirt and sharply contrasted with the little bursts of heat igniting all over my body. My mouth was insatiable, desperate. I had never needed physical touch so intensely, so frequently. I didn't know what these impulses were from, or why I acted on them, but in this moment there was no room in my head for anything but Julian.

My hands slid into his hair and his lips moved over mine in a dance of teasing brushes before he deepened the kiss. An ache bloomed in my chest, some unnamed emotion that was equally painful and satisfying. This connection was nourishment for my soul, feeding a starving part of me that I didn't know existed. I was absolutely breathless with want, with need, with something.

The gravity of our rapidly developing connection forced me to pull away first and I sucked in a breath of clean air, filling my lungs. Panic pricked just below the surface but I didn't pull away from his body completely, just enough to rest my head on top of his shoulder. My hands slid down his back, eliciting a shudder from him as I reached my hand out blindly for the beer I'd set down. When I gained purchase of the cool bottle, I took a large swig, fully aware of Julian's eyes on me.

The hand clutching the beer bottle was dripping with the cooled condensation, so I switched hands and ran the wet hand down my throat, cooling the fire that burned just beneath my skin. I still sat straddled in Julian's lap and became aware of the part of his body that was pressing against my shorts.

Julian must have realized the same thing because he shifted and winced, taking a pull from his beer. As I watched his Adam's apple bob in his throat, mesmerized, I whispered, "What are you doing to me?" My eyes swung up to his, and I searched his dark eyes for an answer.

Julian finished his swallow with a slight smile and brushed his free hand down the side of my face. Leaning forward, he nuzzled that same side of my face, stubble against my smooth skin. I sucked in a breath, suddenly reminded that my attraction to him wasn't something that could be turned on or off. It was always on, and just heightened when he touched me. I felt his cool lips at my ear. "I was going to ask you the same question."

A small part inside me cautioned against letting this continue. I thought I could keep my physical connection to Julian casual. But I was realizing that being around him was both soothing and enlivening. I was driven by feeling alive. And being with Julian fueled that larger part, the more dominant part of me that craved being free. So I muted the small part that protested and turned my face to his cheek, kissing his stubble.

I pulled away and smiled softly at him, taking another sip from the beer. I looked at our surroundings. With the sun starting to heat the earth, the sounds of wild birds cawing, and the smell of Julian, all sandalwood and cinnamon, I felt safe.

"Open," Julian whispered, breaking me out of my trance. I looked quickly at him and saw the cracker topped with cheese in his fingers.

I locked eyes with him as I opened my mouth. Being this close to him, with the sun lighting up his face, I made out slivers of gold and green in his brown eyes. He had a beautiful face with strong eyebrows and a strong nose. As my eyes traveled down his face, I noted his perfect Cupid's bow and licked my lips. Desire sat in the front seat of my mind, aching with each tease.

He placed the cracker in my mouth and I closed it, snagging the tips of his fingers in the process, again. I smiled slyly as I slowly chewed. The cracker was buttery and hinted of onion and some other spices. Combined with the pepper jack cheese, it was delicious and elicited a small moan from the back of my throat as I closed my eyes, chewing.

Swallowing, I opened my eyes and saw Julian watching me, intently as always. "Good?" he asked, his voice gruff.

I nodded and licked my lips. "Very."

"I love watching you eat."

I bit my lower lip to hold back my Cheshire cat-like grin. "So you've mentioned before."

Julian reached out and brushed a finger over my lip ring. "I like this."

"It's my only more radical piercing. I used to have my nose, but that was more annoying than anything."

"Ears?"

I nodded, pulling my hair to one side. "I have five piercings in my left and three in my right. But that's it for piercings."

"I know about the Queen tattoo, but do you have any others?"

"Yup. Sure do," I replied with amusement.

Julian looked at me a moment. When he realized I was making no move to show them, he smirked.

"Maybe you'll get to see them later," I teased, sliding off his lap. I took another pull of my beer and lay down on my back, staring up at the sky. It was as if we belonged in the same magnetic field. Even with the distance I'd put between us, I still felt his presence next to me.

I soaked up the sun's warmth and closed my eyes, completely at peace. "Tell me what growing up with four sisters was like."

I could feel my body relaxing, partly thanks to the beer and mostly thanks to the company. I listened to him tell stories of his sisters, and laughed at their shenanigans. His voice was maple syrup, coating me with warmth.

I didn't realize I'd drifted off until I heard Julian's voice at my ear. "Andra. Wake up."

I soaked up the last bits of my nap, savoring the luxury of it, before I eased my eyes open. He was leaning over me, blocking the sun from my eyes. His eyebrows were scrunched together in concern. "Was I asleep that long?"

He leaned away from me and ran a hand through his hair. "No, just an hour." He didn't look at me again and I felt uneasy. I sat up and pulled my knees up to my chest, hugging them.

Whatever had darkened Julian's demeanor was gone in an instant and he stood up, holding a hand out. I noticed our picnic had been cleaned up and the cooler was missing.

"I brought it back to the campsite. Come on, let's go out on the lake." I shook off the unease I'd felt and followed him, hand in his. About a hundred feet down the beach was a narrow dirt trail. Julian motioned for me to stay put while he jogged up the trail, weaving around large rock formations and brush.

I turned towards the water and took in the calm. I slipped my boots off and then my socks before wading into the water. The water was cool, evidence of the spring temperatures and the snow run off of the mountain keeping the water cold, but not unbearably.

I dug my toes into the sandy bottom, enjoying the feel of the grains sifting through my toes when I lifted them back up. I did it three more times before I heard Julian coming back down the trail. Keeping my toes in the sand, I turned my head towards his direction. He was carrying a beat up canoe. I couldn't tell if it was supposed to be blue or white. Weathered with time or neglect, the paint was chipped all across the planks that held it together.

Julian's grin was reminiscent of a little boy and I couldn't help but smile back as I turned around fully to face him. He kicked his tennis shoes and socks off before sliding the canoe in the water, gesturing towards me to hop in.

He rowed us out towards the middle of the lake while I looked out and around. The lake wasn't huge, but it was surrounded with rock and trees, and situated at the base of a valley that butted up to mountains on one side. It was private, peaceful, and one of the most beautiful places I'd laid my eyes on.

"Tell me about one of your books." I was turned around, facing Julian, one hand trailing across the surface of the lake.

Julian had an eyebrow raised. "Really? That's what those little paragraphs on the back of a book are for, you know."

I lifted my hand and flicked drops of water at his face. "No, you don't say?" I said with mock surprise. "You know I don't own any of your novels. All I know is that you write mysteries." I stretched my legs across one of the benches in the boat while we softly rocked in the middle of the lake.

Julian pulled the oars into the boat, grazing my bare thigh with one of the wet paddles. I knew he'd done it on purpose, in hopes that I would be annoyed, but he was sorely mistaken. Dirt, slime, grease – none of it bothered me. I was meant for this environment.

He eased back and lifted his legs to rest beside mine on the same bench, shoving his hands into the pockets of his dark grey cargo shorts.

"The book I'm working on now is about a single mom who lives a modest life. No frills. She never eats out, doesn't own anything of value. She has one child, the love of her life." He pulled one hand out of his pocket and ran his fingers through his hair, then back again, scratching the strands back into a messy style. "What no one knew was that she was sitting on a massive estate. Over a million in the bank."

"How? And why was she living so modestly?"

Julian shrugged. "It's rumored that her parents were millionaires. She inherited their fortune in a trust. And no one knows why she chose to live modestly. There are theories that she didn't want anyone to know, that something would happen to her. Another theory is that someone found out, because she was murdered, leaving her child an orphan. The mystery part of my novel is who did it and why."

"Well that's no happily-ever-after story, Julian."

He laughed and shook his head. "I don't write happily-ever-afters. I write tragedies."

Silence hung between us then. I pulled my hand out of the water and shook it, releasing the drops that clung to my fingertips. I looked out towards the sun, squinting. "Why?" I asked, swinging my head towards Julian.

Julian looked as though he'd been lost in thought and stared at me, confused.

"Why do you write tragedies?"

"Why don't you read tragedies?" he asked in response. His eyes were guarded, trained on mine, compelling me to release a secret.

I narrowed my eyes. Because I've lived through my fair share of tragedies. I didn't say this out loud, but the look on Julian's face told me his answer was the same. He stared at me, unsmiling. So I chose to say something else.

"Because I prefer love stories."

He tilted his head to the side, and released the tension that had formed around his mouth before he smiled crookedly. "Which is interesting, because you don't seem like a sappy kind of girl."

I shrugged. "I'm not. But I like knowing that life isn't always cruel."

"Ah," Julian said, leaning back. "Who said love can't be cruel?"

"People can be cruel. They make choices to be cruel. Love is not a choice. It's a force of nature." I folded my arms across my chest.

"I disagree." He faced me and mirrored my pose.

"Tell me a story then, storyteller. Tell me a story where love was cruel."

"You're asking for a tragic love story then. Something reminiscent of Romeo and Juliet?"

"Love wasn't cruel for Romeo and Juliet. They were practically babies and their families were comprised of assholes. Tell me something new."

Julian glided a hand along his jawline, his long fingers scratching the stubble that grew there. "Okay. Have you heard the story of Heloise and Abelard?"

I shook my head. "Tell me."

"This is a true story. And I may be a little rusty on some details, but you'll get the idea." He rubbed his hands together and told the story of Heloise and Abelard.

"Heloise was a brilliant woman who lived in the early to mid-twelfth century France. She was considered to be of a lower social standing, and she was a ward of her uncle Fulbert, who was a priest. Fulbert loved her. She was his pride and joy, and he ensured that she received the very best education. She was a scholar and well renowned throughout Western Europe for her intelligence. And not only that, she was considered to be very beautiful as well – a complete package." Julian winked at me and I laughed before motioning for him to continue with the story.

"So then comes Peter Abelard, a philosopher and considered one of the greatest thinkers of that time. He was of nobility, but had chosen to be a philosopher instead of accepting knighthood. He was also a priest, like Fulbert, and was wowed by Heloise, by her intelligence. He persuaded Fulbert to allow him to teach Heloise. He couldn't afford to live in his current home while studying, so he told Fulbert that he would offer tutoring to Heloise in exchange for room and board. Abelard was more than twenty years Heloise's senior, but that didn't stop them from developing feelings for each other.

"Unfortunately, Fulbert discovered their affair. He was grief-stricken and separated the two lovers. It was discovered that Heloise was pregnant and Abelard sent her to his sister's house for the remainder of the pregnancy and delivery. Abelard went to Fulbert and begged for his forgiveness and asked for permission to marry Heloise. Fulbert agreed, but Heloise did not want to marry Abelard."

"Why? Didn't they love each other?"

Julian nodded. "But Heloise loved Abelard selflessly. What penalties, she said, would the world rightly demand of her if she should rob it of so shining a light? See, she would rather be lonely and socially disgraced than allow Abelard to marry her, worried that their union would distract himself from studying. But Abelard insisted and Heloise relented to a secret marriage after their son was born. Heloise left her son with Abelard's sister and stayed with her uncle while Abelard went back to teaching. But Fulbert was still angry and spread word of what really happened, which caused great embarrassment to Heloise. Abelard brought Heloise to the convent where she'd been brought up to protect her. When Fulbert heard he had brought her there, he was enraged, assuming Abelard had brought her there to get rid of her, forcing her to become a nun. He plotted revenge with his friends and his friends broke into Abelard's room one evening and castrated him."

I nodded, understanding the significance. "Because to them, that part of his body had caused great embarrassment for Heloise?"

"Yes. And Abelard was, understandably, filled with shame, so he became a monk while Heloise became a nun. They lived separate lives, and were never together until death, when their bodies were buried next to one another."

I sat back and frowned. "Well that's depressing."

Julian laughed, his features relaxing after telling the story. I'd seen several of the expressions that his face held, but this, this carefree and happy face, was my favorite.

"Yes, it's sad. But Abelard and Heloise wrote each other beautiful letters, and never married anyone else, unless you count their marriage to the Church."

I chewed my lip in thought. "So they had a short time together and then nothing? Spending their entire lives apart? That has to be torture. Death to one of them would have been kinder."

"See? Love can be cruel. The love for his niece drove Fulbert to strip her lover of the part that made him a man."

I digested the story for a minute. "Man," I said, stretching my arms down my legs and scratching my ankles. "Love can be a bitch, can't it?"

"You say that as if you haven't loved."

I bristled at his words. "Of course I love. I love Rosa, my brother, the ranch." I scrunched up my nose. "I love the grass under my feet and the air in my lungs." I met his eyes. "I know what love is, what it feels like."

"But romantic love? Have you been 'in love' before?"

I crossed my arms over my chest again. "Well this is getting rather personal, isn't it?" The direction this conversation had taken made my legs itch to run. Too bad I was in the middle of a large body of water.

"Is it?" Julian asked, leaning forward, encroaching on my space. I backed up as far as I could go, which was another six inches in this small canoe. He loomed over me, casting a shadow over my face. All I saw was his face. He wore a lazy smile, the dimple dipped deep in his cheek.

"Yes." I licked my lips. The movement drew his gaze there and my breathing picked up speed, my chest rising and falling. My sensory system was completely wrapped up in Julian. His sandalwood and cinnamon scent invading my nose and my heart's rapid beating in response to his proximity drowning out all other sounds. The feel of his fingers pushing back the tendrils that clung to my cheeks and the way he looked down at me, as if committing my face to memory. The only sense being deprived was taste.

As if he could sense my thoughts, Julian brought his mouth down to mine, just resting his lips against mine for a minute. My heart shuddered. Julian slowly tilted his lips up, lightly grazing them against my top lip. My eyes were closed, relishing this moment.

The kiss was a tease; the lightest caress of his mouth moving over mine. I felt him move right before I felt his lips on my forehead. "Come on," he whispered, his hands finding mine. "Let's head back for dinner." He helped me sit up before grabbing the oars and sliding into the water.

He always seemed so calm, so collected, while hormones raged within my body. I stared at him in annoyance before he smiled and winked. "You do use kissing as a weapon. You asked a personal question and then kissed me brainless," I said indignantly.

"Don't be cranky, Andra." When I glared at him, he shrugged his shoulders. "You didn't answer my question anyway."

"No," I said, trying to soften the frustration that climbed into my voice. "I haven't been 'in love' before." It was on the tip of my tongue to direct the same question back to him, but I bit my tongue instead. Julian watched me carefully, knowingly, a small smile on his lips as he rowed us back to shore.

I helped him pull the canoe back to the spot he had hidden it. He had told me it was his canoe, but he left it here for others to use. It hadn't been stolen yet, so he counted himself fortunate.

We walked back up to the camp and ate roasted hot dogs and coleslaw on paper plates. I hadn't looked at my watch all day until now. "I can't believe it's already three. But at the same time, I can't believe it's only three."

Julian looked up from his paper plate and glanced at his watch. "This is a late lunch. I have kabobs and s'mores on the menu for dinner tonight."

I was struck by the thought he'd put into this date and all the preparation. I stood up and dragged my camp chair closer to his. "Thanks."

He looked at me quizzically.

"For this." I gestured my paper plate at our surroundings. "I haven't been camping in years and even then, I can't remember it being this easy, this relaxing."

Julian leaned forward, bracing his elbows on his knees, bringing his face closer to mine. "I enjoy this too you know. It's not all for your benefit."

I looked at him a moment, contemplating. His smirk at his sarcastic comment made me feel justified in grabbing a handful of coleslaw from my plate and smearing it on his face. So I did it. Unfortunately for me, Julian didn't miss a beat and smeared a handful of coleslaw in my hair, gliding his slimy hand over my face at the end.

Out of coleslaw, I improvised. I picked my hot dog out of its bun and slapped him in the face with it, sending splatters of ketchup, mustard, and relish everywhere.

Julian's expression was perfection. Laughter bubbled up out of my throat as I stood up and backed away, still clutching the hot dog in my hand. Julian looked around before dunking what remained of his bun into his red solo cup of water. He then squeezed the soggy bun in his hands for effect, letting me see the gooey mush seeping between his fingers. I backed up and held the hot dog out in warning.

"You got me twice, Andra. It's payback time."

"Nuh-uh." I was shaking my head back and forth, walking backwards. He advanced towards me, an animal stalking its prey. His stride was longer than mine, so I turned away from him and took off running down to the water.

He caught up to me in only two heart beats and then one heart beat later, my face was plastered with soggy hot dog bun. I was laughing so hard that I had to grip onto his waist to keep from doubling over. A moment later, he picked me up and hauled me over his shoulder as he walked into the water before unceremoniously dunking me under.

I came up sputtering, still laughing. Julian was laughing too, his face a mixture of coleslaw and streaks of red and yellow. "You've got something on right here," I motioned, pointing at my cheekbone before dramatically waving my hand all over every part of my face.

"Oh right here?" Julian asked playfully, wiping the smear of coleslaw in his hairline. "Did I get it?"

I bit my lip. "Yeah, you're good." His eyebrows were filled with ketchup and mustard, his scruff sprinkled with relish.

Julian swam closer to me in the chest-deep water. "You've still got some on your face. Let me help you with that."

I held my face up towards him and a second later a heavy splash of water hit my face. My eyes were closed, but my mouth was not, so I ingested a significant amount of lake water. I opened my eyes and narrowed them as Julian laughed. "Oh, you're gonna get it."

My prior self-defense training came in handy as I reached a leg out, curled it around his and yanked, causing him to lose his balance and go under the water. I felt hands grab my legs under water and I went under a moment later.

When we both surfaced we were laughing. Julian grabbed my hands and pulled me towards him. I went willingly and looped my arms around his neck, his arms around my waist.

"That was the most fun I've had with a food fight," he said while brushing the hair off my face.

"You like being smacked in the face with a phallic object?"

Julian smirked. "Who doesn't?"

I rubbed a thumb over his eyebrow, removing what remained of the condiments before gliding my nails through his stubble. Julian's eyes closed, his long black eyelashes brushing the top of his cheekbones, water streaming down his face. I was suddenly overcome with how truly attractive he was. Strong cheekbones, wide, almond-shaped eyes, strong eyebrows. I let my fingers graze over his features and then brushed the tip of my thumbnail over his lips.

His eyes opened and I saw the heat in them as he stared at me. "You're beautiful," I whispered. I swallowed back the feeling that had settled in my throat.

He gazed at me for a moment before leaning forward and pressing his lips to mine. We were chest to chest, hearts beating in time. His hands cupped my jawline before he gently tilted my head back, dropping kisses down my throat. A moan trembled out of my throat before his lips moved to my collarbone while his hands moved to my shoulders. I felt his stubble brush my sensitive skin and my body shuddered.

He kept his lips chaste, never moving lower than my collarbone. My hands gripped his shirt under the water and I tightened my hold. I wanted to pull him even closer. I wanted him to feel the way my skin felt under his touch.

I moaned his name, involuntarily, and that seemed to snap him out of the spell he was under. He planted one innocent kiss to my nose before I opened my eyes and looked at him with confusion. "Why did you stop?"

He sighed and moved his hands under water, linking with mine. "You are like a drug to me. Dangerous. Addicting. I can't get enough of you." He brought our hands above water and kissed one of my hands, linked with his. "But I want more, more than just a night, more than just a few touches. And I have a feeling that once we cross that line, you will run away."

I didn't bother protesting. He knew my M.O. "You're a puzzle to me. All the pieces that make up who you are – they intrigue me. I want to figure out a few of those pieces and I want some time to understand you before we take this further."

"What about the sleeping bags then, the ones that zip together?" I asked, teasingly.

"Body heat. Do you know how cold it gets here at night? We're going to want to get up close and personal tonight to keep from losing feelings in our toes." As if to emphasize his point, his toes curled over mine in the water. "Come on," he said, tipping his head towards the shore. "Let's get some dry clothes on. I need to start marinating the meat for the kabobs." He pulled me with him out of the water, still holding my hand.

He had me change first inside the tent so I switched to my sweats and a long sleeved tee. The temperature was dropping behind the mountains that surrounded the lake, which meant it would get cooler sooner. Since my sneakers were wet, I slid my flip flops on.

When I emerged from the tent, he was stoking the fire in the fire pit. Water was dripping down his arms, traveling his taut muscles. Water darkened his hair, dripping down the back of his neck to disappear under his tee. I let out a breath I didn't know I was holding.

He looked up at me; his eyes traveled the length of my body, alighting with warmth. "Warmer?"

I nodded and tugged on my sleeves before sliding into one of the camp chairs he had set up around the fire. The cooler was open beside him, and I saw he had already mixed the meat in a bag of some kind of marinade. The wooden skewers were submerged in the water at the bottom of the cooler.

"Do you cook often?" I asked when he had returned from changing inside of the tent. He was also wearing sweats that hung off of his hips and a fitted thermal shirt.

He shrugged as he sat into the chair beside me and handed me a beer from inside the cooler, popping the top off for me first. "I was the oldest child in a house of girls. My mom worked a bunch of jobs, so it was the least I could do to help out around the house."

My brow furrowed. "What about your dad?"

Julian took a pull from his beer. "My parents divorced while my mom was pregnant with my youngest sister. I didn't see him much after he moved away from Colorado."

I didn't remember Julian talking about his dad before. "Do you talk to your dad?"

"Oh yeah. We actually talk a lot. Now that he's accepted I don't want a football career, he helps me brainstorm all the ideas for my novels."

I took a sip of my beer as I contemplated that.

"What about your parents? Do you get along with them?" Julian started peeling the label off of his beer absentmindedly.

Ah. The question I avoided like the plague. I felt the lie crawl up my throat and a moment before I spoke, guilt settled in my chest. "We are estranged. I don't talk to them."

I felt Julian turn his head to face me as I started peeling the label off of my beer too. "Why?"

I settled my lips into a thin line at the prospect of further developing this lie. Lies were not tangible things, but they still made an impact. Once they passed from your lips, you couldn't take them back. They settled in the space that trust was built on, rotting the foundation of the human connection. Stacking lies on top of each other meant adding more rot to what could be something good.

I was not inherently good. I knew that. My past was tainted. I didn't spend time developing stable romantic relationships. My body had been treated like a toy, damaged. Yes, it was true that I didn't believe in spending time with someone in the long run because I couldn't take the constant lying. But a part of me also believed I didn't deserve it. If someone else had treated me like I was nothing, why should I believe I was anything more than that? I was willing to have short term sexual relationships because that was easy, something that had been taken from me. So now, that was a choice for me to give. Anything deeper than that was unfair. I was dark. I was rot, corroding the good in others.

Don't get me wrong, I didn't think I was a terrible person. I was a good friend, a good worker. But I couldn't give anyone more than what they saw on the surface. Lies were more frequent than truth. I would lie for the rest of my life. How could I share a life with someone who didn't know me, who believed the vinegar I spoke?

No, this was easier.

"Andra?" I was startled out of my thoughts.

I shook my head, clearing away my thoughts. "Sorry." I took a drink from my beer and reminded myself of his earlier question. But before I could speak, he interrupted.

"We don't have to talk about it."

This was my out. I knew I should take it, but I felt guilty. He'd shared about his family. Would it be better to tell him nothing or tell him a lie?

"Rosa is like my family. Everyone at the ranch, they are more than I deserve." A truth.

"I don't believe that," he replied. I couldn't help the bubble of laughter. He didn't believe the one thing that I'd been truthful about. He looked at my quizzically at my outburst. "What makes you think you deserve any less than what you have?"

Oh. I hadn't meant to let that part slip from my lips. I wracked my brain for an answer. "I'm just not an emotional person. I don't let people in." Another truth.

I watched Julian chew on his lip, deep in thought. He leaned back into the camp chair and rubbed a hand over his chin. I heard the rasp of his fingers against his stubble and flashes his stubble rubbing against my skin invaded my mind.

"Why don't you let people in?"

I took another sip of my beer. Julian was unknowingly prying some of the first truths from my lips. "Because it's easier not to."

Julian didn't reply to that, just finished his beer before getting up and heading to the tent. Before I could ask what he was doing, he returned with the guitar case. My heart thudded in my chest.

"Do you mind?" he asked as he pulled the guitar out of its case. I shook my head and watched, enraptured, as he started tuning the guitar.

A moment later, he started playing. The intro sounded familiar, but I couldn't place it.

And then he started singing. His voice was soft, yet full-bodied. It was deep, clean, and clear. He had no trouble when the pace of the song picked up. I knew he was singing the song he'd said was his favorite, "Name." I listened closely to the lyrics while he strummed along on the guitar. I shivered, feeling transparent. Thankfully, he wasn't looking directly at me while singing, so he didn't see the nerves that flooded me, making me want to itch my skin.

When he finished, his eyes met mine. He smiled sheepishly. "I love that song. First song I learned to play."

Not wanting to dissect the lyrics, I tried diverting the subject. "How long have you been playing?"

Julian's hands roamed over the neck of the guitar, a movement that made me antsy. "About ten years."

I'm sure my eyes betrayed how surprised I was at that, because he laughed. "Remember how I told you I played football all throughout high school?" I nodded. "I joined the team to impress a girl I had a crush on. But turns out she was more into music than sports. So I joined a guitar class in high school. I had grand ideas of wooing her with music."

I laughed. "So? Did it work out for you? Did you woo her?"

Julian laughed with me. "No. She saw right through me and was not impressed, to say the least."

"What?" I was surprised. "What girl wouldn't be impressed that you went out of your way to romance her?"

"Well that was part of the problem, actually," he said. He set the guitar with its back on his legs. "She thought I was stalking her and spoke to a guidance counselor. Kind of embarrassing, actually. That killed my affection for her."

"Maybe she was onto something." I lifted my arms to emphasize my point. "You always manage to find me. Perhaps you are a secret stalker."

"Nah, I think it's just that you want to be found."

His eyes met mine and though he was teasing, it felt like there was a double meaning to his words. I tried to play it off with a smile. I pointed to the guitar. "Do you do requests?" I batted my eyelashes, really playing up my question.

Julian puffed out his chest in complete exaggeration. "Sure do."

"Hmm…" I narrowed my eyes in contemplation and tapped a finger to my forehead. "How about some Poison?"

Julian's lips spread into a boyish grin as he launched into "Every Rose Has Its Thorn." I sang along with him, adding as much drama as possible, and did the air electric guitar at the appropriate parts. It was more fun than I'd had in a long time, and Julian didn't pause before he moved from song to song. He played a few songs I didn't know, so I just leaned back and basked in his voice, in the sky darkening as the sun slid down the sky. His voice when speaking or when singing moved me.

He sang "Cannonball" by Damien Rice for his last song and his voice took on a different quality. Gone was his clear, crisp voice. He had more of a gravely sound, whether by design or from overextending his vocals, I wasn't sure. But as with everything he did, I was mesmerized. It was at the end of that song that I felt goose bumps prickle my arms and something squeezed in my chest.

After he finished "Cannonball" he offered me the guitar so he could skewer the kabobs. I plucked the strings, not playing any particular song; just playing random chords.

Julian set a grate over the fire and let it warm up for a few minutes. He laid the skewers on the grate and then sat next to me while they cooked. Steak, peppers, onions, and mushrooms. I barely resisted licking my lips. "Those smell amazing."

Julian nodded and washed his hands with water from the cooler and some hand sanitizer before grabbing the guitar from me and putting it back in its case inside the tent. "The marinade is one of my secrets, a concoction I made after countless attempts in the kitchen."

I tried to imagine what it was like growing up with so many siblings and so much responsibility. "Were you in charge of your sisters growing up?"

Julian offered me another beer before grabbing one for himself. "Pretty much. I was the man of the house when dad moved out. We spent those first few years with the same thing for dinner every night: mac and cheese. When I was sixteen, I started doing the grocery shopping and watched a lot of cooking shows. Then we started eating food that didn't come from a box. It was a revelation."

He checked on the kabobs, turning them on the opposite side. I felt my mouth water at more than just the scent of the food. He was bent over, the shirt riding up an exposing part of his lower back. Just that tiny bit of exposed flesh was enough to make me tingle with need. I felt out of control of my body's reactions. I knew what I was feeling, both physically and emotionally, was an anomaly for me.

Julian wanted more from me, I knew. I could tell when he lifted his head and looked directly into my eyes, his eyebrows drawn together. He wanted a peek inside my head. And the strange thing was, I wanted to allow him that peek. But at the same time, I knew allowing him in would only cause harm to us both.

"This is almost ready."

That snapped my head out of its internal warring. "I cannot wait."

Julian grinned, his funny little boyish grin. It was one of his many smiles, all of which tugged a reluctant smile from my lips in response.

"Do you like s'mores?"

"Don't you remember? I would insert a feeding tube of chocolate if it were possible." I settled into the chair, enjoying the warmth of the fire as the evening cooled.

"Of course I remembered. It's unlikely I could forget. You are something else, Andra Walker."

The compliment was unexpected, but appreciated. "Well you are thorough and thoughtful, Julian Jameson. What's the catch?"

Julian looked at me in mock seriousness. "I'm afraid I'm a terrible kisser," he said, sighing dramatically.

"Well I know that's a lie," I replied, sipping on my beer.

"Okay. I'm a shit writer."

"Doubt that. I looked you up. You're kind of a big deal."

Julian seemed uncomfortable. "I'm just me."

A thought occurred to me. "Why do you go by J.J.?"

He grabbed a couple paper plates and crouched by the fire, turning the skewers once more. "Because I wanted to disconnect my personal life from my professional one. J.J. is elusive. He's kind of a dick, to be honest."

I laughed, slapping my hand over my mouth to contain the noise. Julian looked at me with an eyebrow raised. "What?"

"That was the impression you gave off in your first email to the ranch about booking. I swore you'd be an uptight asshole."

Julian didn't seem surprised. "I wanted you to think that. Believe it or not, I don't make a habit of letting people in. I'm closed off, like you," he said, meeting my eyes, the challenge in them daring me to disagree with his assessment.

I shrugged. "It's not that I'm hiding anything. I just don't feel the desire that everyone else feels; the desire to tell everyone everything about your life."

"Which is why you don't have a Facebook, I guess."

Of course he searched for me on Facebook. "That's part of it, yes. I like my anonymity. And besides, I don't have much else outside of the ranch. I don't travel, I don't party, I don't meet famous people – apart from you – so my life would be rather dull to some people. And I don't want people to think that. I love my life. I don't seek validation from anyone but myself."

Julian was looking at me with an expression of complete understanding. "I really respect that about you, Andra." He looked back at the skewers and turned them again. "I value my privacy too. It's why I go by J.J."

"So who calls you Julian?"

He pulled four skewers off and set them on a paper plate before handing the plate to me. "My mom, my sisters." He pulled another four skewers off and set them on a second plate before sliding the remaining skewers to another plate. He settled in the chair next to me and slid a piece of meat off the skewer, popping it in his mouth. He smiled while chewing and looked over at me. "My friends. You."

"You don't introduce yourself as Julian? What about your book people?" I popped a small mushroom in my mouth and closed my eyes, groaning. Lemon, garlic, and pepper burst on my tongue.

"Do you always do that?" Julian asked, his voice husky. My eyes were still closed, but my lips stretched into a feline smile.

"Only when I taste something incredible." I opened my eyes and met his eyes. "This is amazing. You're wasting your talents writing."

He laughed and popped a mushroom in his own mouth. I popped a piece of steak into my mouth and tried to suppress the resulting groan. "Holy shit, Julian."

"I'm glad you like it." He ran his tongue over his teeth, seemingly in thought, before saying, "I hope you let me cook for you again."

"Let you? Hell, I will chain you to my kitchen if it means you'll cook like this for me again."

"Oh, bondage? I can roll with that."

I knew my cheeks flamed red. Me? Blushing? What alternate universe had I just walked into? "You never answered my question, you know," I said, clearing my throat. "Do your book people call you J.J.?"

"Yes. I don't ever introduce myself as Julian."

"Interesting." I chewed another mushroom. "Would you prefer that I call you J.J.?"

"No." The answer was quick and firm. I raised an eyebrow. "You're more than an acquaintance, Andra. And you haven't even read my books." He laughed and tossed his finished skewer into the fire.

"True." I chewed thoughtfully. "So, Heloise and Abelard. Why do you know so much about their story?"

"I've always found tragic love stories fascinating, believe it or not. I don't subscribe to the belief that every love story is meant to have a happily-ever-after ending."

"Why not?"

"Well think about it this way: would anyone care if Romeo and Juliet had lived happily? It was the struggles they faced that made the story iconic. Or Cyrano de Bergerac, another depressing tale of love. Sure, in the end she realizes it was him all along, but Cyrano is dead. Their love story ended the moment it began. Roxanne mourns Christian misguidedly, thinking he is the author behind the letters. But she realizes the truth at the end and now has to mourn another man."

"If you're so enamored with tragic love, why do you write mysteries?" I asked, tossing my skewer into the fire.

"Because I enjoy puzzles. I enjoy challenges. Which," he reached the poker into the fire to adjust the burning logs, "is why I was so drawn to you at first. You made yourself a challenge to me. That's like waving a bone in front of a dog. I had a compulsion to accept the challenge you unknowingly offered. So if you think about it, it's kind of your fault."

"I'm a challenge, a puzzle?" I took a moment to chew more steak. "What happens if you put the pieces together then? You're done?"

Because he was looking at the fire, I couldn't see his eyes. But his lips curved in a small smile. "Your story isn't done. There will always be pieces to put together. See, when I write one of my stories, I know all the pieces to the puzzle. I am the one who separates them. I'm the one who creates and then unravels the mystery for my readers. I know the beginning and the ending." He tossed another skewer into the fire, causing a spark to crackle from within. "I don't know these things about you. You're giving me a glimpse here and there, but you're a mystery still." He took a sip of his beer before continuing. "You're also funny and intelligent. I can see you absorb what I say and reply thoughtfully. You're more than just beautiful. And I've never met anyone like Andra Walker."

Wow. I was speechless. Had that ever happened before?

"So now I'm the one wondering, what's the catch?"

I laughed. "Well I wouldn't call my cooking skills impressive. Or the results even edible."

"That's what I'm here for. Tell me something else."

"I probably smell like horseshit most days."

"False. You smell like clementines."

"You've mentioned that. Okay, I am a homebody. I rarely leave the ranch."

"And why would you? You have peace there. The pond, the woods, and the cabin: they're all parts of you. If someone thinks those are negatives, then they must not like *you*. So why bother with them?"

It was terrifying how well Julian knew me already. And that he even cared to notice these things about me. I knew it was foolish, but I couldn't help but feel even more drawn to Julian. "You're definitely a writer," I murmured.

"I can read your body language, you know," he said, tossing his now-empty paper plate into the fire.

"What is my body language telling you?"

"That my observations make you uncomfortable, but a in an odd way you like it."

"Ha!" He nailed it. That was exactly how I felt. "Well," I drew out, standing up. I threw my empty plate into the fire and stood in front of Julian. "What is my body language telling you when I do this?" I climbed as gracefully as possible into his lap. His arm immediately wrapped around my back.

"That you want to sit on my lap," he replied matter-of-factly.

"And what is my body language telling you when I do this?" I slid my lips up his neck, grazing his veins. I felt his arms tighten around me and he breathed out a deep breath.

"That you want to make out."

"Mm-hmm." I purred alongside his throat, feeling his Adam's apple bob against my lips. His hand grabbed the back of my head, fingers twisting in my hair. He skimmed his lips along my jawline and finally found my lips.

After making out with Julian until it grew dark, we finally separated, a mess of heavy breaths and red skin. Julian grabbed the stuff for s'mores from inside the tent while I added another log to the fire. It was getting late and colder, so I was grateful for the blanket Julian laid on me when he came out of the tent.

"Did you think of everything?"

Julian smiled and handed me a stick. I pulled my pocket knife out and began sharpening the end of the stick for the marshmallows. Slivers of wood landed all around my lap and I wiped them off into the fire pit.

"Are you up for a beverage change?" he asked.

I'd finished my second beer an hour before, so I nodded as I started sharpening the second stick. I heard the unmistakable sound of a cork being released. I whipped my head around. "Champagne?" I questioned, incredulous.

"In solo cups, no less," Julian returned, and handed the bright red cup, fizzing with champagne.

"Is this a combination of your taste meets my class?" I asked, swirling the pale liquid around the cup.

Julian looked at me sharply. "This is more like my taste meets convenience. Glass flutes aren't exactly practical. Fancy clothes and fancy foods don't make you classy, Andra."

I felt scolded. But he was right to say as much. I often found humor at my own expense, and while it wasn't always insulting, my latest remark was.

"You're right," I said before taking a small sniff of the champagne. "But I do enjoy champagne. It accompanies s'mores much better than beer does."

Julian slid two marshmallows onto the tip of each sharpened stick before grabbing one stick from me. We hung them over the fire, the flames just barely licking the white confections. "Shall we toast?" he asked, holding up the cup.

"To what?" I asked, holding up my cup next to his.

"To you. For keeping me on my toes."

I shook my head. "I'd rather toast to you. This is the very best date I've been on."

"I'm afraid we're at an impasse then."

I smiled. "Let's toast to each other then," I offered, tipping my head in his direction. He tipped his cup against mine and then we both took a sip. "Like everything else, this is delicious."

Julian looked into his cup. "Yes, it's one of my favorites."

When the marshmallows were sufficiently brown, we assembled our s'mores and made a mess of eating them. "So," I said, gesturing around the campfire, "is this how you usually woo women? Champagne in plastic cups with s'mores?"

One side of his lips curved in smile. His lips had such a perfect symmetry to them. "I guess I need to know if I'm wooing you before I can answer that question."

"No," I said, biting the inside of my cheek. I didn't meet his eyes until a moment later. "You don't need to woo me. This," I waved my cup between us, "feels natural. Not manipulated by things or words." I took a sip, more for courage than anything. "I'm not used to this. To this type of need." I took another sip, washing down the chocolate and the nerves. "It's only our second date, and I'm feeling…" I searched my brain for words, failing miserably, "things. Stuff. I'm feeling stuff." I met his eyes, embarrassed at my admission.

His eyes reflected the firelight, shadows dancing on his face as the flames roared. He smiled his secretive little smile. "I'm feeling stuff too," he whispered.

"Can I come sit on your lap again?"

"Please do."

I curled up on his lap, his arms around me and the blanket covering us both as we sipped champagne and talked until the fire died out.

Before we went inside the tent for the night, Julian held my hand and led me over to a patch of grass. "Is this okay?"

I looked at him in confusion before understanding what he was referring to. My nightly prayers. I nodded, swallowing the sudden lump in my throat.

He set the lantern he'd brought over down and pointed to the tent. "I'll go get the sleeping bags unrolled while you pray."

I laid in the grass and closed my eyes, breathing in and out for a minute. I took in the sounds, the crickets chirping softly, the sound of the leaves rustling slightly with the night breeze. And then I whispered my prayers.

After extinguishing the lantern, I joined Julian in the tent. He handed me a flashlight. "Here. I'll step out while you change into pajamas. I'll be back in about twenty minutes, I'm going to bring the cooler and our garbage to my car. I don't want to keep food near the tent."

"Okay," I whispered.

I slid my pajama leggings on and then some cotton socks. I stripped off the long-sleeved tee and pulled on a tank top. I carefully packed up my backpack, leaving out jeans and my tee for the morning.

It wasn't until I was climbing into the sleeping bag that I remembered that tomorrow night, I would be falling asleep in Michigan. Dread sat like lead in my stomach. While I tried to focus on other things, the tent unzipped and Julian stepped inside. The tent was dark, since I'd turned off the flashlight. He handed me a bottle of water. "Here," he said. "I don't want you to have a headache tomorrow from the beer and champagne."

Even though I didn't have a buzz at all from the alcohol, I took the water and uncapped it, drinking greedily from it. "Thanks."

Julian stripped off his socks and then pulled his shirt up over his head. Unfortunately, all I could make out was a dark torso. He slid in beside me, his toes playing with mine. "You wear socks to bed?" he asked.

I finished the water bottle and tossed it by my duffel, rolling onto my side to face him. "I do when camping. I don't like chilly toes." I rubbed my toes over his before he trapped one of my feet between both of his. My eyes had adjusted to the dark enough that I could make out his features a little bit better.

"Today was really fun," I whispered, inching closer to him. The rustling of the sleeping bag gave me away, and I was able to make out Julian's white teeth flashing in a smile.

"It was," he whispered back before pushing a wayward tendril from my face. "Thanks for agreeing to go on another date with me."

His hand moved from my hairline to cup my jaw and I pushed my face into it, closing my eyes. "Best two dates I've had."

"How many dates have you been on?"

I grinned. "Two."

He laughed, and the sound of it enveloped me inside this tiny tent. His eyes were lit with warmth as he looked at me. His thumb and forefinger held the tip of my chin in place. His face moved closer to mine and I held my breath in anticipation. He moved closer still, until our lips were a breath apart. I felt his warm breath against my lips and my eyes closed. I ran my tongue over my top lip and because he was that close, it grazed Julian's lip too. And then his lips met mine, hungrily.

I slid the hand that wasn't supporting my head over Julian's chest, my fingers tracing the hard ridges of muscle as his tongue traced my tongue. Desire shot through me powerfully, causing me to dig my nails into the side of his stomach. I felt the muscles clench beneath my fingertips. Julian's hand slid down my back before it yanked me closer. I hadn't felt this heady with arousal before. It felt as if I'd been asleep for years, and my body was finally coming back to life, my limbs coming alive with feeling.

I shivered from the shock of my body's reaction. This time, I was the one to pull away first.

Julian held my face in his hands, touching our foreheads together. My eyes remained closed as I breathed in and out, in time with Julian, whose exhalations mingled with mine. My heart was beating hard against my ribcage, my lips trembling with each breath. I felt Julian's lips press against my forehead. "Good night, Andra," he whispered, pulling away slightly to settle on his pillow.

I wavered a moment before pushing my own pillow away and laying my head on his bicep. I felt his arm wrap around my back as he pulled me closer. I felt safe. I felt warm.

I was asleep in minutes.

The following morning, Julian woke me up in the dark. "Andra. Wake up. We need to pack up the tent and get on the road."

I rubbed the sleep from my eyes and sat up, stretching my limbs in the dark. "Brr!" I exclaimed, rubbing my hands down my bare arms. "It's freezing!"

Julian was sliding socks on. "See what I meant about body heat?"

Just as I realized I didn't pack anything heavier than a long sleeve tee, Julian tossed a sweatshirt at me and I quickly slid it over my head. It smelled like him: sandalwood and cinnamon. "Thank you," I murmured, sliding out of the sleeping bag and sliding jeans on over my pajama leggings. I shivered again, sliding a second pair of socks over the pair I wore to bed. Julian handed me my hiking boots before he started unzipping the sleep bags from each other. I grabbed one of them and rolled it up, securing it to my backpack before grabbing my backpack and following Julian out of the tent.

We took the tent down in silence and in relative darkness. Julian had lit his oil lantern and it provided enough light to see what we were doing. When he secured the tent to his backpack, we hiked back to the car.

After an hour of driving, Julian pulled into a small coffee shop off of the highway and we drank tea with bagels before heading back towards the ranch.

Without thinking, my hand found his on the gear shift and he weaved our fingers together. "This was the best date I've ever had," I said, looking at him.

Julian looked at me for a moment before shifting his eyes to the road again. "It was the best date I've had too. And the longest date. You're breaking records, Miss Walker."

I smiled, caught up in this feeling of contentment. As much as I loved working on the ranch, it had been so nice, luxurious even, to get away from the day-to-day, to be in the wild. It was a soothing balm on my soul, a much-needed reprieve from the worries that warred in my head. As the miles to the ranch grew shorter, I knew I needed to tuck this feeling away as the reality of what lay ahead tonight loomed.

Julian dropped me off at my door and said goodbye, kissing me softly. I washed my face in my bathroom and drank another cup of tea before heading up to the big house to start my day, putting away clean dishes and moving laundry along. Then, I stripped all the beds in the vacant cabins and stocked the bathrooms with fresh towels. I dusted all the surfaces and wiped down the bathrooms. I would stock each cabin with a welcome basket the morning they were due to arrive.

I spent the rest of the day helping Rosa with miscellaneous chores inside the big house, trying to avoid looking at the clock. I failed, miserably.

When five-o-clock rolled around, I heard the front door to the main office close, the wooden screen door slamming on its frame.

I closed the lid to the washer and washed my hands, scrubbing them hard enough to make my hands red. I was excited to see Six, but I knew that seeing him would be bittersweet, since the reason for his visit was not a pleasant one. I felt his presence in the laundry room before he said anything.

"Hey kiddo."

I dried my hands on the towel and turned to face him. He was leaning against the doorway, hands in his pockets. I took in his appearance. It had been a while since I last saw him. He was clean shaven, and not just his beard. He was completely bald. He looked tan, fit. I wouldn't have known it was him if it wasn't for his eyes. His eyes were the color of bright green moss.

He wore jeans and a black leather coat, looking like he'd just stepped off an advertisement for menswear instead of off a plane. He looked nearly half his forty years without his usual beard and scruffy mane of hair.

I walked into his arms. Despite the change in his appearance, he still smelled the same. Like leather and spice. I breathed in his scent while he rubbed my back. Six was normally very taciturn; he was not driven by emotions or compelled to share what he was thinking. But with me, he would occasionally drop his guard and allow me the smallest of peeks into his thoughts. "How are you doing?"

I pulled away from him and shrugged. "Where did your hair go?" I rubbed my hand over his shaved head.

He ran his hand over his smooth scalp. "I thought it best that I look…different."

Understanding passed through me.

"I have a disguise for you, too. But we need to wait until we get through airport security."

"I am NOT shaving my head, Six."

He granted me a brief smile. "I'll admit, it crossed my brain. But don't worry, I've something else in mind."

As usual, Six was secretive. "Are you hungry? Oscar made spaghetti and meatballs." Six smiled again. While I had been in hiding at his house, the only thing I could make somewhat decently was spaghetti and meatballs. We ate it twice a week. After I left, in one of his momentary lapses into chatter, he admitted he missed it. I made sure to make it every time he visited.

Six and I were the first to dinner. We sat near the door to the kitchen and ate in silence. I tried to eat as quickly as possible, mostly to avoid running into Julian. I hadn't told him I'd be leaving because I didn't want to lie about the reason for my absence. Lies were becoming harder to tell for me, which meant they were probably harder to believe.

Six raised an eyebrow at me. "We don't have to leave for thirty minutes. You don't have to inhale it."

"I know. I just want to get this over with." That was part of it, at least.

He looked at me suspiciously but finished eating before having a quick word with Rosa while I filled up the dishwasher with our dishes.

"I just need to grab my bag, I'll meet you at the car," I called over my shoulder as I ran out the door. I speed walked to my cabin, grabbing my purse, phone, and the packed duffel bag. I was in such a rush to get out the door that I didn't see Julian in the doorway until my body collided with his. It was the scent that gave him away when all I saw was shoulders.

His hands came up to hold me steady. "Whoa. Slow down, Shorty."

I let out a breath and looked up him. "Hi."

"Hi." His eyes took in my full hands. "Where are you going in such a hurry?"

Before I could open my mouth to reply, I heard Six call my name. Julian's brow furrowed and he turned around to look at Six, standing on my porch just behind Julian.

Both men sized the other up, Six's expression more concerned than Julian's.

"Are you Andra's brother?" Julian asked.

Six looked to me for a minute before letting his features smooth out. He had a lot of control over his facial expressions; it was a skill I'd always envied.

"Yes, I am. I'm Six." He put his hand out for Julian's to shake. I wasn't surprised that Six didn't give him a false name. Six was no more his real name than Andra was mine, but they were both names that no one would connect to our true identities.

"Julian." After shaking hands, both men looked at me to explain the relationship. This was awkward.

"Julian is…" I started, not sure how to continue. Julian looked at me before he interjected.

"A friend."

I watched Six's lips move, and knew that he was running his tongue over his teeth. It was a cue to me that he was thinking. I knew there were more questions in my future once we were alone. He nodded to Julian, his eyes moving briefly to mine.

"Are you leaving?" Julian asked me. I felt both of their eyes on me and fidgeted with the handles of my bags.

"Just for a couple days. I'll be back on Friday," I answered. I hoped he wouldn't ask more information. Thankfully, Julian just stepped back.

"See you Friday, then." He looked like he wanted to say more, but didn't. Six watched our exchange with great interest. I felt my palms grow sweaty.

"Okay," I said as I closed the door to my cabin behind me. When I turned around, Julian was walking back to his cabin. I felt unsettled and handed my bags to Six. "Give me a minute," I said before running after Julian.

"Julian."

He turned around, his expression showing surprise. "Hey."

"I…" I didn't know what to say. I'd run to him on a whim. So, I put my hands on his shoulders and stood on my tiptoes, planting my lips firmly on his. Julian's arms wrapped around my torso, keeping me glued to him, as he kissed me back.

When we finally pulled away from each other, I whispered against his lips, "goodbye."

I felt his lips curve against mine before he kissed me quickly once more and then released me. "Bye, Andra."

I walked away from him, unable to conceal the smile on my face. I climbed into the passenger side of Six's rental car and didn't meet his eyes as I buckled in.

"Are you ready?" Six asked. I nodded and tucked the loose tendrils behind my ear. We were halfway down the driveway before Six spoke again. "A friend, huh?"

The smile tugged at my lips before I could help myself. "We might be dating. It's not a big deal."

"Well Andra, that's the first time you've told me a boldfaced lie to my face."

I looked over at him. "We are dating, believe it or not."

Six shook his head, before turning on the road at the end of the driveway. "I knew that wasn't a lie. The part about it not being a big deal was a lie."

Six knew me well enough to see through any thing I tried to pull past him, so it wasn't unusual for him to call me out. But I didn't think my budding feelings for Julian were that transparent. I didn't say anything else until we were through security and heading to our gate at the airport.

Six stopped me outside of the restroom and handed me the small bag he had carried through security. "I want you to put everything in here on. I'll meet you at the gate." With that he walked away and I sighed, heading into the bathroom and keeping my head down from the people washing their hands.

When I was locked inside a stall, I took inventory of the contents of the bag. There was a red wig, a bob with blunt bangs on top of everything else, so I quickly separated my hair into two sections and wrapped the sections around my head, pinning my hair in place with the box of pins he'd supplied. Luckily, Six had included a wig cap as well as a travel sized bottle of hairspray. I grabbed my compact in my purse to look at my reflection while I pinned the remaining loose tendrils. I sprayed it all flat with the hairspray and slid the wig cap in place. My head was already itching.

I put the wig on my head and left the stall, relying on the large mirror over the sinks to straighten the wig. I opened up the bag Six had given me and applied the heavy makeup he had included before sliding the square wire-rim eye glasses on. The lipstick he'd purchased was bright red, not my color at all, but possibly the color of this red headed mystery woman I was portraying.

He didn't leave instructions, but I'd guessed he would want me to remove my lip ring. I needed to remove all traces of what I looked like now. There was a scarf in the bag as well, which I knew was to hide my neck tattoo. I slid the lip ring into a pocket inside my purse and packed the makeup bag into the bag. I put that bag inside my purse and went back out to find Six.

When we landed in Detroit, we picked up the one case of luggage Six had checked at the airport in Denver before we checked into the nearest hotel. I turned my phone on once we were in our room and Six stepped out onto the deck to make some phone calls.

I whipped off the uncomfortable wig and glasses before glancing at my phone.

I had one text.

> *Julian: Your brother is a bit intimidating.*

I smiled, curled up onto my bed in the room, relaxed against the fluffy pillows as I typed my reply.

> *Me: He's just protective. And hi.*

> *Julian: Hi. Miss me yet?*

I laughed.

> *Me: Terribly. I haven't stopped crying since I kissed you goodbye.*

> *Julian: Wow, that's intense.*

> *Me: Yeah, I will probably need therapy after being apart from you this long.*

> *Julian: What can I say? I am like human cocaine.*

It was funny how accurate that statement was, at least for me.

> *Julian: So listen. I know I'm supposed to wait three days or something stupid like that before asking you on another date,*

but I am asking you now. I know you've got a busy weekend ahead of you, so maybe Sunday?

I figured he had talked to Rosa again.

Me: You know, you can ask me what my schedule is like. You don't have to charm that information out of Rosa.

Julian: Yeah, but I like Rosa. She tells me stuff.

Me: Hmm. Part of me wants to know what "stuff" she tells you and part of me thinks it's best if I don't know.

Julian: The latter.

I groaned.

Me: Okay, Julian. What kind of date?

Julian: I want to show you my house.

I let that stew for a moment. I wish I wasn't such a novice at this dating thing. Was showing me his house a big deal?

Me: Only if there will be food.

Julian: I would never deprive you nourishment. And I wouldn't deprive myself the experience of watching you eat. There will be food.

Me: Okay. Sunday it is.

Just as I hit "Send," Six walked back into the bedroom from the deck. He shrugged his leather jacket off and picked up the suitcase he had checked, plopping it on the bed. I watched the bed bounce while he grabbed his cell phone and touched buttons on the screen for a few moments before setting it down.

"Ready to go over the game plan for tomorrow night?" he asked, one hand on the zippers of the suitcase.

"Yes. Tell me."

"Alright." He sat down next to the suitcase without unzipping it. "We are going to break into the apartment."

I sucked in air in disbelief. I remembered he'd said breaking and entering, but I refused to believe it involved the apartment. My personal hell. My heart picked up its pace, and I counted five beats before he continued.

"Technically, you are going to be the one breaking into the apartment."

"What?!" I exclaimed, jumping up off of the bed. "No. No way in HELL. No. No." I walked around the bed, shaking my head back and forth over and over again.

"Andra." I refused to look at him. "Andra. Look at me." I reluctantly met his gaze. "It's the only way to make this happen. You, unfortunately, know him better than I do. You know where he keeps paperwork, you know his passwords-"

"Yeah, if they haven't changed in the last six years!" I exclaimed. "Why? Why do we need to do this? Why do I need to do this?"

Six sighed and ran a hand over the top of his bare head. "I have reason to believe he is looking for you."

I shook my head. "So? Hasn't he always been looking for me?"

Six motioned for me to sit down next to him on his bed. "Yes, but he never had a clue, or at least he didn't seem to, until now." I looked at him, confused. "He bought a plane ticket for Colorado. Requested leave from work."

I was thankful I was sitting down because this news would have brought me to my knees. "How could he possibly know?" I asked when I was able to breathe again.

He shook his head. "I have no idea. That's why we're here. We need to monitor his online activity better. I need to track his movements. I have equipment in this suitcase. Surveillance. I need you to install a program onto his computer and to find some paperwork in his house. I will keep watch outside." When I started to protest he interrupted me. "No. Think about it – if he were to show up and I was the one inside, how would you distract him from going inside? If he sees you, it's game over. He doesn't know what I look like, especially clean-shaven. If he comes home early, I'll keep him from going inside."

I stared down at my hands, willing them to stop shaking.

"It's our only option. Tomorrow, I am going to follow him. You're going to wait here. And tomorrow night we are going to break in."

"How do you know he won't be home tomorrow night?"

"He's got a date."

I resisted the sudden urge to vomit. "Okay," I said after sighing deeply. "What's the plan?"

We spent the rest of the night going over the plan, repacking the small backpack I would carry. We went over plans A, B, and C until I fell asleep on top of the hotel duvet.

When Six returned the following evening, he didn't say anything, but he seemed to have a lot on his mind. He tossed me a department store bag. "Here. Your cat burglar attire."

I rolled my eyes but went to the bathroom to change. I'd texted him my clothing sizes earlier in the day, in between all the exciting hours I sat in the hotel room, doing nothing.

He'd purchased opaque black leggings, a black long-sleeved tee, black beanie, black socks, and black running shoes. I tried not to think about the possibility of needing to run, but at least I was well trained. And he wasn't joking about cat burglar attire. No normal person would wear all of this at the same time unless they were planning to break a law or two. Before putting the beanie on, I slid the wig over my head and put on the glasses.

I walked out of the bathroom and Six handed me a pair of black leather gloves. "Don't put these on yet. I don't want anyone to be suspicious of you when we leave here."

I looked at him like he was joking and gestured my hand across my outfit. "And head to toe black doesn't scream 'suspicious' to you?" Six's mood lightened and the corner of his mouth lifted in a smile. His smiles were always brief, as if the muscles around his mouth were unaccustomed to such exuberance. The thought made me smile as I slid the gloves into the backpack – also black – that held all my gear I'd need.

Six pulled the beanie off my head. "Here, now you look normal." He tossed the beanie on the backpack. "Or as close to normal as you can get."

I resisted the urge to flip him off and instead glared at him, sliding the backpack over my shoulders.

"Ready?" Six asked, the mood heavy again. I nodded and followed him out of the hotel room.

Six was not driving a rental. This car had Michigan plates and racing stripes down the sides. I knew it wasn't Six's car either. "What's with the car?" I asked when we were on the road.

"Someone owes me a favor. So I borrowed it." With Six, you never knew if "borrowing" was with or without permission. I didn't bother asking, because he would never tell me one way or another.

We were silent until we pulled onto the street I used to live on. I had managed to distract myself on the way here, with colors, or thoughts of my date with Julian. That felt like ages ago now. Six slowed the car and drove around the block a couple times, checking which buildings had lights on. Finally, he parked a few buildings down and turned off all the lights. "Are you okay?"

I nodded, not trusting my voice, knowing it would betray me. My heart was flailing about in my chest, wild, terrified. I reached into the front pocket of the small backpack and grabbed the beanie. I pulled the wig off and slid my cap on my head before sliding the gloves on.

Six handed me a small cell phone. "Put this in your sock. I am the only person with the number to this phone. If it vibrates once, that is your sign to get the fuck out. If it vibrates multiple times, that means to hide. Do you understand?" I nodded.

"How do you control how many times it vibrates?"

Six pulled out his own phone. "I have a draft text message ready to go. If I send it," he clicked send on his phone and a moment later, the phone vibrated once in my hand. "Get the fuck out."

"Okay."

"And," he said, switching to call mode, "if I call the number..." he dialed and pressed send. The phone vibrated in my hand over and over. "Hide."

I swallowed the lump of anxiety that settled in my throat.

"Hey." Six braced his hands on either side of my face. "I will not let anything bad happen to you. Hawthorne will not touch you."

Hawthorne. The Monster's given name. I didn't call him by his given name. That only humanized him. He was a Monster, plain and simple.

"I'm ready," I said. Six would wait in the car while I walked the perimeter of the building before breaking in. I slid the phone into my sock and then slid it under the legging so it was against my skin.

Six nodded. "Good luck."

I exited the car and walked toward the tree line that ran behind the apartment buildings. I checked my watch. 11:42 PM. With any luck, all the neighbors in the Monster's four-plex would be either asleep or have the television on full blast. When I had lived here, the neighborhood was overrun with elderly couples.

When I reached the back of the apartment building, I looked around before creeping up next to the building, pressing my back against the vinyl siding. There was complete silence. Not even crickets chirping. I slowly made my way to the front of the building and looked up and down the street. I couldn't see anyone outside and noticed no vehicles running apart from Six's. His engine was practically silent, and all I could make out of him from this distance was his silhouette in the vehicle.

The Monster's vehicle, normally parked on the street, was nowhere in sight. I slowly climbed up the concrete steps leading to the second floor landing and quietly slid the backpack off my shoulders to grab my lock pick kit.

I inserted the torque wrench in the bottom of the dead bolt lock and turned the lock slightly counterclockwise. Then I slid the rake pick through the top and slid it back and forth, in the hopes that it would release one of the pins for me. I stuck the rake pin in my back pocket while holding the torque wrench in place and put the pin pick into the lock, pushing the pins up. I had to ease up on the tension of the torque wrench for one of the pins, but this lock was pretty easy because it was cheap, apartment-grade. Six had set me up with his laptop the day before to watch YouTube video tutorials on everything I'd need to do.

Once I pushed the final pin up, the wrench slid the lock open easily. I stuck the pin and wrench in my pocket and looked around before turning the handle and entering the apartment.

I was immediately overcome with the smell first. It was stepping back into time. Nothing had changed in the six years since I left. It still smelled like a mixture of his cologne and coffee. He ran the coffee maker all day, every day, so it made sense that the smell of coffee permeated the air.

I closed the door behind me, locked the deadbolt, and slid the lock picking kit back into the backpack before making my way to the third bedroom, his office.

As usual, his computer desk was littered with paperwork. I'd never bothered to linger in here before, so thankfully this room held no memories for me.

I pulled his desk chair out and sat in it before booting up his computer. I pulled the USB drive Six had given me out of my backpack and unfolded the instructions that were wrapped around it.

Luckily, his computer was not password protected, so I was able to access his desktop immediately. I inserted the USB drive and followed the instructions Six had typed, installing the remote monitoring software he had loaded onto the USB.

While it installed, I stood back from the desk and took photos of his papers with the pocket camera in the backpack. The Monster was a creature of habit, almost OCD with his compulsions and how he kept things ordered. I had a feeling he'd know if papers were moved, so I first took photos a few feet away from the desk, to copy the positioning before I left this room. Then I got closer and took close up photos of some of the papers. I didn't bother to read a lot of what they said, it looked like a lot of legal documents.

The papers were littered with bright sticky notes, with scribbled questions on them. "Who requested inquiry?" "See Ralph." And one sticky note named several places. "Boston, Denver, San Fran, Chicago." Chicago and San Fran were crossed off. I shivered the fear off and moved on.

My eyes caught on one red folder. I recognized the name on the label. Mayberry Law Group. That was the name of my mother's attorney. It confused me, because my mother had been dead for years, and yet here was a folder on top of other folders which meant that it had recently been reviewed.

I lifted the folder open, expecting to see a copy of her will. Instead, there were scores of printed emails, some highlighted. I skimmed over the emails, reading a handful of the highlighted words:

"trustee," "beneficiary," "POI," and "refusal to support allocation." My former name stood out among these papers, a name I never said aloud until now. "Cora," I whispered, running my fingers across the four letters. Over and over my name repeated, in every page.

I took photos of each page before moving on, hoping Six could make sense of it all. The program was still installing, so I shuffled the papers back into the position I found them in, according to the photos I'd taken.

I checked my watch. 12:13 AM. The program was about halfway done installing. Six hadn't given me any real rules for what I could do while I was in the apartment so I made a spontaneous decision to go to my old bedroom.

The door was shut. I made a mental note to remember to shut it when I left. I turned the tarnished, chipped, brass knob.

The first thing I registered was the creak that door made. It was the same creak I heard in my nightmares. *Push it back, Andra,* I told myself. I eased myself in the room and looked around. He hadn't removed one thing from my bedroom. My curtains still hung, partially open, allowing moonlight to spill across the floor. My flowered comforter was spread, taut, across my mattress, my pillows placed in the same positioning I'd always placed them. My dresser was still the resting place for the small chest that I knew had held my mother's jewelry. Beside it, my hairbrush sat, untouched. Like the rest of the apartment, my former bedroom remained unchanged.

It was a museum of a dead girl. Home to the girl I was before, the girl who existed in the memories that haunted this room. My fingers grazed over the comforter as I walked around the room. Flashes of my nightmare returned in bits and pieces as I looked at the bed. No.

I refused to be reminded of those memories as I strode to my dresser, anger driving me to pick up my jewelry box. I had left this behind before, intentionally, to help give weight that I was not a runaway. I eased open the lid and breathed a sigh of relief. It looked like everything was still there. I ran my fingers over my mother's pearl earrings, her sapphire lariat, and her Claddagh ring. These were all I had left of my mother apart from my memories.

I felt my ankle vibrate once. The phone. I froze. Then it vibrated again. And again. It didn't stop vibrating.

HIDE.

I quickly closed the lid of the jewelry box and picked it up, whipping my head around in desperate search of a hiding place. I heard the pounding on the concrete steps outside. "Fuck fuck fuck fuck fuck!" I exclaimed under my breath. I didn't have time to panic. I reached the bedroom door and closed it quickly before dashing into the closet.

As I closed the bi-folding doors, I heard the sound of the front door being unlocked right before the swish sound of the door swinging open. It was at that moment I remembered my backpack in his office, the USB still plugged into the computer. My entire body went still at that moment, except for the boom-boom-boom of my heart. I prayed harder than I ever had for a miracle.

I peeked through the slats of the closet doors, seeing the light from the moon slashing a stripe across the dresser. It illuminated the now-empty space where my jewelry box once sat. An unmistakable square of dustless space signaled that something was missing. I'd grabbed the box on a whim, not realizing until now that it was my intention to bring it back with me.

I heard the sound of keys hitting the entry table before I heard the door to the freezer open in the kitchen and checked my watch. 12:20 AM. My right leg started dancing up and down, a definite sign of nerves getting to me. A moment later, I heard the unmistakable sound of a glass bottle being set on the counter. Then, the creak of a cupboard and the sound of a lighter piece of glass being set on the counter. Vodka and his shot glass. I couldn't help but think of the frozen chicken I had purposefully avoided so many times and wondered, momentarily, if it was still there.

Unfortunately, the dust that had settled in the closet from my absence was sprinkling the air around me, disrupted by my movements. I felt my nose twitch from the tickle. Shit. I covered my free hand over my nose and mouth and prayed for quiet.

I sneezed.

I wasn't sure how loud it had been, but I knew soon enough that it had been loud enough to alarm the Monster.

I saw the hallway light turn on, illuminating the space between the door and carpet. My heart was beating like a jackrabbit's. I wondered, briefly, if I could see my heart beating right through my shirt. Panic squeezed my veins. There were no colors to name off in the dark to calm me. Any moment now I would go into shock from the fear of coming face to face with the Monster. Nearly seven years and I was still crippled by anxiety. I willed myself to be brave, to be strong, but my body betrayed me. Sweat prickled my palms.

I saw a shadow of his steps to the door and sucked in shattered breath. It hit me then that I was breathing in the same air as the Monster once again. Bile rose up into my mouth and I swallowed it back. This was reliving one of my many nightmares, but worse. I closed my eyes, praying this was just another nightmare. Praying this wasn't real.

A second later, I heard pounding on the front door. Adrenaline was still coursing through my veins, choked by the panic that squeezed them. But the panic eased as I saw the shadowed steps stall, and then grow fainter, lighter, as the Monster headed towards the front door.

"I'm so sorry, but I think I just hit your car." Six. I almost sobbed with relief, clamping a hand over my mouth. His voice, at this moment, was the most beautiful sound I'd ever heard. I was not alone. I was not alone.

The Monster didn't say anything for a moment before I heard Six's voice again, more insistent. "I can't afford my insurance to go up again. Can I just give you a thousand cash and call it even?"

I knew this would have the Monster's interest. I would bet whatever piece of shit car he was driving now wasn't worth half that. I heard his voice, the voice that echoed over my nightmares. "Let's see what the damage is, and then we can talk price." The door closed and I held my breath for a few seconds, making sure he had left the apartment. Muffled voices and heavy footsteps descended the stairs and then my ankle vibrated once.

Get the fuck out.

Carrying the jewelry box to the Monster's office, I started shakily putting it into the backpack. I clicked "Finish" on the program installing and shut down the computer, removing the USB drive. I put everything back into the backpack and headed to the kitchen window, looking out. The Monster's back was to the window. I could see Six's face, lit by the exterior lights.

He handed a stack of something to the Monster. I presumed it was money by the way the Monster started to count it. Six's eyes flicked up to the window and narrowed. I knew he was pissed that I was still inside. I looked back at the front door, knowing that an escape was out – the Monster's car was parked right out front. I moved towards the door in the living room, the door to the deck. It was my only option, short of climbing out of a window.

The deadbolt was secure on the deck door. There wouldn't be a way for me to relock it when I was on the porch, so it would likely alert the Monster to someone having been in the apartment. I couldn't dwell on that, however, so I unlocked the door and went out onto the deck. I quietly closed the door behind me and leaned over the railing. There were no lights lighting up the grass, telling me that the neighbors below were asleep.

I swung a leg over the railing, and then the other, and turned my body so I was facing the door to the deck. I held onto the railing firmly and then let each leg swing loose, one at a time, gradually bringing my hands down from the railing to the spindles. I heard the front door inside the apartment open and I let go of the spindles hastily, falling to the grass below. Immediately, pain bloomed on my left cheek and I knew I had caught it on the wooden ledge when I had jumped. I placed a gloved hand to my cheek and winced. Now was not the time to think about it.

I saw the light turn on from the living room inside the Monster's apartment, so I dashed along the side of the building, my back to the vinyl siding. I breathed in through my nose, exhaling out of my mouth a moment, calming my racing heart. And then I ran behind the dumpster, the same dumpster that had been the beginning of my escape the first time. Without looking back, I ran into the woods.

Per plan C, Six's car was waiting about a mile into my run on a road that intersected the woods. I slowed my pace, my overworked muscles warming me despite the cooler temperature outside. I slid into the idling car and buckled up before Six sped off.

Anger and frustration were radiating off of him in waves. Ten minutes into silence, Six slammed his brakes, steering the car off the road and throwing it into park.

I felt his palm on my raw cheek and chanced a glance at him. "What happened?"

"I fell off the deck and must have caught my face on the wood."
I flipped the visor down to finally see what damage I'd done.

My entire cheek was flamed red, swollen. The abrasion itself was
bleeding, my skin looked torn up. I could see small slivers of wood in
the injury and hissed as I reached a hand up to pull one out.

Six slapped my hand away. "Don't. I'll clean it."

It was silent for a moment. I saw Six's hands grip the steering
wheel tightly. A moment later, he smacked his palm on the steering
wheel. Once, then twice, then a third time.

I didn't say anything. This amount of emotion was something I'd
never seen from him before.

"Did he see you?"

"No." I didn't bother mentioning that he nearly walked into the
bedroom I was hiding in. "Sorry you had to damage your friend's
car."

Six swung his head towards me. "Do you think I give a fuck
about this car?" He was yelling. Angry Six was intense.

I didn't know what to say, so I said nothing, just slid the gloves
and beanie off.

"Besides, I hit his car with a tire iron. I couldn't risk impairing
our getaway car." His voice was calmer, his anger subsiding.

"I hope you hit it hard."

"Oh, I did. I beat the shit out of it." I attempted a smile, but it
hurt to stretch my injured cheek. "It was that or his stupid face."

"How much did it set you back?"

"Fifteen-hundred. Worth it."

Yikes. That was a lot of money. "I can pay you back. I have
savings."

Six grunted. "Good. That you have a savings. Keep it. I don't
need your money." When I started to protest, he held a hand up and
spoke forcefully, allowing no room for argument. "No. What I
should have said was that I don't want your money. I don't need it, I
don't want it, and I won't take it. Fifteen-hundred is nothing. So drop
it."

Wow, that was practically a speech coming from him. "I didn't
realize you were so loquacious."

Six granted me one of his brief smiles, but kept his eyes on the
road. "Only when you say stupid shit."

We were still in Michigan, which meant I would be more easily recognized from all the MISSING posters years ago. News of my disappearance had mostly died down, the case having gone cold. But once every year, the story popped up in the news again, highlighting the anniversary of the day I went missing.

Six stopped at a drug store and came out with a bag of supplies that he tossed into my lap before driving off to the hotel. I peeked inside the plastic bag and noted tweezers, ibuprofen, gauze, rubbing alcohol, a squirt bottle, antibiotic ointment, and band-aids. "Gonna perform surgery on me, doc?"

Six looked at me with exasperation written clearly across his face. "I wouldn't need to if you didn't eat it while escaping."

Oh, was Six teasing me? This was new. "You know I'm naturally clumsy. I'm lucky I didn't blow my ankle when I landed."

Six pulled into the parking lot of our hotel. "Yeah, instead you merely fucked up your face. It's a shame; you didn't look too bad before." He exited the car and opened my door.

I rolled my eyes and grabbed the plastic bag and the backpack, tossing the latter at him with more force than necessary. "Here. There's lots of dirt on him in here." Six slung the backpack over his shoulder.

"There's a lot of dirt in your face. Let's get you cleaned up."

Six directed me to wrap myself in robe and sit on the edge of the tub of the hotel bathroom while he got everything ready. He came back into the bathroom and tossed a small bottle of vodka at me.

"Mini bar," he answered my unspoken question. "This is going to hurt like a bitch, so drink up. Just don't pass out on me."

I unscrewed the cap of the bottle and chugged, watching Six scrub his hands with soap and water, supplies laid out on a towel next to the sink. I watched him set the temp of the water before filling up the squirt bottle and then he looked over at me. "The scrape is close to your eye, so you're going to want to keep them closed while I clean this. I need to flush the dirt out before I go in with tweezers."

I nodded and swallowed hard. He sat on the lid of the toilet seat and cupped my jaw with one free hand, gently tilting my face to give him better access to my cheek. I closed my eyes and felt the warm stream of water over the wound. That didn't feel too terrible. Water dripped down my face, collecting in the robe.

"You can open your eyes now. I'm going to get the splinters out."

I opened my eyes and rubbed water from the left eye.

Six handed me a hotel washcloth. "Bite on this." I rolled it and stuck it in my mouth while Six doused the tweezers in rubbing alcohol. This was going to suck.

I bit down hard the moment the tweezers touched the raw flesh. I probably said every swear word ever invented and then made up a few more as Six picked out the slivers and wiped them on a washcloth he'd soaked in rubbing alcohol.

When he'd finished, I felt hot tears tracking down my cheeks. Six pulled the washcloth out of my mouth and asked, "Do you want some water?"

I nodded, not trusting my voice to radiate strength. I gulped the water he handed to me as he refilled the squirt bottle.

He crouched in front of me. "Are you okay?" Six was normally so distant, emotionally-speaking, so to see him with concern and regret in his eyes was a new experience for me.

"Yes," I croaked.

He moved back to sitting on the toilet seat's lid. "I'm going to flush it again, several times, and then clean around it with soap, then flush it again. Then I'm going to put pressure on it for a few minutes to stop the bleeding." He held up the antibiotic cream. "Then I'll apply some of this and then we'll bandage it, okay?"

"Is it pretty bad?"

Six shrugged and put the cream back on the counter. "You look like you rubbed your face up against some bark, so you'll need a more realistic story. It's definitely noticeable. And it'll be more so with a giant bandage over it. Now close your eyes again."

I did. Six chose this moment to ask, "So, you're dating?"

I was caught off guard. "I've gone on two dates with Julian." I felt water from the squirt bottle spray down my cheek.

"How do you know him?" Six was unusually inquisitive.

Eyes closed, I frowned a little. "He's a tenant at the ranch."

"What does he know?"

My frown only deepened. "Why? It's not like I've told him I'm really Cora Mitchell, that girl that went missing from Michigan in 2003. He knows my favorite color and that I like to eat." I knew I sounded defensive, but I didn't understand or even like Six's questioning.

"I saw how you looked at him. How serious is it?"

I pushed Six's hand away from squirting water on my wound and opened my eyes. "Why the interrogation?"

Six sat back and twisted the towel in his lap over and over. He didn't meet my eyes. "I just worry. You're all the way in Colorado. Maybe we should move you somewhere else."

That really set me off. "Are you kidding me? What gives?" My voice raised several octaves. "I'm not a child. I'm not an object. You cannot just 'move' me."

Six sighed. "Calm down. I told you, I just worry."

I ran my tongue over my teeth. It was a habit I'd adopted from Six. "I appreciate the concern, but I'm a big girl, Six."

"Stop frowning, you're making it hard to clean this boo-boo, big girl."

I huffed out an annoyed breath and allowed him to finish. Six flushed the wound several times before cleaning around the area with soap. The alcohol was starting to kick in on my empty stomach, so the pain wasn't as intense as before. He pressed a square of gauze to the scrape and had me hold it while he cleaned up the mess and then washed his hands.

"I want you to wear your hair in the beanie when we get to the airport, and the glasses too. Once we get through security, I want you to put the red wig back on. You're going to stand out with this bandage on your face, so we need to make you less recognizable." He dried his hands and then grabbed the ointment and the band-aid before crouching in front of me again.

He peeled the gauze off my face and applied the ointment on the scrape and then on the center of the band-aid before pressing the band-aid in place.

"It's two in the morning. Our flight leaves at six. You have two hours to get some sleep. Go."

I stood up and stretched, wiping the excess water away from my neck. I walked by him on my way out of the bathroom but stopped short and turned around. "Thanks Six."

He was bracing both hands on the bathroom sink, his head down. He looked at me and sighed, turning to me and opening his arms. I stepped into them and hugged him tightly. I felt him kiss the top of my head briefly before loosening him arms and shooing me off to bed.

I crashed onto the bed and fell into a dead sleep, only to fall asleep again in the car on the way to the airport. And the moment the plane took its ascent into the sky at 6 AM, I was asleep once more.

We landed in Denver at 7 AM thanks to the change in time zones and were back at the ranch by 8:30. Six didn't stay, choosing to drop me off and leave once again for the airport.

That morning I aired out the cabins and placed welcome baskets in each one. After that, I helped Rosa set up the few rooms in the big house that would be used for guests. Rosa didn't ask about the trip. The moment she'd seen me, she'd wrapped me up in a big Rosa hug, clucked over my bandage for a moment, and then helped me get started on work. Rosa knew me. She knew that I needed to have something to focus my energy on. If I got bored, I wallowed.

When the family reunion pulled in that afternoon, I helped them get settled into their cabins, only chancing a glance at Julian's cabin. I hadn't heard from him since we'd texted that Wednesday night. I figured he'd been on a writing spell. Better that he not see me with the large bandage on my face anyway. I wasn't in the mood to fabricate lies. I was sleep deprived and still tingling a bit from anxiety. I wondered if Six had started monitoring the Monster's computer.

While heading back to my cabin for lunch, I detoured and walked to Julian's cabin. I pulled my hair down over the bandage and then knocked on his door, hearing something fall from the other side before the door swung open.

The first thing I saw was his face. He was wearing black glasses, the frames rectangular. His hair was totally disheveled, like he had run his hands through it over and over in frustration. He was wearing a tee shirt that had seen better days; it was full of holes and the logo on the front was almost completely worn off. He wore flannel pajama bottoms and his feet were bare. My eyes swung back to his face, taking in the surprised smile and tired eyes and the hand he was rubbing through his hair.

"Hi," he finally said. He leaned in as if he was going to give me a kiss before he pulled back, alarm in his eyes. "Wait. I've not brushed my teeth yet today." He gestured me to follow him in while he walked back to the bathroom. It was dark, the shades drawn and only a lamp lighting the space. And every single surface was covered in soda cans and paper.

So he does have a flaw after all. "It's three in the afternoon," I said, taking in the mess all around his cabin.

"I haven't gone to bed yet," he answered, peeking his head out of the door of the bathroom.

"It's three in the afternoon," I repeated, confused.

"I've been awake since yesterday. Got some kick ass writing mojo around eleven last night and couldn't stop."

"Until now, since I've interrupted you and made you brush your teeth."

I walked around his bed, which was still made, the cover rumpled a little, loose papers and sticky notes scattered across its striped surface. I picked up one of the yellow sticky notes. "Timeline – check 4." It made no sense to me, but I decided to avoid it, being reminded of the Monster's office in Michigan and all the notes across his desk.

Julian returned from the bathroom and strode straight for me, his hands cupping my jaw as he kissed me hello. My hands gripped his wrists, holding him still, while he kissed me thoroughly.

"Hi," I whispered when we were separated. I slowly opened my eyes and met his, mirroring the smile that stretched his lips.

"Hi." He kissed me again. His thumbs gently rubbed my jawline when he deepened the kiss, relaxing my mouth to open and allow him inside.

I felt us move closer to one another, and my arms moved to encircle his back, holding him still. He kissed me the way he breathed, as it if was the most natural, the most essential thing in the world. And I kissed him the same way, because it did feel natural. Our connection was not just chemical. There was that element, but under the surface was something more. His lips didn't just move my lips, they moved the part of me that ached to be connected to him. The blood that rushed to my head was chemical. But the feeling that settled over my heart and moved from his fingers and into my skin, pushing into my bloodstream, was more. But I wasn't willing to put a name on it right now, worried that labeling whatever this was would force it into a corner, keeping it from expanding. And I wanted it to grow, I wanted to see where it took us. I was making a conscious decision to let this go forward, to open myself up to Julian. It was a profound and scary decision, but at this point it felt inevitable.

He pulled his lips away just slightly, so that they rested against mine. "Andra," he breathed, the word sliding from his lips and through mine. His fingers moved higher, and I could tell the moment they brushed against the bandage. I opened my eyes.

He was looking at me with concern. His thick, straight eyebrows were drawn together and his mouth was set in a firm line. "What's this?"

"I'm vertically challenged." When his face displayed even more confusion, I elaborated. "I'm taller than I realize. I fell, scraped my face." At least I wasn't lying.

He didn't say anything for a minute. His fingers played with a corner of the bandage. "Can I look?"

I nodded. I felt the bandage tug against my skin right before I felt the air that hit the scrape. I saw Julian's jaw clench. "That looks rough. You're probably going to scar."

I shrugged. "Scars don't scare me."

Julian settled the bandage back in place and gently cradled my cheek in his hand. "What does?"

"You," I answered without hesitation. I rubbed my cheek against his palm.

"Ah." He brought his other hand up to push the hair from my face. "You scare me too."

With my eyes closed, I smiled and answered, "Good."

I heard his chuckle and reluctantly stepped back to get my bearings. "I just wanted to say hi. I've got a busy day ahead, but there's a small concert on the outskirts of town tomorrow night. Local bands in a park sort of thing." I pushed a lock of hair behind my ear. "Wanna go?"

Julian's smile was wide and the corners of his eyes crinkled behind his glasses. "I'd love to. What time are you going to pick me up?"

I laughed. "Seven."

He stuck his hand in the pockets of his pajama pants before nodding. It struck me then how different he looked from all the other times I'd seen him. "You'll want to wear actual pants, though," I commented, eyeing his clothing.

"Pants are overrated."

I looked up at his eyes, noted the suggestive waggling of his eyebrows. "The glasses are sexy. You look very academic."

He frowned comically. "I think 'hot' is what you meant to say."

I shook my head no and bit my lip, which drew his attention to that direction. "What happened to your lip ring?"

My hand immediately went to the side of my lip, touching just the skin there. "I took it out and forgot to put it back in, I guess." I tried to remember where I had put it.

"Well, I like it. It suits you."

"Noted." I made my way back towards the door of the cabin. "I'll see you tomorrow, Julian."

He followed me to the door, opening it just before I reached the handle. I turned to him and pressed a quick kiss to his cheek.

"Looking forward to it, Andra."

Later that night, I was in my office in the big house, catching up on paperwork when I heard a voice call out from the main office.

I turned my monitor off and walked out, peering my head around the corner. There was a woman there, about my age, running her fingers over the books on the shelves by the door.

"Can I help you?" I asked, moving to stand by the check-in desk.

She whipped her head in my direction, pale blonde strands of hair flying around with the movement.

"Yeah," she answered hesitantly, moving closer to the desk. "Are those books for rent?" she asked, motioning a thumb over her shoulder to the books she was just perusing.

"Well, we don't really rent them out. They're here for guests to borrow and we welcome books that are left behind. But we don't police it or anything; it's a really loose library system."

"Okay." She tugged one long strand behind her ear before coming closer to where I stood. "I'm the only twenty-something in my family that remains unmarried and childless, so there's not a whole lot for me to do here. I'm trying to pass the time, I guess."

"Oh, well would you like some suggestions?" I asked, moving around the desk towards the shelf. She followed me like a shadow, stopping just a few feet from me at the shelf as I gave her some recommendations.

When she had a small stack in her hands, she turned to face me, her smile grateful and friendly. "Thanks," she said, smiling. A second later, she squinted her eyes and slightly cocked her head in one direction. "Do I know you from somewhere?"

"Probably not," I smiled, hoping the nerves I felt at her question weren't visibly straining my lips. I moved away to head back to the check-in desk.

"Are you from here?" she asked, coming closer. I fiddled with the computer to avoid looking at her.

"Yes," I started. "Well, I'm originally from California."

"Huh," she said, still looking at me like she was trying to place me.

"Where are you from?" I asked.

"Chicago." Worry instantly climbed up my back at that one word. That was close enough to the area from which I'd gone missing. Shit, shit, shit, shit. My mind raced.

"Oh, that's nice." It was all I could come up with.

"What's your name?"

"Andra."

"Really?" I looked at her at that, my back up in defense.

"Yes, that's my name. Do you want to see my drivers' license for proof?" I knew I said it rudely, but her line of questioning was becoming too personal.

She bristled and stepped back for a second. "I guess you just look familiar."

"I get that a lot." I stepped away from the desk. "I've got to get back to work now. But if you need anything, just holler."

I heard the screen door shut, the wood rattling against the frame just as I entered my office and let out a relieved breath. I wasn't lying when I'd told her I got that a lot. I did. But never from someone as persistent as she was. My hands shook as I turned my monitor back on and when I climbed into bed two hours later, I knew I'd have another nightmare.

A hand was clamped over my mouth. All I could taste was the salt from his sweat. I gagged and bile rose from my stomach, but with no way to release it, I had to choke it back down. Tears streamed from my eyes. His weight pressed against me, into me. I shook my head back and forth, frantic, scared. But it was too late. Pain lanced into me and my body recoiled, my tears forming rivers, my mouth sobbing. I couldn't fight my way free, I couldn't move. My body eventually stilled, waiting for it to be over. I let my head rest to the side, looking out the window. And then he moved away from me. He'd won. It wasn't the first time or the last time.

I woke up crying, sobs violently shaking my body as I curled up on my side. I bit my knuckles to keep the sobs from becoming too loud, from letting my emotional response to the memory become more powerful than it was.

The Monster had taken much from me: that was true. But I was strong now, brave. A lot of my bravery was cloaked with lies, but it was still mine. I shook myself from the nightmare and climbed out of bed, stripping off my sweat-soaked clothing and slipping on an oversize night shirt instead. I walked to the kitchen and filled a glass of water before walking back into my bedroom and digging for the bottle of pills I kept in my nightstand.

Sometimes it was easier to feel nothing. To have a void within you that drowned all the happiness, all the sadness. You could climb into that void and feel safe from it all. It was another escape for me, another thing that separated Andra from Cora. I wanted to be untouched from pain, from cruelty, from love, from goodness. Sometimes, like now, I needed to climb into the void and have my mind erased. I needed to just not feel.

I swallowed the small pill with a sip of water and climbed back into bed. A few minutes later, my mind went blank and I fell into sleep, without a thought to occupy my mind.

I poured myself into work the next day. I cleaned the stables, cleaned the chicken coop, skimmed the pond for trash, and remade the beds in the big house. I avoided Rosa like the plague, avoided all human interaction, and worked until my muscles ached for rest. It was my usual MO after a restless night's sleep. I was no longer numb to emotion, which meant I was in a vulnerable state, dangling precariously on the edge to another crying jag.

At noon, Six texted me.

> *Six: What are you doing this weekend?*

> *Me: I have plans tonight and tomorrow. But I'll be around. Why?*

It took him a few minutes to answer.

> *Six: Keep your phone handy.*

> *Me: Why?*

> *Six: Because I've told you to.*

I rolled my eyes. He was so bossy and secretive. I chose to push it from my mind as I cleaned up the lunch dishes, avoiding Oscar's questioning eyes as he prepared dinner and dessert for the large family reunion.

"Do you have a bug up your ass?" he finally asked, when the silence was becoming unbearable, even for me.

I turned to him and gave him a dirty look, flipping him the bird with a soapy, gloved hand.

"No thanks, you're a little too young for me," he said casually, dicing red peppers.

"It wasn't an invitation. Why can't you be a normal person and ask if I'm okay?" I asked, annoyed, scrubbing the dish in my hand with more force than necessary.

"Because normal is boring. But since you're testy this morning – are you okay?"

"Just peachy," I said, rinsing the plate and setting it firmly to the dish rack.

"Yeah, you're a ray of sunshine this afternoon. Get out of my kitchen."

I turned to him, my hands dripping with soapy water. "Why?"

"Because you need to cool off. Your rage is going to be absorbed in my peppers and you'll ruin what could be a tasty meal. Also, I don't hold hands or give hugs, so you're not going to feel any better being in here. Go," he reiterated, pointing his knife to the door, his eyebrow raised to show how serious he was.

I snapped my gloves off, biting my tongue from spewing an unnecessary retort. I slapped the gloves onto the counter and strode out of the kitchen, into the big room.

Frustration at my bad temper and childish behavior was moving through my veins like electricity, leaving me unable to sit still as I whirled around before I stalked off the patio door, heading to my cabin. My feet moved faster than the workings of my brain and I didn't have a clue where I was headed until I was at my cabin door.

I reached a hand into my pocket for my keys and then realized I left them back in the kitchen. I cursed a few words, my frustration now peaking, when I heard my name being called.

I whipped my head to the left and saw Julian standing just off his deck, one hand in a pocket and the other raised in greeting.

"Trust me, Julian, you don't want to be around me right now."

He walked across the grass towards me. "Why would you say that?" he asked, strolling towards me, acting as if he had all the time in the world. There was something off about his demeanor, almost like he was approaching me with caution. But he was still approaching, and at a steady pace.

"Because I'm really pissed off right now."

"Why?"

I shook my head and ran both hands through my hair. "I don't know. Because I have irrational anger sometimes, I guess?" I was lashing out, my words full of all the frustration I was feeling. I didn't speak to him kindly. I knew part of this was a side effect of the medication I'd taken last night. And another part, probably the more dominate part, was all the blackness inside of me. It was easier to hurt with words than it was a knife, but they cut just the same, under the skin. Knives left scars on the surface while words left scars under the epidermis, on the soul. And words were not used as a weapon to protect me, but instead the hurt was to protect those around me.

"Wanna go for a run?"

"What?" I looked at him like he was speaking another language.

"When I am working through a scene that I can't get just right, I go for a run. The frustration leaves and the words pour from my fingers onto the page. I just thought a run might help you sort out whatever is battling inside that brain of yours."

I digested his words before nodding. "Are you going to run with me?"

"Of course. I think I recall you saying you don't run very fast, so I'll try to take it easy on you."

I narrowed my eyes. "I don't need you too, but thanks. Give me ten minutes to get my keys from the big house and I'll meet you back there." I pointed to the tree line behind the cabins.

When he nodded, I turned around, heading towards the kitchen to grab my keys.

Julian and I were over two miles into the run and so far, we were both keeping the same steady pace. His breathing was even and I noticed he didn't bring headphones along for the run. We were nearing the meadow so I kicked up my legs, pumping them faster, harder. When Julian noticed the gain I was making on him, he picked up speed and we raced each other until I slowed, the meadow coming into view. Julian looked over at me, questioningly. I tilted my head towards the clearing that we could just barely see through the trees and he nodded back at me, slowing his pace. By the time we reached the meadow, we were both walking, breathing heavily. Blood was roaring in my ears, so I abruptly sat in the middle of the field and then laid my head back, settling against the tall grass. I closed my eyes and pulled in a deep breath, inhaling the earth, the heat from the sun, the scent of the grass. They were my favorite smells.

I felt Julian lay next to me and heard him breathe it all in. I opened my eyes and looked around us. Thanks to the height of the grass, we were completely hidden from anyone or anything that walked out from the cover of the tree line. There was comfort in that, being hidden out in the open. We existed in that small patch of earth and no one knew.

I turned my head to Julian and took in his profile. His nose was strong, proportionate. His facial hair had grown a little in the past couple days, reaching a length that said it was intentional, instead of the product of several days of no sleep. Men were like that. They didn't require any real grooming as long as they kept their hair at a manageable length. They could run their fingers through their hair and it resembled an actual style. Doing the same with my own hair made me look unkempt, homeless.

Julian's eyes popped open and he turned them towards me. "Feel better?" he asked.

"Yes. Instead of being annoyed at nothing in particular, I'm annoyed at you."

His brown crinkled with his frown. "Me? Why?"

"Because you always look so effortless. Like you wake up looking good. And I know for a fact that you do look good when you first wake up. And that pisses me off."

He laughed and rolled onto his side, facing me. "You look good when you wake up. I know *that* for a fact."

"After I've brushed my hair and scrubbed the sleep from my face, I'm sure I look presentable."

"Okay, when you first wake up you look sweet, as if the world has not touched you yet. Sweet like a kitten, purring contently. Which is the exact opposite of how you looked thirty minutes ago, with your talons itching for flesh to pierce. Like a dragon."

"Like a dragon, huh?" I asked, amused. "Don't they breathe fire?"

"Why do you think I didn't come too close when I was talking you into this run?"

I laughed then. "I'm glad you did. I have missed running the past few mornings. I'm sure that's put me on edge." I sat up and brushed the dirt from my bare arms. Julian sat up and faced me, leaning back on his hands.

When I caught him staring at me, I crawled over to him and slid into his lap, chest to chest. I linked my arms around his neck and cocked my head to the side, licking my lips. Julian's hands slid to either side of my waist. I let my fingers play with the hair at the nape of his neck. The tank top I was wearing slipped down, exposing a part of my chest. I saw his eyes land there and realized my bra was more revealing than the bikini top he'd seen me in the week before.

He moved a hand to my collarbone before moving his hand down my chest. I held my breath as his fingers traced the script written there. It was written over the curve of my left breast, just one word: free. He didn't comment on it, merely traced the word with his fingertip, slowly, carefully.

"Do you have more?"

I nodded. One I couldn't show him, but I could show him my other one. I hiked up my shorts, pulling them up high enough to show the quote I had inked on my skin.

"'There are far, far better things ahead than any we leave behind,'" he said, once again running his fingers over my skin. He looked up at me. "C.S. Lewis?"

"Yes." I was mildly surprised he knew.

He stared at the tattoo for a minute, not saying anything. He left his fingers there, resting on the words I lived by. "Do you have any tattoos?" I asked, trying to break the silence.

"No. I haven't found anything I need to etch permanently into my skin, yet."

I chose to put my tattoos in places on my body that were often concealed from others, because their meaning was to me. Though I rarely saw my Queen tattoo due to placement, I knew it was always there, right behind my throat. I'd left much of Cora Mitchell behind when I left that apartment years earlier, but I couldn't replace my love for my favorite band. This tattoo would be a dead giveaway for those who knew me, knew me as Cora Mitchell. All my other tattoos were for the after, the word "free" inked on my chest to remind me of what I was, that my choices were mine. The words on my leg to remind me to keep putting one foot forward, to move on from the things that haunted me.

"I like your ink," Julian said, pulling me from my thoughts. "I like that they have meaning. I'm quite fond of words, if you didn't know."

I smiled. "You make your living from them, so you should like them."

He shook his head and ran a hand through his hair. "My stories aren't profound. They're words I manipulated into emotion. Once I finish a story, I don't think about it anymore. They're mysteries. Once the mystery is solved, the story is over. The words I'm fond of are the ones that we inherently know what they mean. We don't have to influence them to mean something. They stand on their own."

"Okay, what words are those?" I was still sitting on his lap, his fingers still resting on the words on my thigh.

"For example: hate. That's a word you feel. If you hate something, that's some kind of power. Often, people hesitate from using that word because of its power, the depth of what it means to hate anything, anyone." His fingers moved from my thigh to my waist, rubbing his thumb over the thin fabric of the tank top. "Love is another one. You don't need to be taught its meaning. How could you teach that? I remember when my youngest sister, Annemarie, was about two or three years old. I was in high school, already driving. I was going through a phase where I resented my mom, resented her working all the time, resented being responsible for my sisters. And as I grabbed my keys to go for a drive, Annemarie came into my bedroom and asked me to play with her. I was upset, impatient, and I told her no. I told her to get out of my room, to go find one of our other sisters to play with. I looked back at her, saw her eyes welled up with tears. 'But I want to play with you,' she said, her bottom lip trembling. 'I love you.'"

Julian picked a piece of grass with his other hand. "That was a profound moment for me. How did she understand what love was? We hadn't sat down and discussed the definition of it, and even then, who would understand that? Love isn't taught; it's felt. But my toddler sister understood it, felt it, she knew what it was without explanation. Love and hate, those are my favorite words. They stand on their own. They don't need to be defined."

"Perhaps you should have them etched into your skin then," I suggested, trailing my fingers down his arm.

"Perhaps," he agreed, leaning in and peppering kisses across my collarbone. I closed my eyes and tilted my head back, allowing him more access. Sitting in his lap gave him better access to my throat, and he took advantage, gliding his lips up my neck, nipping at the skin between my neck and my chin. His hands moved up to frame the sizes of my face as he pulled my face towards his. The way he held my face in his hands was my favorite, as if he wanted me to be aware of only his presence. I was always aware of his presence though, my body drawn to his like a magnet.

Using his thumb, he gently pulled my chin down, bring my lips closer to his. "I can't stay away from you, Andra," he breathed, pressing soft kisses against the corner of my lips. I was intoxicated, pulled under by his touch. "The way you move, you're water. You're fluid. When you're wrapped around me, I'm drowning." He pressed his lips just above mine, nibbling on my cupid's bow. "You consume my thoughts." He pressed his lips against mine for a brief moment and pulled away. "My hands instinctively reach for you when you're in the vicinity." He pushed his fingers back into my hair, rough hands pressing into my scalp. He brushed his nose just behind my ear. "Do you understand?" he whispered into my ear, the bite of his facial hair scratching my face. His words were fingers, trailing over my face, reaching inside of me, drumming against my heart beat. "Do you understand?" he repeated.

I couldn't speak, my entire throat burned with desire. I nodded, swallowing, hoping to cool that fire.

"As much as I hate to say this, we need to get back. I'm sure you have things you need to do before we go to the concert tonight."

I sighed, my body wavering between ignoring my chores and falling onto Julian. My loyalty to the ranch won out. "Yep, you're right." I stood up and wiped the dirt from my legs.

"Here," Julian said, putting a hand on my shoulder. "You have grass in your hair." His fingers tugged my hair, loosening the pieces of grass. When he'd pulled the last piece, he ran his fingers through my hair like a comb. "I like your hair."

"You like my ink, you like my hair. What else do you like?" I asked, looking at him over my shoulder.

"I like your eyes. And not just their shade, which is remarkable itself. I like how much you reveal yourself through your eyes. Your lips are beautiful too, but the words that come from them can tell a story or tell the truth. Your eyes, though, they can't lie."

I frowned and started walking through the meadow into the tree line, heading back to the ranch. "Okay, what don't you like about me?"

"You snore in your sleep."

My eyes were wide when I turned to him. "I do not snore!"

"Your face is really ugly with that bandage." I knew he was saying it just to get a rise out of me.

I reached up and yanked the bandage off, exposing the scrape underneath. "Is that better?"

Julian looked shocked that I'd pulled it off. Then he shrugged. "You look more badass now."

I laughed. The air actually felt good on the scrape, I'd just have to get used to the pain I felt whenever I smiled or laughed. "Now that I've fixed that, what else don't you like?"

He laughed. "I don't like that you lie."

I stopped my stride and turned to him. "Elaborate." It wasn't a question.

He held up his hands in surrender. "Okay, when we talked that first night I met you, you told me don't run very fast. That was obviously a lie." His eyes were aimed at mine, daring me to disagree.

I let the tension subside and nodded, pursing my lips. "Okay, you're right. I lied. I can run pretty fast, actually." And so I did.

After I'd finished the rest of my chores, I hurried back to the cabin to get ready for the outdoor concert with Julian. It was a weekly thing in the summer months, local bands performing on a cement slab in a park. People gathered with blankets and coolers, and stayed out until the last band finished their set. I'd gone with Dylan a few times but because Dylan wasn't as naturally drawn to music as I was, he didn't hold too much interest in going. I knew Julian loved music, and would appreciate it, so inviting him had been a no-brainer.

I wore my skinny jeans and a pair of boots, an old, threadbare Queen tank, and pulled on a black zip-up jacket in case it got cold when the sun went down. I put a few things into the cooler and dumped my entire ice tray into it, so I wouldn't have to stop for ice. I grabbed a couple flannel blankets and stepped outside, locking the door behind me.

I took the top off of the Jeep and drove to Julian's cabin. He stepped out and laughed. "I didn't expect you to actually pick me up," he said while climbing into the passenger seat. "But thank you for not opening my door."

I drove slowly down the gravel road, increasing the speed when I reached the main, paved road. Our town was tiny, but there were three other neighboring towns that worked together to organize these weekly concerts. Everyone paid a $5 fee to cover the bands' charge and to help pay for the permit for the land.

After paying the fee, I parked the Jeep just off the road and hopped out, heading to the back of the vehicle to grab the cooler and other things I'd packed. Julian took the cooler from me and I grabbed the blankets. Then we both walked up the road, past cars that had arrived earlier than us. I could hear the sound check up ahead.

Julian reached his free hand for mine, grabbing it and entwining our fingers. He walked more closely beside me and we both slowed our steps, his fingers squeezing mine. My hand was warmed by his, by knowing that he wanted connection just as much as I did.

When we reached the field in front of the concrete stage, I led Julian to the left of the stage, the side that, to me, had the best acoustics in relation to the trees and the mountains around us. I spread out the larger blanket and plopped down, both of us turning on our sides to face on another. The first band was still setting up so we had time to talk. Once the music started, it would be too loud to hear each other without yelling.

"This was a great idea," he said, scooting closer to me.

"I hope you like the music. They usually do a lot of covers."

"I'm sure I will." He pushed the hair away from my shoulder. The jacket slipped over my shoulder with the movement and Julian wasted no time running his fingers over the bare skin. "I can't not touch you. I'm not going to be sorry for it either."

I raised an eyebrow. "Did you see me complaining?" I asked, reaching out to grab a handful from the center of his shirt. I pulled him closer. "I don't like the space between us," I admitted. I propped myself up on one arm and looked down at him. His head was cushioned on his bent arm, his biceps flexed from the positioning. His hair was deliciously mussed up and his lips were in a contented smile. That smile was one of my favorites, knowing that I helped put it there.

I leaned down, allowing my hair to become a curtain around us, nuzzling my nose against his. I could tell that he was holding back, allowing me to take control of this situation. I peppered his facial hair with kisses, loving the bite against my lips. I kissed his lips quickly once, and then twice, and when I tried to pull away the third time, his hands came up and held my head in place, kissing me at his leisure. He was careful not to brush the scrape on my cheekbone.

Not sure about the PDA that was allowed at the park, I pulled away and off of him and laid flat on my back. I blew out an exaggerated breath. "Does it always feel like this?" I asked without thinking.

"No. I can say that it definitely does not always feel like this. In fact, I'd go as far as to say it never feels like this, or at least it never has for me before."

I turned my eyes to his. His eyes were running over my face. It made me feel self-conscious. "Why do you look at me like that?"

His eyes met mine. "I'm memorizing your face." He said it nonchalantly, as it that was the most obvious answer. Before I could ask why, the music started, drowning out my voice. We both turned our heads to the stage to listen. At some point, Julian had curled up behind me, allowing me to use his arm as a pillow, his other hand running down my waist, over the curve of my hip. Some of the songs, he used my hip as a guitar, plucking his fingers against the material in time to the band. I was sure it was innocent, but the repetitive motion was driving me crazy. As a result, we made out for all of the songs, pausing to catch our breaths, laugh, or have a sip of soda. Being around Julian was like being alive. I was more aware of my heart beating, challenged to evaluate myself, and I laughed so often my cheeks hurt.

When the third band played and Julian and I had each finished our second sodas, the sky had grown dark. The only lighting was around the stage and on the road, leaving those of us on the grass in complete darkness.

When the band played a song that was a bit sappy but still upbeat, Julian hopped up to his feet and reached a hand down to me.

"What are you doing?" I asked, suspicious.

"I, Julian Jameson, am asking you, Andra Walker, to dance with me to this happy song." He seemed upbeat, and while I wanted to protest, I found myself placing my hand in his and standing up.

He led me towards the tree line, completely out of sight from the other concert-goers. It was absolutely black except for the stage, so I took comfort in knowing that no one else could see us. We could live in this square of trampled grass off to the side of the actual concert, and only acknowledge each other. Julian danced with me in time to the beat of Jason Mraz's "I'm Yours" in the grass, spinning me away from him and pulling me back with drama. It was funny and fit the mood of our night together. The song blended into the next one.

"OneRepublic," I whispered, my lips against his hair. "Your band."

I felt his lips touch the shell of my ear as he sang along with the lyrics to "Stop and Stare."

He serenaded me in the dark, his hips pressed against mine, the hand he held to my back tenderly tracing my spine. Every few chords, he would press his lips to my earlobe, in a kiss as soft as his voice. He didn't withhold anything from me, whether it was his words or even his touch. He gave me everything.

And for the first time in my life, I fell in love. I fell in love with his hand on my waist, under the stars, while we danced to borrowed words. I fell in love with his breath at my ear, his cheek pressed against mine, with his body pressed tightly to mine. I fell in love again when we laid on the ground, my head on his chest and his hand in my hair. His heart beating in my ear was the loudest sound, my favorite sound.

Not for the first time, I knew I was in trouble.

When we made it back to the ranch, Julian asked me to come with him to his cabin. I was sleepy, sated, emotionally drunk from spending the evening in his arms. I agreed and followed him in.

Julian disappeared into the bathroom, so I crouched down to the small table that held the television. He'd stocked it with a few DVDs. The two DVDs stacked on top of the DVD player were The Goonies and The Princess Bride. My heart did a somersault in happiness.

I didn't hear him come out of the bathroom as I read the back of the DVD cases for the movies I didn't recognize.

"Cora."

"Hmm?" I murmured, absent-mindedly. An instant later, my brain woke up. I spun to face him. I was certain my face displayed shock. "What did you call me?"

Julian took cautious steps toward me. "Cora. Cora Mitchell. That's who you are."

I was in absolute disbelief and I shook my head back and forth as fast as it could move. "No. That's not-I'm not her." It was my worst attempt at lying yet.

Julian moved closer and I backed up, my knees bumping into the television stand. Julian put a hand up, likely in an attempt to calm me. My eyes bolted towards the door but before I could make a move, Julian stood in front of it.

With his hands held up, he spoke softly, calmly. "I'm not going to corner you. But I don't want you to leave until I explain."

If I had opened my eyes anymore, I was sure my eyeballs themselves would roll right out of their sockets. I was shocked, scared, and absolutely speechless.

"I've known you were Cora since our first date, though I've suspected it far longer."

I shook my head, shaking his words from my ears. "How?"

"I told you my father moved away when my parents divorced. And I told you he helped me with my novels. I didn't tell you that he's a police officer." He paused. "In Michigan."

My jaw lost control of itself, and I knew my mouth hung open. I had no words for what this felt like.

Julian gestured me to sit on his bed. I didn't have much choice, my knees were wobbling, unable to bear my weight. I sat hard on the bed, noticing for the first time that he'd cleared the room from his earlier mess. There was a short stack of papers on his desk. I finally let my eyes fall upon him again.

Julian moved away from the door, just a few feet towards me. "He's a detective, actually. And he's assigned to cold cases. Some of my books are modeled after cases I know he's worked on. I still fictionalize the stories, but he gives me inspiration."

I nodded, my first acknowledgement that I was listening.

"About two years ago, we got to talking about a case of a missing girl. A seventeen year old who vanished. It'd been eating him alive and he joked that I should use some of my internet prowess to see what I could dig up. He never shared details with me that hadn't already been leaked to the press. So I didn't have an extra advantage.

"Well, I made a trip to see my dad last year and while there I snooped around, did some research. And while the entire internet believed the uncle was responsible, I didn't. I did some digging. He lost a lot of money when she disappeared."

I looked at him with a question in my eyes.

"I'll get to that part," he answered. "I looked up Cora's history, delved into her life before she became an orphan." I swallowed hard then, reminded of my mother. "I found Six that way. Or, as he's legally known, William." I cringed, knowing Six hated that name. "I followed the trail to California, thinking you might be with him. Of course, you weren't. I got to thinking about you, how you were orphaned after you mother passed away. And I felt that Six would leave you with someone motherly." Julian took a deep breath, as if admitting to the lengths he went to find me had weighed him down. He continued, "So I looked up his mother. I checked out her Facebook. I looked through all her friends, and you weren't on there. So I checked out her friends. She had only about thirty friends, and maybe ten that she interacted regularly with. One of those friends was Rosa."

I had calmed down slightly, and I was able to finally form words again. "She has a Facebook account mostly to maintain the ranch's Facebook page."

"Bingo," he said, his voice soft. "There are a lot of photos of the ranch on its Facebook page. Photos of every single employee-"

"Except me," I interrupted.

"You don't have an individual photo, no. But the photo of Oscar, in the kitchen. Behind him, out of focus, is a woman, her head bent, hair fanned to conceal her face. It's entirely innocent, except for the comment on that photo."

"Show me."

Julian pulled out his laptop, a slender rectangle of silver, and sat next to me on the bed. He booted up the machine and a moment later he turned the laptop to me. I saw the photo of Oscar, knife pressed to the cutting board, his usual scowl evident. The photo was captioned "Oscar the Grouch, Chef Extraordinaire." And over his shoulder, on the opposite end of the kitchen island was me. My hair was indeed covering most of my face, and because I didn't remember the photo being taken, it was likely a quick candid. I was definitely out of focus, but I knew it was me. It wouldn't have been so clear to anyone else.

I scrolled down to the comment section and instantly recognized Dylan's model looks as the author of the comment. "Haha, is this supposed to be Andra's employee photo too?" it said.

I handed the laptop back to Julian and ran my tongue over my teeth. Dylan didn't know my past, knew nothing about Cora Mitchell. I couldn't be mad at him for a seemingly innocent comment. He didn't know. I looked at Julian. "But you said it yourself, I'm out of focus. How did you know it was me?"

Julian clicked on Dylan's profile. "When I saw the comment, Dylan had a different profile photo up." He clicked on Dylan's profile pictures album and scrolled until he found the right one. It was one of me and Dylan, right after I'd gotten the Queen tattoo. Dylan had his arm around me and we were standing in front of a mirror. Off to the right, in the reflection, you could make out the ink on the back of my neck, the skin red and irritated. But our faces were in focus, and I had one eyebrow raised while Dylan made a goofy face. I dragged the memory out of the cobwebs of my brain. "I took this to send to Six," I said, touching my hand to my neck in remembrance. "He told me not to get tattoos, so naturally I did." I bit my lip, my lip ring still missing. "I got my lip pierced later that day.

Julian went back to Dylan's albums and opened one up, navigating quickly to the photo of me, coyly smiling at the camera, pointing two fingers at the fresh piercing, challenge evident in my eyes. I was obnoxious. And I was on Dylan's profile, in at least two photos.

"Dylan texted the photos to me so I could forward them to Six," I explained. "I honestly did not think he would post them to his Facebook page." I felt like a total idiot. "And Dylan has all his photos public?" I asked, incredulous.

Julian nodded. "He didn't make it hard for me to find you." He closed the laptop and turned to face me. "When I stepped out of the car and saw you, my heart stopped in my chest. But it wasn't from recognition, Andra. Or, at least not the recognition you think. Frankly, I was dumbfounded. You stood in the sun, wisps of hair framing your stunning face, legs up to your neck. And then you stalked towards me with such purpose. You had that teasing smile on your lips, eyeing me haughtily, not taking my crap for even one second. When I stepped into my cabin and closed the door, I had to shake my head to clear my thoughts. It was then that I remembered I'd come here to find you. To see if you were Cora."

I absorbed his words like a sponge, soaking up the knowledge he was so freely giving. "You acted pretty damn sure of yourself when I first met you."

"I've told you I enjoy a challenge. I don't find pleasure when women bend to my will so easily. I want them to want me to work for it, to match them in wit. I want to compete with a woman, even if we're hoping to win the same thing. When you spoke to me with challenge right away, it was second nature to challenge you right back, to get on your level." He ran his hands through his hair, frustrated. "Maybe I'm not explaining myself well. I met you, was immediately intrigued and captivated by you. My entire focus had been finding Cora – I hadn't planned further than that. But then I met you and I didn't care if you were Cora or if you weren't, but I needed to get to know you." He stood up and walked away before turning right back around and grabbed my hands, pulling me to standing.

"When I look at you, into your green/gold/hazel eyes, something settles, comfortably, in my chest. Every single time. I see stubborn bravery and sorrow in those big eyes of yours, and they both inspire me to be a better man so that I am deserving of knowing the secrets you keep, of seeing into the pieces of your soul that you're willing to share with me." His eyes were earnest, his hands open. "I want to take the sadness away from you. Not all of it, because I know the experiences you've had have made you this person, this wonderful, intelligent, incredible person. I just want to take the parts that burden you. I want to free you."

With those words, my heart somersaulted in my chest, a heavy lump settling in my throat. I was wholly overwhelmed with all the information, and his admission. Though I knew my feelings for Julian were of the strongest variety, I still felt that urge to push him away, to keep the blackness I nurtured from touching him.

I wanted my words to be sharper than a knife, and I wanted them to hurt, to push away his goodness before I turned it black from my secrets. I mustered all the anger I felt, let the words crawl from my throat, let their lies serrate my heart. There would be no taking it back, no way to swallow them once I let them free. I swallowed and turned my face away from him. "I told you this was casual, Julian. That's all I've ever felt." Lie. "You were fun to be around, but I didn't take this seriously." Another lie. "I don't want to see you again." The lies were beginning to choke me on their way up my throat, so I closed my mouth and walked towards the door.

"Stop." His voice was soft, but firm in its request. I turned to look at him.

Julian moved closer to me. One step. Two steps. Three steps. And then he was right in front of me, his harsh breathing disrupting the air around me. Sandalwood and cinnamon assaulted my senses and I squeezed my eyes tight, unwilling to look at him. Unable to look at him. He knew me; he knew the parts where Cora Mitchell and Andra Walker intersected. The parts I tried to hide the most. So he would know I was lying to him, see the fear at losing him reflected in my eyes.

He didn't say anything for a moment, but I could feel the turmoil, the rage, rolling off of him in waves.

"You think you don't deserve to share yourself, your secrets. You think you burden people with your darkness. But you don't. You're not dark. You're light. You're warmth. You're good. God. Andra," his voice broke, "you are so good."

My entire body trembled, a need to hold him warred against my stubbornness. And yet, I couldn't believe the words he was saying.

How could he believe I wasn't dark? If your soul was comprised partly from experience, then my soul would at the very least be some shade of grey. And each lie I told hung heavy on the dark side, slipping the gradient scale more towards the dark. I didn't believe light and dark could exist without the other. It was the absence of light that made us dark in the first place. And while I wasn't wallowing in some emotional self-pity, I knew my soul was more dark than light. I was more bad than good. And it was with that realization that I made the choice to walk away from Julian. Not because I was dark, but because he wasn't.

My heart felt heavy in my chest, weighed down by my decision. I turned away from him, towards the door. My hand gripped the handle and I reached to pull the door open. I felt his hand slam against the door, right next to my face. I looked over my shoulder at him and tried to keep my face calm. "Let me go."

"No."

I gritted my teeth. And pushed his hand from the door. "I told you, I don't feel the same."

"Stop lying."

I ran my tongue over my teeth, contemplating. "What can I do to make you believe me?" I asked, staring at the door, my voice completely calm.

"Look me in the eyes and tell me I mean nothing to you." His voice was smooth, as if he didn't think I was capable of lying to his face. "And make me believe you," he added.

"Okay," I said, forcing annoyance into my voice. I turned around and time felt as if it had slowed down significantly. Meeting his eyes was harder than I expected. I felt my heart thundering painfully in my chest and willed it to calm. But it was futile. My heart beat harder whenever I was in his presence. I was betrayed by its reaction. I swallowed.

"You mean nothing to me," I whispered, my voice strangled.

"Look me in the eyes when you say it."

I swallowed again and finally looked him in the eyes. I was surprised to see his face completely calm, no trace of the anxiety I was feeling at all. *Probably because he knows you're a big, fat liar, Andra,* I told myself. I opened my lips, but no sound came out. I tried again. This time I formed the words. "You mean nothing to me," I repeated shakily. My voice was siding with my heart, both of them betraying me, making my voice weak.

Julian braced his hands on either side of my face, against the door. He leaned in. "Make me believe it."

I closed my eyes and let my head fall back against the door. I summoned all my courage and opened my eyes. "You mean nothing to me." My voice sounded foreign even to me.

"Again," he said. He was scarily calm.

"You mean nothing to me." If anything, my voice was getting weaker and weaker. I saw triumph in his eyes and gritted my teeth again. I pushed against him, pushed him away from me. "Fuck you, Julian," I spat. Frustration simmered just under the surface of my words.

"Now that I believe. I really felt those words. Now say it again, and maybe you can try to sound less like a dying robot."

"Fuck you."

"I told you, I believe that. Make me believe I am nothing to you."

It was a pang to my heart just to hear the words from his lips. My natural instinct was to deny it, but I sucked the words in. I blew out a breath and met his eyes once more. I mustered everything I had left and opened my mouth. The words refused to form this time and I pushed him again. "Damn you, Julian," I growled, frustration finally boiling over in the form of tears streaming down my eyes. "I can't say those words with meaning, and you know it." I slid down the door until I was sitting on the ground. "But it doesn't change anything," I mumbled, wiping the tears from my face.

Julian crouched in front of me. "Yes it does. You can't push me away. I won't go quietly."

I shook my head and covered my face with my hands. "You don't get it. I can't go back to that life. I can't be Cora Mitchell again. As far as I'm concerned, she's dead."

"What are you talking about?"

"Your father. You found the lost girl. He's going to want to close that case."

Julian pulled my hands away from my face. "My father has nothing to do with us. Cora Mitchell is not his only cold case."

"I won't go back, Julian. This is my home." This time, my voice was strong.

"I don't want you to go back. Are you serious? You think I'm going to report your location to the police, so they can send you back to your uncle?"

"I don't know! This is all kind of overwhelming right now. Isn't finding me kind of thrilling for you, the mystery author?" I said it snidely, I knew, but I couldn't help it.

"Look. I don't give a fuck that you're Cora Mitchell. Are you listening to anything I'm saying? My feelings for Andra Walker, for you, they're stronger than any feeling I've ever had. From the moment I overheard you praying in the grass, finding Cora Mitchell has been secondary to getting to know you, Andra. I don't feel like I've won a prize for finding Cora Mitchell, the missing girl. I feel like I've won something far more profound for falling for you, Andra, stubborn, sarcastic, warm, beautiful, intelligent, funny woman. I want Andra, I want you. I want everything you're willing to give me, and I want the parts you don't want to give me."

"You don't know what you're taking on, Julian," I answered, wearily.

"Then tell me. Tell me everything. The bad, the good, the mundane."

So I did. I told him of growing up without a father, but with a devoted mother. I told him of my mother's death, of having to live with my aunt and uncle and then later, her death. Then, with a deep breath and a heavy heart, I told him all about the abuse, not leaving out a single detail. After, with a lighter heart, I told him of the escape and my life since. And while the tears flowed from my eyes, Julian held me and let me unload all of it. I purged everything until I was empty, until my voice was hoarse.

Not for the first time, I fell asleep secure in his arms. But, for the first time, I felt peace settle over me like a warm blanket, and I slipped into sleep without the threat of a nightmare looming.

I awoke disoriented. I looked to my left and then to my right and remembered where I was. The bed was empty on the side that Julian had slept on so I stretched my limbs and sat up.

He was in the kitchen, shirtless, humming along with the radio he had playing on a low volume. I heard sizzling and crackling and realized he was cooking. I watched him dancing and humming as he transferred something from the skillet to the waiting plate. He poured water from a kettle into a mug and turned around, seeing me awake.

He carried the mug over to me and sat on the edge of the bed. I watched him set the mug on the end table before I felt his fingers on my face, cradling me as he kissed me.

"Mmm," I murmured against his lips. "I have morning breath."

Julian's eyes were tender. He brushed the bed head hair from my face. "Don't care," he whispered before kissing me again. How could I pretend I felt nothing for this man? How could I pretend for even a second? His lips moved to my cheek and then he handed me the steaming mug. "Tea," he explained before standing up, brushing his lips over the top of my head. "Hungry?" he asked as he walked back into the kitchen.

"Yes, very." I sipped the tea. It was raspberry, my favorite. The man didn't miss a thing.

A moment later, Julian returned with breakfast: a mound of fluffy scrambled eggs, bacon, and toast. I took the plate from his hands. "Thank you," I smiled up at him.

"It's my pleasure." He kissed the top of my head again before returning to the kitchen.

I dug into the hot food. "These eggs are delicious."

"One of the quickest and easiest meals to feed a group of people."

His sisters. "Well, you've impressed me with your chef skills thus far."

He grinned at me as he loaded up another plate and came towards me, sitting next to me on the bed.

"Today's your day off," he said, in between bites.

I swallowed the bite of bacon. "Yes, and I think I remember you mentioning bringing me to your house."

"I did. I was thinking we could head over there in a few hours."

I stretched my back and took a bite of toast. "What time is it?"

"Almost noon."

I nearly choked on the toast. "Noon? How did I sleep so late?"

"You were exhausted, obviously. I let you sleep in."

I let that sink in. I ate my toast silently. "I'll just need to shower and change and I'll be ready." I stood up to bring my plate to the kitchen, but Julian stopped me.

"I'll take that," he offered, taking my plate and standing up. He set it on the kitchen island before following me to the door.

"I still have things I want to tell you," he said when we stopped at the door. "Things about Cora, and things about you. But today, is it okay if we just live in a bubble, not let the troubles of the world touch us?"

I nodded, swallowing hard. "That sounds perfect to me."

He leaned in, wrapping an arm around my waist. He pulled me against him and I found myself wrapping my arms around his neck. "I'm sorry I kept secrets from you," he whispered in my ear.

"I kept secrets, too." I gripped him tighter. "I don't want to anymore."

"Good." He kissed the skin right next to my ear. "Come back when you're ready."

"Okay," I breathed. And just like that, he forgave me for the lies, for the secrets. My fingers found his facial hair and I lifted my lips up to kiss him. It was different this time. Kissing Julian was existential.

I walked back to my cabin with a lighter heart.

When Julian pulled his convertible up the long driveway to his home, my mouth fell open in awe. It sat back off the driveway, built into a hill, with large windows facing the trees. The entire second floor was glass, the windows separated only by some support beams. The house was made of log, glass, slate, and stone, with a tall pitched roof capping it off. The main floor had glass doors onto a stone patio and on one side of the house was a stone stairway, providing access to the garden that was built into the hill. The house had a two-story wing off the other side, with a stone bay window on the ground floor and all glass bay window directly above it on the second floor, to match the large picture windows that stretched from side of the second level to the other.

The house was built into a clearing of trees, so it was surrounded on all sides by tall pine trees. And I imagined with the abundance of windows, it made one feel like they were in the woods themselves. I couldn't wait to find out.

Julian opened my door and held a hand out for me. Holding my hand, he led me into the ground level entrance, his hand on the small of my back, guiding me through the door. The main floor was a mess of construction equipment everywhere, completely bare of furniture.

"Come upstairs," he said, tugging on my hand. In the back of the house was a grand staircase. The staircase was curved, wrapping around a stone wall. It was like something out of a medieval castle. Two different wood tones made the steps up to the second floor.

The second floor was lit up from the floor to ceiling windows that dominated the living area, where rich, brown leather sofas sat. They were covered in a sheer sheet of plastic. You could tell the interior was still being remodeled, with boxes of wood flooring sitting up against walls, hammers strewn about. There was a large fireplace on one side of the living room and Julian moved to light it. I watched him crouch down, lay a couple logs into the grate before crushing the newspaper he grabbed from the basket on the side of the fireplace. I watched his arms, the muscles stretching the sleeves of his shirt. My body started humming, the desire to be wrapped in his arms growing stronger by the second. I turned away and walked to the windows, breathing a sigh at the view. There were trees for miles, in every direction. You couldn't even see the main road we'd entered from. It was truly like living in the forest.

I felt Julian come up behind me, heard the crackle from the fire he'd made. He put hand on my waist and without a second thought, I pulled his arm forward, wrapping completely around my waist. His other arm wrapped around me and we stood at those windows not saying a word, our arms tangled, the only sound from our hearts beating. I relaxed more fully into him, his chest at my back. I felt his chest expand slightly with each breath he took and it was such a good feeling, to feel him breathing against me, his warmth wrapped around me.

I felt his chin come to rest on my shoulder. "What do you think?"

"I can see why you bought it."

Julian tilted his head and kissed my neck once, softly. "I've always wanted to live in the woods, surrounded by quiet."

I leaned into his lips at my ear, felt him kiss me again. "I kind of have a thing for the woods," I said, tingles running down my neck from his kiss.

He murmured something intelligible against my neck before bring his lips to kiss just behind my ear. "I kind of have a thing for you."

I couldn't help the smile. "I kind of have a thing for you, too."

"That's convenient," he muttered under his breath before tightening his arms around my waist. His lips moved along the angle of my jaw and I exhaled a breath.

"You make me forget who I am," I admitted, closing my eyes to savor this moment. "You make me feel like I'm lost and found, at the same time."

"I'll always find you," he said into my neck.

I couldn't believe I'd only known him for nine days and already felt this way for him. Knowing what he knew now, how he felt about me, was freeing in a way I didn't expect. I'd unloaded on him, told him everything, and he was still here, happily. I felt the itch in my nose that signaled tears. I turned around, facing him, and brought my hands to his face. His trimmed beard was prickly against my palms, and his eyes were on mine, searching. I felt his arms wrap around my waist. We were close, his chest pushing into mine with each inhale. "Thank you." It was simply said, but I hoped he understood why I was thankful.

His brows drew together as he brought a hand to my face, pushing the hairs away from my eyes. "Andra." And then I knew, because he felt the same way. The way he said that one word told me everything.

"Can I see your kitchen?" I asked, my fingers playing with his hair.

"Yeah, come on." His hand slid from my face, down my arm, and clasped my hand as he led me through the open doorway into the kitchen. The dark wood cabinets were in, the silver and gold granite counters were glossy, reflecting the light that streamed through the windows.

I let go of Julian's hand to get a little breathing space. I walked along the kitchen island, aware of Julian's focus on me.

My heart was starting a slow strum in my chest, my body attuned to his. I opened his refrigerator under the guise of being nosey. I saw Julian move around the kitchen island out of my peripheral vision. I eyed the contents with a detachment, my attention more focused on the man advancing towards me.

I reached in and yanked out a water bottle before slamming the door shut. Julian was a few feet away. He was looking at me with a hunger in his eyes. It was both intimidating and thrilling. I backed up until I hit the counter behind me. Why was I so nervous?

I twisted the lid off of the water bottle, never once breaking eye contact. I hesitated a moment before bringing the bottle to my lips. I took a small sip, pulled back, and then a longer sip. The coolness of the water did nothing to extinguish the heat that was traveling across my body.

Julian's lips were set in a firm line, his eyebrows drawn together. As with every other time I caught him looking at me, his stare was intense. But this time it had the added sexual tension simmering underneath, causing a small tick in his jaw. He gave me the briefest crooked smile as he stepped closer, slowly.

My pulse picked up tempo as the distance between our bodies decreased. I took a hurried sip of the water before Julian was close enough to take it from me. Keeping his eyes locked on mine, he took a deep sip of the water. When he pulled the bottle away, I couldn't remove my eyes from the tiny droplets that remained on his upper lip.

The hair on my arms stood on end, as if his nearness was causing a magnetic reaction. The air was thick with our heavy breathing, but we weren't even touching. Yet.

He took another pull from the bottle before setting it on the counter my back was up against. He moved closer still, close enough that I swore I could feel the warmth of his body despite not being physically touched by him. Sandalwood swirled in the small space and it was all I could breathe in. I was becoming intoxicated by his presence.

Fuck, I thought. His lips curved, the skin at the corners of his eyes crinkled in humor, and then I realized I'd actually spoken the word out loud. *Fuck*, I thought again, this time silently.

Julian lifted a hand up and I sucked in a breath as he ran the back of it down my arm, surely feeling the gooseflesh that had popped up all over my skin. When he reached my wrist, he traced it with just a fingertip. My hand unclenched its fist and I closed my eyes. How had I become so sensitive to such an innocent touch?

I felt him lean forward until his mouth was at my neck. He paused a moment, his breath warming my skin, before pressing a kiss softly against the spot just under my chin.

My breaths at this point were coming in fast, uneven, as if my lungs were constricted.

He dragged his lips down my neck, stopping along the way to press a kiss here and there. I felt his hands go to my shoulders and slide in, towards my neck. Julian's hands gently bent my neck in one direction, giving his lips more access to my flesh. He slid his hands into my hair and cupped the back of my head, manipulating my neck to accommodate the path he traced along my throat.

I shuddered a breath loose from my lips. Time felt suspended, like nothing else in the world could be happening at this moment. I couldn't think outside the space we occupied. It was equally the most terrifying and most sensual moment of my entire life.

He held me as if my bones were made of glass, as if my skin would tear beneath his lips if he applied too much pressure. When his lips pressed against the pulse at the base of my throat, I wondered if he could feel the power in my pulse, the power he was solely responsible for. As if in answer, his hand moved from my neck to my chest, resting over the space that contained my heart. There was something beautiful and intentional about that gesture, like he was acknowledging the mortal part of me that reacted so restlessly to his touch.

He looked up after my heart thudded several times beneath his palm, brown eyes penetrating into my own. We stared at each other for a few more thuds before I lifted my hand tentatively, placing it on his heart. I felt the power of his muscle, the muscle that gave him life, the muscle that pumped the blood through his body. This was more than the sexual tension that flowed around us; this was tenderness. This was the defining moment. My body was no longer a pendulum, swinging to and from Julian. I leaned into him in acknowledgement of that fact. I'd fallen in love with him at the concert when we danced under a dark sky. And still, I was falling headfirst into love, real love. I knew feeling so deeply was not without risk or fear, but it was there regardless. Julian had broken through the barriers I'd set in place, though admittedly, I hadn't resisted too much. He knew my secrets and yet, despite losing the security blanket my secrets provided, I'd never felt more safe with someone.

He brought his other hand to mine, the hand over his heart. Slowly, with care, he removed my palm from his shirt and brought it to his lips. His eyes never left mine as he kissed each fingertip once, ending with a kiss to the center of my palm.

My heart tripped over itself. This man would definitely be my undoing. Desire bloomed deep in my belly.

Before I knew what he was doing, he reached behind me. I heard a soft click and then a crackle as speakers turned on. A second later, piano played softly, and then the vocals came in, "come away with me in the night." The soft vocals and sleepy melody was perfect for this moment.

His fingers intertwined with mine, and the hand over my heart moved to the curve of my waist. He gently pulled me forward until we were chest to chest, hip to hip. My free hand found his shoulder as Julian led me away from the counter, moving slowly against me to the rhythm of the song.

"Norah Jones, huh?" I murmured against his face.

I felt the movement of his smile from the scratch of his stubble on my forehead. "Norah Jones," he repeated.

I closed my eyes to better soak in the moment. The song was romantic, sleepy, and sweet. Her voice was silky, like a slip of smoke curling around us.

We danced in his kitchen, across ripped up flooring, surrounded by tools and boxes of tile. There was nothing but Norah Jones and the scuff of our shoes on the dusty floor as Julian slowly moved with me back and forth, rubbing his stubble against my hair.

"I love dancing with you," he said after a moment, his voice soft.

"I'm growing quite fond of it myself." I rubbed my head against his. "Why this song?" I whispered.

I felt his lips press against my hair. "Words are what I know," he murmured. "I'm good with words; I turn them into sentences and into paragraphs and eventually into novels. The words don't have any deep meaning to me, they're just words." I felt the hand at my waist squeeze once. "But you?" he asked, his voice taking on a deeper quality. "You burrow down, underneath all that bullshit, down to the core of who I am." I felt my throat constrict with feeling.

Julian nuzzled against my hair. "You aren't impressed with my words. I'm not J.J., the writer, to you. I'm Julian." He pulled me closer, close enough that not even the threat of air would be able to separate our bodies. His arm was now snug around my waist, wrapped from one side of me to the other. I was trapped, but I wasn't scared. I was safe, in his arms, wrapped up with his words and his presence.

"This song?" he continued. "These words have meaning. These words echo how I feel for you. I'm no song writer, nor am I a poet. I'm just Julian." He pulled back slightly, just enough to stare into my eyes. He brushed the tendrils away before framing my face in his hands. "I'm just Julian. And you're just Andra. And my words usually hold no meaning, but these do: I'm falling for you. Hopelessly, hurriedly, and freely falling for you."

My entire body shuddered, igniting a smoldering fire inside of me. I couldn't look away even if I wanted to. His eyes were so earnest, so humble. I felt like I was having an out of body experience. I parted my lips, but before I could push any words between them, his lips closed on mine.

He kissed me softly at first. But that fire inside of me was starved, and I reached out, gripping onto his shirt, trying to grasp anything to keep me grounded.

I felt myself being lifted up onto the kitchen island. This position put me up higher than he was, so I cradled his jaw in my hands and deepened the kiss. Julian's hands were on my waist, tightening and loosening his grip intermittently. I leaned back and whipped my shirt over my head. His fingers glided up from my waist to my bra, bypassing my breasts completely as he traced the straps on my shoulders.

I watched him, enraptured. "Beautiful," he whispered while trailing his fingers down the straps, over the cups of the bra. I tried to steady my breathing as his fingers traced the edge where skin met satin. Up and over one curve, tracing my tattoo, before he moved his fingers to the under band. He slid his hands to the wings on the side and in an instant, his fingers were under the material, touching my skin, gripping around my ribcage. He brushed his thumbs over my nipples, which were pebbled and protruding slightly from the thin satin.

I shuddered again.

Julian moved his hands over my upper arms to my shoulders again before I felt him tug the straps away from shoulders. A second later, he released the straps and there was a very satisfying slap sound from the straps connecting with my shoulders again. The sensation was just another jolt to my desire. I felt his fingers hook in the front center of my bra and he tugged me forward before lifting me down from the kitchen island.

My impatient hands grasped the bottom hem of his tee before I lifted it up. He took the shirt from my hands and flung it over his head, tossing it somewhere behind him.

I hadn't forgotten how sculpted his torso was, but it was still another shock to my over-aroused body. My fingers had a mind of their own and immediately rested upon his chest. I traced the hard lines of muscle there and met his eyes. His eyes were heady with desire, his bottom lip wet from our kiss. His face was the most sensual part of his entire body, hard lines and eyes burning with need for me. I was drunk off of the way he looked at me. Keeping my eyes locked with his, I deliberately bit my lip before brushing a finger nail down the line that separated the halves of his six-pack.

He narrowed his eyes in response before picking me up and tossing me over his shoulder like I weighed nothing. I thought he was headed back to the island but he strode down the hallway to a dark room. Upside-down, I could see barely more than long, dark wood flooring, then a shaggy cream rug. I made out dark wood posts of what I assumed was a bed before Julian tossed me onto it, confirming my guess. I quickly glanced at it, noted the dark wood of the four-poster style bed. I was on my back, my legs hanging off the end of bed frame. I moved my eyes to stare at the shirtless man watching me silently from between my hanging legs. There was challenge in his eyes and I smiled playfully before scooting backwards towards the head of the bed.

I didn't make it far.

He grabbed my ankles and with one yank, tugged me back down the duvet to the foot of the bed. He smiled, his sexy, pleased-with-himself smile. I quickly unsnapped the button on my shorts and slowly tugged the zipper down. His hands landed on mine, stalling me. His eyes told me he wanted to be in control of this part and I let him.

He grasped the waistband of my shorts and I lifted my butt off the bed to allow him to pull them down and off. He tugged my flip flops off along with my shorts and then looked down on me.

The room was dark, and only half of his face was highlighted by the muted lights of the hallway. His eyes slid up my legs to my underwear, over my bare stomach and bra, before they met mine. Something shifted then, turning something that was playful into something serious. I felt my heart thud, painfully hard, in my chest as we stared at each other silently. Those nerves returned, reminding me that this man was different. This was obviously much more than sex, for both of us. It was the first time that I'd felt anything more than a desire to scratch an itch.

This was the first time I had an emotional attachment to the person I was going to be physically intimate with. That realization took my breath away.

Julian nudged my legs apart before starting to climb onto the bed. I scooted back towards the pillows, giving him room and laying my body more fully on the bed.

He leaned over me, his face tender. "Are you ready for this?"

My heart settled in my chest as I smiled up at Julian. I reached a hand to his face and gently rubbed my fingers against his stubble. "I've never been more utterly unprepared for this. But," I said before he moved away, "I've never wanted this more, never wanted another man more than right now."

Julian leaned down until his face was in my neck. I heard him release a breath as if in a sigh. His warm breath fluttered over my neck and I wiggled a little in reaction. "God," he said. He pulled his head up, supporting himself on one arm while his free hand cupped my cheek. "Do you know how enchanting you are? What kind of magic are you conjuring up, Andra?"

"You've charmed me too, Julian." I whispered.

His lips moved down the center line of my chest. Light kisses peppered my skin until he reached the center of my bra. He looked up at me and as if I was reading his mind, I arched my back off the bed, allowing him to reach under me and unclasp my bra. He tugged the straps off my shoulders and pulled them down my arms, releasing the bra from my breasts while doing so.

He sat up and looked down at my bare skin. I was breathing heavily, my breasts heaving with the exertion. Julian reached down and traced just one finger over the curves of my breast, tracing the word I'd tattooed there. "Your skin is like silk."

He leaned down and traced the same path, but this time with his lips. I writhed under his touch, impatient for more. He chuckled against my skin, rubbing it with his facial hair. I squirmed more when he rubbed his face against my nipple, scratching with his facial hair. "Julian…" I said, on edge.

I felt two fingers press against my lips, pushing me so that I lay my head on the pillow. His lips moved down my body, along the waist of my panties, while his fingers glided up and down on my inner thighs. His knuckles brushed against me through my panties and I nearly bucked off the bed.

Julian eased the sides of my panties down. I felt him stop after a couple inches and I looked down to see what had stopped him.

He was staring at the initials I'd inked under my hip bone. CM. The one tattoo I hadn't shown him. His eyes lifted up, his eyebrows drawn together. Locking eyes with me, he placed his lips on the CM. My breath caught at the tender gesture, and it only further enhanced the ache I felt to connect with him.

A moment later we were stripping our underwear off of each other with hurried movement, in between multiple, one second-long kisses.

When we were both completely free of clothing, Julian leaned down and placed a kiss over my heart, as he had placed his hand once before. It produced a calming effect, stilling my heart's ramblings. I barely registered the moment he leaned over me to slide the condom on.

He climbed back over me, pushing just the tip of himself against my opening. Our eyes connected in the dark as he slid slowly into me, making sure to watch my face the entire time. I gripped his upper arms, adjusting to the sensation and the size. I felt completely stretched, whole. I smiled at him and nodded, urging him to continue.

It started slow and sweet, similar to the dance we'd shared in his kitchen earlier. Once I became accustomed to his size, it quickly became frenzied, his thrusts faster. My nails dug into his arms and my legs gripped his waist in a crushing hug. I was overcome with the physical sensation of being connected to Julian finally, and all the ways it made me feel. I could no longer hide myself from him. As my body climbed, so did the rush of emotions and I couldn't prevent the tears that slipped from the sides of my eyes, gravity pulling them into my hairline.

Julian's eyes narrowed in concern and I shook my head quickly, smiled, and put my fingers on his lips, halting whatever he had opened them to say.

It was raw, and real, and desperate. My heart became a jackhammer in my chest, quickening as I lost control of myself beneath him, my body trembling with the climax. Dimly, I heard his shout shortly afterwards before he collapsed on me, being careful to brace his weight on his forearms.

Julian's cheek was against mine, his breaths fast in my ear as his body settled. I could hear the faint dim of Norah Jones serenading us from the kitchen.

It was as if my heart was made to react to him, to beat for him. Everything my heart was doing in his presence was so foreign, like it recognized him as someone significant and reacted as such. I likened it to an animal greeting its owner after their absence. Julian owned me, he owned my heart. It was beating strong, steady, just for him. And more than anything, I wanted to be strong. I wanted to be steady. I wanted to give Julian the pieces of me that weren't dark. But part of me wanted to give him the dark pieces too, to see what he could make with them. And I knew that Julian wanted that too. He wanted to remove the burdens that my soul had carried for so long.

My tears came again, flooding my eyes. I tried to blink them back, but a tear slipped out of one eye, stalling when it connected with his cheek.

I held my breath as I felt him move and then saw his face above mine. I searched my brain for something to say, but faltered. How could I explain that I'd felt unburdened? He had promised to relieve me of the weight that sat heavy on my chest, and he did just that. The impression from the weight was still there, but it was easing. I was no longer handicapped by secrets. I was free. And it was all because of Julian.

Instead of asking why tears leaked from my eyes, he seemed to understand. "I'm not letting you escape from my bed easily you know," he said, casually wiping away the second tear that slid down, this one in relief. He grinned down at me before kissing my lips once, then twice, then over and over until I pushed him off of me while I laughed.

"You'll have to feed me at some point," I said.

"Of course." He slid off the bed gracefully and yanked up his previously discarded board shorts. "We'll need to keep your energy up for the rest of the night." He winked before strolling out of the room.

I laid back into the pillows, getting comfortable. I couldn't articulate how at ease I finally felt. Guilt had dominated my life for so long, and I'd wrapped myself in it like a security blanket with each lie I spoke. I'd found comfort in my guilt, knowing and accepting that I had a dark soul, tainted by circumstance and secrets. Security in that I didn't have to burden anyone with who I truly was. I'd lost a bit of myself, of Cora, shoving her aside to embrace the life of Andra: hard worker, compulsory liar, lonely girl. And Julian had found her, had found Cora. Literally and figuratively.

Before the tears could threaten again, I looked around the bedroom, taking in the sparse furnishings. The bed itself was beautiful, rich espresso-colored wood. The headboard was carved with a giant tree, gnarled-looking with twisty branches and devoid of leaves. But the carving was intricate, delicate. I ran my fingers over one of the branches when I heard Julian's bare feet on the wood floor. He had a glass of water in one hand and our clothes from the kitchen floor in the other hand. He tossed the clothing at the foot of the bed.

"That's custom," he said, walking over to the side of the bed I lay on.

"Tell me about it?" I asked, wrapping the tangled sheet around my upper body.

He sat on the edge of the bed next to me. "I found this wood near where we camped. Someone had just disposed of it, dumped it. It was a bunch of logs, so it may have been a camper who didn't want to be weighed down with logs when he left, but I don't know," he shrugged, and seemed self-conscious. "I felt bad. This wood was supposed to serve a purpose and then its purpose was gone. It was just wood, dumped on the ground. And it was good quality too. So I carried it all back to my car and commissioned a local woodworking artist to make my headboard from it. He leveled all the logs together so it was flat and then started carving." Julian brought his hand to rest on mine, tracing the carving with our fingers.

"Did you choose the design?"

"I can't take credit for that. But I think he knew what I wanted. He told me he made the tree angry, angry for being cut from its life only to be discarded. But it's still beautiful, the wood and the tree he carved. You just need to see the beauty in the ugliness. Or vice versa."

"That sounds suspiciously like a metaphor." I looked sideways at him.

"Because it is." He regarded me for a moment, wanting the significance to sink in, before he handed me the glass of water he had set on the nightstand. I took a large sip before he took the cup from me and set it back down. "What are you in the mood to eat?"

I leaned back into the pillows while I contemplated. "What do you have? Or, more importantly, what are you capable of cooking in that construction zone?"

"I think I can manage some pizza. I have a couple in the freezer. And beers of course."

"Yes and yes."

Julian smiled and leaned forward, brushing a kiss over my lips. "I'll be right back."

I was jolted out a sleep and sat up straight in bed. My eyes had to adjust to the darkness as I realized I was still in Julian's bed. I looked over and saw Julian next to me, sleeping peacefully.

What had interrupted my sleep?

A moment later, I heard my phone chiming from the kitchen. I'd left my purse there earlier.

Carefully, I pulled the sheet back and set my feet on the wood floor, warmed from the heat of the fireplace. At the foot of the bed, I picked up Julian's tee and slipped it on, smelling sandalwood and Julian on the soft cotton.

I peeked at the bed and was reassured that I hadn't disturbed Julian. He still slept peacefully, his face completely relaxed.

I padded quietly down the hallway to the kitchen and snagged my purse from the middle of the island. I pulled my phone out and glided my finger across the screen, waking it up.

I had four missed calls from Six. Just as I was about to dial him back, another call from him came through. Fear fell into my stomach.

I walked to the sliding glass door to the deck before answering.

"Hi," I breathed.

"Where are you?"

I didn't like the sound of his voice. "I'm at Julian's home."

"Yeah I know, I'm already in the town. What's the address?"

I told it to him before I was full awake. "Wait, why?"

"I'm coming to get you. We need to get the hell out of Colorado. Now."

My throat constricted and I reached a hand up to massage the fear free. "Why? What is going on?"

"He knows, Andra. Hawthorne knows where you are. And he knows about Rosa."

"What?!" My voice rose several octaves from a whisper. "What do you mean, he knows?"

"He figured out that you were in Colorado. I don't know how. But it's only a matter of time before he figures out about Julian. And then what, Julian's sisters? You weren't his last victim, you know. You need to leave Colorado until we can get a handle on this. Before he gets too close. He's on his way to the ranch now."

I wasn't his last victim? Six knew about Julian's sisters? We needed to leave, right away? My mind was filled with questions. "Are you fucking kidding? We can't just leave! What about Rosa? What about the ranch? No. No, Six."

"ANDRA!" His anger was loud through the phone. I had to pull it away from my head, wincing at the volume.

I glanced at the house while my mind raced. It was information overload. I tugged my hair on my head with my free hand, hoping to relieve some frustration. "Julian won't let me just leave."

"Then you can't tell him you're leaving. Just leave a note or something, but tell him not to seek you out."

I choked on grief. I couldn't leave Julian. My stomach pitched and I leaned over the railing of the deck to vomit. Tears streaked my face.

"I have people on their way to the ranch. They'll stay there. I've already talked to Rosa. It's handled. You need to get out of there. I'm fifteen minutes away. How far is the house from the main road?"

I wiped the back of my hand over my mouth as I looked out into the trees, despair causing my tears to well up. I couldn't imagine leaving now. My life had just shifted, my heart was beating a beat for someone else. Walking away would be cutting out all the good and leaving the bad.

"Andra. Focus. Name your colors if you need to." Six's voice was insistent, his patience wearing thin.

"It's the middle of the night, goddamn it. Everything is black as fuck," I growled.

"Good, work with that anger and get dressed. Now, how far are you from the main road?"

I stared out through the trees. "Half a mile, maybe."

"Can you run?"

"I brought flip flops."

I heard him sigh. "Well you're going to have to run regardless. Get dressed. I'll keep an eye out for you on the road. Hurry." The phone went silent.

I breathed out a deep breath. A million things ran through my head, crowding my space to think. I pulled on my hair in frustration, squeezing my eyes tight. I needed to move.

I opened my eyes, saw I was wearing Julian's shirt. I could work with this.

I quietly reentered the kitchen and tiptoed down the hall to his bedroom. He was still asleep.

I pulled my shorts on and tucked the shirt into them. I slid my feet in the flip flops and chanced a glance at Julian again. His face was so settled, his features relaxed in sleep. I bit my lip as the pain surfaced. I couldn't write him a note. I couldn't look at him without wanting to say "to hell with it all." But that would be selfish in many ways. The Monster finding me would have a ripple effect to all of those who had come in contact with me over the years. It would negatively impact Rosa, possibly criminally, and definitely her business. It would bring negative press to Julian. And Six would definitely go to jail.

I turned away from the bed and walked into Julian's closet, hoping for a sweatshirt. I found one and threw it on in the dark before grabbing my purse and leaving the bedroom. I felt like I was leaving a trail for Julian, leaving behind the pieces of me I wanted to share with him.

When I entered the kitchen, I heard a noise behind me. My heart stopped and I looked over my shoulder, towards the bedroom.

Julian's feet came into view. "Andra?" he called out, his voice hoarse from sleep.

I hesitated for only a moment before I bolted out the door and ran, down the steps, across the yard, and into the trees.

My heart was actually aching, not from exertion, but from feeling. I knew tears streamed from my eyes, whipping into my air from the speed at which I ran.

"Andra!" his voice was loud and I knew he was on the deck. A sob wrenched, unwillingly, from my mouth and I clamped my hand over it as I stopped to catch my breath, leaning my back up against a tree, out of sight from Julian.

When I'd gained control of myself, I peeked around the tree and saw Julian running down the stairs, wearing tennis shoes. That gave him the advantage.

I started in a sprint, my arms pumping as I ran, harder than I'd ever ran before. I heard Julian call my name again, this time with fear wrapping his voice. It was harsh and broken, and though it pained me, it meant I was losing him in the darkness of the woods. I reached the road in record time and ran down it, to avoid Julian reaching the same spot and finding me waiting for Six. When I'd crossed the road into the tree cover on the other side, I pulled my phone out and dialed his number.

"Where are you?"

I was out of breath from the run, wheezing. "I'm hiding in the trees across the road from his house. Drive by and flash your lights and I'll come out."

There was silence on Six's end, until I heard him rev his engine. "What do you mean you're hiding?"

"Julian chased me." I winced when Six blasted a stream of swear words. "Just hurry. I'll keep running north." I closed the phone and took off in the direction I hoped was north, taking care not to let Julian's distant voice call me back to him. Oh, it hurt. The pain in his voice matched the pain in my heart, the pain I was trying so hard to push aside. My heart betrayed me, flashing images of Julian across my brain. I tried to focus on colors, but in the darkness all I could see was black and dark green.

After I'd run for ten minutes, I heard the purr of an engine approaching. The lights were flashing erratically, so I peeked out from the trees. The silver car stop abruptly in the road. The passenger door opened. "Get in."

Six. I ran to the car, my muscles aching from running in flip flops on uneven ground. I slid into the passenger seat and closed the door.

"Seatbelt," Six muttered before speeding off. I slid the seatbelt on. As my hand brushed the pocket of my shorts, I remembered I had my phone. I could send Julian a goodbye note that way.

When Six saw the phone in my hand, he rolled my window down from his side. "Toss it."

"Not yet. One text. I didn't get a chance to tell him not to pursue me."

He held up one finger. "One, Andra. And then the phone is gone." I nodded.

I opened up my phone and pulled up the thread of texts Julian and I had exchanged. I ran my fingers over the screen for a moment, wishing it was his skin instead. And then I composed my message.

> Me: *Julian. There is danger. You can't return to the ranch for a little while. You have to pretend you never met me. Don't look for me.*

I paused before continuing, blinking back the tears that made my vision go fuzzy. Swallowing the lump that would more than likely permanently live in my throat from now on.

> Me: *This is so hard to type. I wanted to say goodbye to you, but I knew you'd never let me leave. You'd face this nightmare with me. But I can't let you take this on too. You've given me too much already, and I want to give you something. I'm in love with you, Julian. Oh, do I love you. When you placed your hand on my chest tonight, my heart belonged to you. I want to figure this out and come back to you, if you'll have me. I don't know how long it will be, but I've left a part of myself with you — I will return to you. I'll find you. I love you.*

I pressed "Send" and waited until the message went through before I tossed the phone out the window and silently rolled the window back up.

I settled in for the drive, closing my eyes and turning my face away so Six wouldn't be witness to the visible effects of my heart breaking.

OCTOBER 16, 2010

My life was in another stage of before and after. After meeting Julian, after leaving the ranch. I missed the before. I missed it with each breath I took, inhaling a different air.

I pushed my bare feet against the railing, which caused me to lean further back in my chair, balanced on only the two back legs, before I let my feet slide down, causing the chair to slam back on all four legs. After, I repeated the process. Over and over.

This was what I had been doing every single day. Sitting on the back deck of the lonesome little beach house, testing this thrift store chair's limits waiting for…what, exactly?

I missed the big house, the warmth of the logs in the fire and the view from the large picture windows. I missed the horses, I missed Dylan, and I missed Waffle Wednesdays. I missed my little cabin, my collection of cast iron, my bookshelves. I missed Oscar and Clint and even Farley. I missed Rosa. Oh God, did I miss Rosa. I missed her cooking, her warmth, her laughter.

And when I am not trying to distract myself with the colors I'm surrounded with – white, yellow, blue, green - I miss Julian. My breath still catches in my chest when I think of him, of how I left. That lump hasn't left my throat. It's anguish, and it lives in my throat, choking me when I think of him. And I think of him all the time.

The change in my surroundings had changed only the location of my body, my breath. My life itself was thousands of miles away in a small Colorado town. When the anguish was especially unbearable, I imagined Julian lying under the stars the way I showed him, whispering prayers the same time I did. It brought me some comfort, knowing that the same sky covered us.

Now that I was thousands of miles away, I realized that there was only one thing I truly feared. And it lived on repeat in my nightmares, which no longer consisted of the Monster, but of the moment I walked away from my life.

In a way, it was a good thing. My fear of the Monster was eradicated. In fear's absence, rage took up residence, churning in my stomach whenever I thought of all the choices he'd taken from me, again. He was no longer a Monster; he was just Hawthorne. Hawthorne the murderer, abuser, vile human. He was nothing and everything at the same time. And I wanted to kill him.

This was how I spent my days. Every morning, sat on the deck, trying my damnedest to break this ugly chair with as little force as possible, thinking of the people who lived their lives without me in them, and plotting ways to kill Hawthorne.

My only reprieve from these four walls was each time Six came and allowed me out of the house. This was a repeat of seven years ago, except I had no losses to mourn then. Six spent his days working as best as he could, despite the remoteness of our surroundings. When he returned from working each day, he seemed haggard, weighed down by obligations. Or, rather, one obligation: me.

Which is why I was trying to break this chair without seeming like it was on purpose. I needed to get out of this house. I rationalized that if the chair broke, Six would either let me wander down to the shore or send me into town for a new chair. One way or another, I'd get out of this cage. He didn't want the neighbors to see me, to have them become curious about the new neighbor, which I always laughed at. Our nearest neighbors were a mile down the beach. And they were retirees. It was Bingo and bedtime before sun down for them.

I treated this time like prison; I worked out every single day. Six bought me a treadmill, probably sick of me lamenting my lack of opportunity to run outside. I hated the treadmill. I was a rat in a cage, running on a revolving track, running until I couldn't run any more, but going nowhere.

Six positioned the treadmill to face the window that faced the ocean. The world outside mocked me when I ran, logging miles with an unchanging landscape.

Rage fueled my workouts. I ran, I lifted, and I pushed, snarling with the anger that coursed through my veins. Because if it wasn't rage pulsing through me, it was grief. And grief labored my breathing worse than physical exertion, grief weighed my legs down with excruciating sadness, and then I absolutely could not run.

But I needed to run, I needed to lift, I needed to push my body to its breaking point. My one and only goal was to see Hawthorne dead, and I couldn't fight him if I was curled up into a ball of sadness and weak with sorrow.

After Six had placed the treadmill in front of the window, I'd sent him to the local home improvement store with a list. He'd delivered my supplies and during one of my sleepless nights, I had dipped the paintbrush into the paint can and let the wall bleed with the color of rage. Now, the wall with the window that faces the sea was a deep, blood red. And it was a rage red, so when my feet were aching and my muscles were strained and my mind started slipping into memories of the people I'd left, I'd yell "RED!" at the top of my lungs.

RED.

RED.

RED.

I leaned back again in my rickety, wooden lounge chair, with my feet resting on the railing of the back deck. The sound of the waves rolling over each other roared in the distance while the smell of sand and sea blew through my hair. It was peaceful and quiet, the calm only occasionally interrupted by the sea gulls that cawed as they clambered for washed up trash. The beach was beautiful, but it wasn't home. It was a different kind of calm, of quiet, foreign to me. I hated it.

Six knew I hated it, but there was nothing he could do about it. As soon as we'd left Colorado, we'd traveled by car all the way here. We had moved in under the cover of darkness, though there wasn't an active neighbor for miles. We didn't talk much, Six and I. He knew I hated it here, but so far the only knowledge he had imparted on me had been that he'd looked into Julian's background, to make sure he was good for me. I hadn't told Six that Julian knew who I was, so Six didn't truly understand how important Julian was to me.

Six didn't tell me anything about Hawthorne. Once we got here, he didn't talk about why we came here. A week earlier, he'd shown me the pistol he kept under the loose floorboard of the bottom step of the stairs. He'd shown me how to use it, but hadn't told me why.

It made me feel antsy, knowing that gun was under the stairs. Not because guns made me uncomfortable, but because I wanted to use it. I wanted to find Hawthorne and take his life. That scared me a little, the intensity of my desire to kill him. But I felt justified in taking his life, when I strongly suspected he'd taken my mother's.

It'd only taken me a month or so after I arrived to this beach house to reflect on the nine days I spent with Julian. I recalled all our conversations. One that stood out in particular had been when he'd told me about his new book, while we rowed on the lake. A book about a single mom, living a modest life, despite having a fortune in the bank. And then she'd died, leaving her only child an orphan. Except in Julian's words she'd been murdered. Not the presumed suicide of my memories. My mother taking her own life had never made sense to me. And since I knew Julian's novels were partially based on truth, I searched my brain for more clues.

I remembered the papers I'd found in Hawthorne's office when I'd broken in. There was correspondence from my mother's law office. Why else would Hawthorne be contacting them if there wasn't a trust of some kind set up?

And when Julian admitted that he knew I was Cora, he'd said Hawthorne had lost of lot of money when I'd disappeared. What else could he have meant by that, if there hadn't been a trust in place, with Hawthorne receiving allocations for my living expenses? The more I thought about it, the more I believed that Hawthorne had killed my mother. I wasn't sure how. But I could figure out the why. It only made me wish more that I had Julian to turn to for answers.

When the breeze blew in harder, I stood up and walked back into the house, running up to the second floor, where my treadmill sat. I eyed it with contempt but slipped my tennis shoes on and began my run. I ran until sweat ran down my legs, soaking my socks, until the sweat ran into my eyes, burning them to the point of tears.

After showering off the sweat, my limbs felt wobbly, so I grabbed one of the books from my bedside table and curled into bed. It was one of Julian's novels. I'd read almost all of them since leaving Colorado.

I awoke in the dark. Something had roused me from sleep. I heard a noise outside. Six?

I reached for my new phone. Six always texted when he was on his way back to beach house.

There was nothing on my phone. I rolled over on my stomach and pulled myself up, gripping the wrought iron headboard. I pulled the blinds down. There was a car in the street, black, large. It didn't belong to Six.

I heard the noise again, and a then low voice. My stomach clenched in fear and I rolled off the bed. The moment my bare feet hit the wood floor, I was running towards the stairs.

I heard the squeak of the screen door opening. The trespasser heard it too, and they returned the door to closing. I crept down the stairs, jumping down after the last step and crouching in front of the hiding place.

I pulled out the handgun and the magazine, my hands shaking as I slid the magazine into the butt of the gun. With my back to the wall opposite the stairs, I walked down the hallway towards the front door, carefully putting my ear to the wood. There were no sounds. It was completely silent. If anything, that only quickened my heart rate as I tiptoed to the living room, adjacent to the entryway. I slowly approached one of the windows and quickly peeked through the blinds.

I saw nothing, no one.

I held the gun in front of me, pointed to the ground as I crept towards the back of the house, into the dining room. The entire bottom level of this beach house was made up of four rooms, entryways connecting one to the other. When I couldn't make anything out in the darkness of the windows there, I walked across the hall that separated the living and dining room from the kitchen and den. I passed the staircase in the hall and kept going, peeking out the kitchen window. When I still saw nothing, I started to really feel the panic. My heart thundered, my hands shook. There was someone trespassing on the property and I couldn't find them.

I heard my phone ringing upstairs and cursed myself for not bringing it with me. Without thinking, I dashed up the stairs towards my bedroom. I dove on my bed and ran my hands over the sheets, searching for my phone. I had a missed call. It was Six.

I frantically hit the call back button, holding the phone to my ear as I climbed off the bed and pressed my back against the wall next to my bedroom door, the gun in my free hand. "Hurry up and answer!" I whispered under my breath.

"Andra," his voice answered.

"Where are you?" I hissed.

"What is it?"

"Someone's here," I whispered.

There was silence for only a moment. "Grab the gun," he said, his voice harsh.

"I already have it. Are you far?"

"About twenty minutes away. Where are they?"

"I'm not sure. They tried coming through the front door, but now I can't find them. I don't know where they went."

"Fuck!" Knowing that Six was worried was more concerning to me than a stranger trying to enter the house.

"Do you know who it could be?"

"No," he said, vehemently. "It's probably a burglar." I heard the unmistakable sound of the back door opening. I'd forgotten to lock it after coming into the house.

"Shh," I hissed. I tiptoed away from the door, towards my bedroom closet. "They're inside." I said it so quietly, I couldn't even hear myself over the pounding in my ears.

"What?"

I breathed hard into the phone. "They. Are. Inside."

I could practically feel Six's panic through the phone. "Don't hang up the phone. Put it in your pocket and hide."

I didn't say a word, just did as he asked. I couldn't hear any noise downstairs. I sat crouched in my closet for several minutes, until I heard steps ascend the stairs. Each step creaked under the intruder's weight.

I decided I couldn't cower in my closet and wait to face them. I stood, albeit on shaky legs, and took small steps from the closet, along the wall to the door.

I kept the gun pointed to the floor, closed my eyes and breathed in through my nose. The gun felt like a hundred pounds of dead weight in my hands. I heard the intruder reach the top of the steps. I could hear breathing and knew it wasn't my own.

I realized then that I hadn't prepared the gun to shoot. I knew pulling back the slide would signal my presence, but it was do it now, or wait until I was face to face with the intruder. My hands were already slick with sweat so waiting would only make my actions less successful. I lifted one shaky hand and placed it on the barrel, feeling the grooves beneath my fingers. I sucked in a breath and quickly pulled the slide until it stopped, then released it, chambering a round.

The noise was loud and unmistakable. There was no way the person at the top of the stairs couldn't have heard it.

"Andra." The voice was soft, almost overpowered by the sound of my strained breathing.

And then I smelled him. Sandalwood and cinnamon. My heart tripped over itself, beating to another beat and I knew.

"Julian." It wasn't a question. With shaky legs, I crouched down, setting the gun on the ground. I heard his steps approach my doorway and I stood back up, the blood coming back to my legs. Holding onto the wall for support, I stood in the doorway and squinted my eyes into the darkness. There he was. "Julian," I said again, this time with relief, with gratitude. With love. He stepped out of the darkness and I leapt onto him, our arms crushing each other, his body rocking with me.

He found me.

THE END...FOR NOW.

ACKNOWLEDGMENTS

First and foremost, I must thank my husband Stephen for encouraging me to continue, even when I felt defeated. Also, thanks for all the meals you prepared alone and all the nights you fell asleep with the light of my laptop glaring on your face. I hope you look forward to doing it again!

In the same breath, I need to thank my two baby boys. You are my light, my love, my inspiration. Thank you for suffering through a month of grilled cheese and cereal dinners. And thank you, Dub, for the high-five when I told you I was writing a book.

I want to thank my family for their support, especially my mom. Thank you for reading early, messy drafts, and for your honesty. You taught me to read, thus you taught me to write.

This book would not have come to fruition were it not for the encouragement of Christine Janes. Your belief in my ability gave me the courage to put words onto paper. You listened to me bitch and moan and gave me a Starbucks gift card – the caffeine from that gift inspired some of my favorite scenes in this novel. I appreciate your advice and your friendship more than you know.

To Sona Babani, my best friend and the most honest and hilarious person I know. Thank you for every positive thing you said, and for the dozens of screenshots of my many mistakes. Thanks for being excited for me, for reading every draft I sent you and the incredible amount of feedback through every step of the way. Our fourteen year friendship is one of the most treasured things in my life and I cannot imagine my life without you in it. Can't wait to tackle you again.

To Wilma Bristol, my supervisor and friend – your enthusiasm for this project made a huge impact on my desire to finish. I can't tell you how much it meant to me whenever you were giddy with excitement to read more, especially knowing that you do not like to read. Thank you for treating my family like your own and for celebrating every small step I made with his book.

Early drafts of my book were sent to only a handful of people, but one of them, Tracie Ingram, returned an email LOADED with important feedback. I was feeling so much conflict with some parts of Chapter Two and Tracie, your suggestions were invaluable. Thank you for reading this and providing me your thoughts along the way, and for making me feel like I could do this.

Thank you to my good friends for your encouragement and excitement, especially my Army wife friends. Debbie Snyder, thank you for delivering me Twizzlers in my time of need and for going to the movies with my boys so I could write uninterrupted. And for being such an excellent human being in general.

Tarryn Fisher, you don't know me, but you inspire me. I read Mud Vein towards the end of finishing this manuscript and felt ripped open. I fueled that pain into one scene in this novel and walked away feeling free. Thank you for inspiring me, for unknowingly making me try harder, do better. Your talent for writing is unparalleled, your storytelling is flawless. I have this feeling that you radiate power, and I hope to meet you one day and feel it for myself.

I thank you, the reader, for picking up my book and giving it a chance. I know there are so many novels out there to read, and I'm honored you chose mine. Please email me if you want to talk, and I hope you follow me along this ride.

And finally, I have to thank my Savior above. I hope to always seek you, and to always grow in my relationship with you. Thank you for my many blessings.

Made in the USA
San Bernardino, CA
12 July 2016